Dear Reader,

They say that p[...]
Whether it's a sm[...]
town nestled in th[...]
along the Western[...]
hopes and dreams[...]
we cry—and, of c[...]

It is this universal experience that we at Jove Books have tried to capture in a heartwarming series of novels. We've asked our most gifted authors to write their own story of American romance, set in a town as distinct and vivid as the people who live there. Each writer chose a special time and place close to their hearts. They filled the towns with charming, unforgettable characters—then added that spark of romance. We think you'll find the combination absolutely delightful.

You might even recognize *your* town. Because true love lives in *every* town . . .

Welcome to *Our Town*.

Sincerely,

Leslie Gelbman
Editor-in-Chief

Titles in the Our Town series

⚮ OUR · TOWN ⚮

THE LIGHTHOUSE

LINDA EBERHARDT

JOVE BOOKS, NEW YORK

THE LIGHTHOUSE

A Jove Book / published by arrangement with
the author

PRINTING HISTORY
Jove edition / February 1997

The Putnam Berkley World Wide Web site address is
http://www.berkley.com/berkley

ISBN: 0-515-12020-0

A JOVE BOOK®
Jove Books are published by The Berkley Publishing Group,
200 Madison Avenue, New York, New York 10016.
JOVE and the "J" design are trademarks
belonging to Jove Publications, Inc.

PRINTED IN THE UNITED STATES OF AMERICA

10 9 8 7 6 5 4 3 2 1

To Jason and Julia,
my pride and joy,
for their forbearance

To George,
for allowing me the opportunity
to pursue my dream

To my mother, Rosemary,
for believing in me

To the staff of the Lighthouse Museum
in Michigan City, Indiana,
for all their help

To my fellow authors and critiquers,
Anne and Cindy,
for their support and hard work

To Jim,
my friend, adviser and champion,
for being there

❖ 1 ❖

THE CLANG OF the harbor bell was the only sound heard over the gale-force winds that wrapped Fiona Cleary's lightweight summer skirt around her ankles and swirled her thick auburn hair wildly about her face. She ran toward the lake, intermingling with members of the rescue team—weary men in oilskin coats and hats, anxious women carrying blankets, medical supplies and coffee—all roused from their beds in the predawn hours of the warm July morning to answer the bell's summons.

Fiona did not continue down to the docks with the rest. She turned right instead and dashed up the stone path toward the lighthouse sitting atop a dune, her heart racing in dread. Her younger sister, Deirdre, met her at the door, her small, pale face pinched with worry, her arms protectively cradling her pregnant belly. "Oh, Fiona, it's terrible. Another shipwreck; two in less than a month's time."

Fiona shut the door and latched it, then turned to face her sister. She forced her voice into a calmness she didn't feel. "The beacon was on all night, wasn't it, Dee?"

Deirdre wrung her hands and bit her lower lip. "I don't know, Fiona. But it was Da on duty, not Carvey."

Fiona let out her breath in a rush. The ship had struck through no fault of the lighthouse keeper. Her brother-in-law, Carvey Gannon, was fairly new to the job of assistant lighthouse keeper and could possibly have fallen asleep and forgotten to check the oil at midnight. But her father would never let the light go out.

"We can praise the saints for that, Dee, but why did Da take Carvey's watch? He's too old for a double shift."

Deirdre sank wearily to a chair and dropped her head into her hands. "Because—" Her sister sniffled and her chin began to tremble, a sure sign of tears to follow. "Because Carvey had a terrible bellyache in the night and Da had to take over his watch for him. And it's my fault." Deirdre laid her head on her arms on the table and began to sob. "It was my cookin' that caused his belly to roil. I'm just no good at cookin'."

Fiona sighed in frustration. Deirdre rarely had to cook for the family, and it was only because Fiona had gone into town the day before to stay with their ailing Aunt Tullia that her sister had had to cook at all. "All right, Dee, next time *you* can go sit with Aunt Tullia when she's having one of her episodes and *I'll* stay home and cook."

At a fresh outpouring of sobs, Fiona relented and began to smooth her sister's honey-brown hair. "I didn't mean to be cross with you, Dee. You, Jamie and Da ate the same food as Carvey, didn't you? Are any of you ill?"

Deirdre's reply was broken and muffled. "You know—I have—a weak stomach—when I'm carrying."

"Well then, how about little Jamie? Is he ill?"

"I don't know. I put him to bed directly after supper." Deirdre looked up, panic flaring in her light blue eyes. "Oh, Fiona, you don't suppose Jamie's dead and I don't know it?"

Fiona resisted the urge to shake her sister and instead threw up her hands in resignation. "By all the saints in heaven, Dee! Your man complains of a bellyache and you've got your child dead from food poisoning." She headed toward the staircase that led to the tower. "I should never had stayed at Aunt Tullia's last night. Put the kettle on. I'll be needing some tea to wake up."

"It's already heated. Oh, Fiona, you don't suppose Da let the light go out, do you?"

Fiona gave her sister a reproachful look. "Da wouldn't let the light go out, Dee. You know that."

"But he did before," Deirdre persisted.

"That was years ago, and we both know the reason for it. Now I won't hear another word on the subject."

Dee just isn't thinking straight, Fiona told herself as she climbed the tower's spiral staircase. Carrying a babe always made her too emotional for clear thought. Finn Cleary was strong and capable, with only two incidents in twenty-five years to mar his excellent record as lighthouse keeper. Above all else, her father knew that if he let the light go out and caused a ship to wreck, he'd lose not only his job, but also any pension he would have received as well. If that were to happen, there was no telling what would become of her sister's family, either. They might very well end up penniless and without a home. No, Fiona thought, pressing her lips together, her father would never allow the beacon to go out again.

She stopped midway up the tower to glance from one of the narrow windows. Lanterns bobbed in the gray dawn below as the lifesaving teams prepared to launch their rescue boats into the choppy waters of Lake Michigan. She whispered a quick prayer for the brave men who manned the gigs, crossed herself and continued up the tower steps toward the tall, circular room at the top of the lighthouse.

Fiona breathed in the smell of kerosene, a scent as familiar to her as it was distasteful. She had grown up in the lighthouse, and at the age of fifteen, after her mother's death, she'd had to shoulder the responsibilities of managing the household, caring for a younger sister and assisting her father as keeper of the light, an arduous task even for a man.

Fiona had an older sister as well, Ena Cleary Murphy, wife of the town's undertaker/cabinetmaker, but Ena had never been of help. As a child, Ena had refused to involve herself in the lighthouse duties. She had considered it a very lowly occupation and had moved out as soon as she was able. Ena now had a fine, roomy house in town, although she and her husband had no children of their own.

"Praise the saints for that," Fiona muttered under her

breath. "As full of themselves as a pair of peacocks." She shuddered at the thought of any offspring those two might produce.

It hadn't been until Carvey had taken over the role of assistant lighthouse keeper that the burden had been lifted from Fiona's slender shoulders. At once she had taken the position of schoolteacher, saving every penny she could in the hopes of one day leaving New Clare. But the closer she came to seeing her dream realized, the more she feared something happening that would prevent her from leaving.

Such as her father losing his job.

Fiona stepped into the room and quickly surveyed it. Carvey stood at one of the windows, his tall, spare frame ramrod straight, his hands jammed deep into his pockets, his bright red hair tousled from sleep as he watched the efforts of the rescue teams below. Her father sat slumped in a chair, his heavy shoulders sagging as he stared sightlessly at the wooden floorboards. In the center of the small room sat the immense fixed light, its many glass prisms gleaming in the first rays of morning.

"Da?"

Finn Cleary lifted his grizzled head and gazed at Fiona through weary eyes. "Mornin', Fiona."

She saw Carvey glance over his shoulder and mumble a greeting to her. His face looked haggard and gray and his eyes had a strange, haunted look to them. With a worried frown, Fiona knelt at her father's feet. "You must be bone tired, Da. Why don't you come down for breakfast and then go to bed?"

Finn rubbed his eyes with his thumbs and answered in a listless voice, "I'll wait until the rescue boats come back. How's Tullia?"

"As stubborn as ever. She swears I'm the only one who knows how to ease the aches in her joints."

"There's truth in that, Fiona. You're the only one who'll take the time to help her. Those big, ugly sons of hers only help when they need her money."

"Da!" Fiona tried to give him a reprimanding look, but ended up hiding a smile. As her father said, there *was* some truth in it. Tullia Brody had spoiled her two sons silly, and where it hadn't seemed to have affected Tom, Devlin was as self-centered and pompous as they came. Of course, there was no love lost between Tullia and Fiona's father, either. Finn had married Fiona's mother, Tullia's younger sister, against the family's objections and the battle between them had never ceased.

Fiona pushed to her feet. "Are you coming downstairs to eat, Carvey, or is your stomach yet too weak?"

Carvey turned to face her, a startled look on his narrow face. "What?"

"Dee said you had a stomachache during the night."

"Oh, yes. Yes, I did, Fiona, but it's some better now. I'll be down directly."

Fiona glanced at her father before she left. He was sitting as she had first found him, head bowed, shoulders slumped. A tiny worry tugged at the edges of her mind but she quickly shoved it aside. It was only natural that her father be upset. He had been a sailor once and knew better than anyone the devastation a shipwreck caused for the families of the drowned crew.

When Fiona reached the kitchen, she could hear Deirdre moving around in the bedroom behind the kitchen. Her sister had gone there, no doubt, to reassure herself that her three-year-old son was merely sleeping and not dead.

Fiona had just finished preparing a batch of biscuits and ham for the men when she heard the cries of the women on the dock. She slipped out the door and hurried down the path to join them as the rescue boats returned. Standing on the pier with the others, Fiona spotted her cousin, Tom Brody, the town's blacksmith, who was coxswain on one of the two gigs.

Tom was a large, robust man with curly brown hair, a high forehead, broad face, prominent, bulbous nose and engaging smile. There was a strong resemblance between Tom and Devlin, except that Tom lacked his older brother's cruel streak.

"What's the news, Tommy?" she called.

"Fiona, is that you? Not good news, I'm afraid." He waited while one of the men tossed the rope to someone on the pier and tied up the small craft. "She's a large steamer. The *Thomas E. Paine* is her name. Probably had at least a twenty-man crew. No survivors that we could see. We pulled three bodies from the lake."

One of the women crossed herself and another whispered, "God rest their souls."

Fiona watched as the two boats were unloaded of their gruesome cargo. She followed her cousin to where the women had set up the coffee, waiting until Tom had a cup in his hand. "What caused the wreck, Tommy? Surely her captain saw the light in time to steer away from the sandshelves."

"My guess is that she got stuck broadside in a trough and was carried onto the sandbar, same as the last wreck. The waves destroyed her pilothouse and deckhouse. Skylights above the engine room were crashed in and the room was flooded. We found two empty lifeboats floating near the ship. The bodies will wash up eventually."

Fiona stared up into his ruddy-complexioned face. "You said she was a big steamer. She would have been heading for Chicago Harbor. What was she doing this far south?"

"Most likely she was blown off course by the storm." He turned to survey the progress of his crew and began issuing orders.

Fiona clasped her hands together as she stared out at the abandoned ship in the distance listing drastically to the starboard side. She had seen many a wreck in her twenty-three years, yet she felt each one as profoundly as though it were the first. Until the fate of the crew was known, her stomach knotted in dread and then she ached with grief for lives lost. Every wreck seemed to take a little more out of her, until Fiona worried that one day there would be no emotion left. It was one of the reasons she wanted to leave New Clare.

Yet Fiona knew the men and women who risked their lives to aid the stricken ships were just as affected by the tragedies as she was, if not more so. Because of their compassionate natures and because many had close connections with crews of the ships that plied the lake waters, the rescuers treated each victim of a wreck as a loved one. Every member of the rescue team had been personally touched in some way by a shipwreck.

Fiona glanced at Mrs. O'Donohue, who was gently covering one of the dead sailors with a blanket. Mrs. O'Donohue had lost her husband when his ship went down in a sudden winter squall on the lake. Beside her stood Brian Kelly, whose father's ship had sunk to the bottom of the lake in a spring storm. And even Father Patrick, who stood now praying over the dead, had lost his only brother in a shipwreck.

Fiona turned abruptly and walked to the end of the pier. Strong gusts of wind billowed her skirts and tugged at the pins holding her hair. She paid it no mind as she gazed out at the whitecaps, hating, fearing, the awesome power of the seas. She knelt and cupped a handful of lake water, spreading her fingers wide to let it trickle through. "By every drop of blood that flows through my body," she vowed fervently, "I'll *never* let you take my loved ones from me."

"Fiona?"

Fiona let her hand drop to her side and wearily pushed to her feet. She turned to find Tom's wife, Pegeen, behind her, a worried frown creasing her plump face, her dark brown hair coming loose from its pins.

"Are you all right, Fiona?"

Fiona put her arm around the shorter woman's shoulders and they started back together. "I could use a cup of coffee, Peg, if there's any left."

Fiona drank a cup of the steaming brew while the rescue team packed up their supplies. After so many years of witnessing their efforts, it still never ceased to amaze her how quickly the jolly, leisurely paced town of New Clare changed personalities when disaster struck. Employers and employees worked together as equals, quarreling neighbors set aside their differences, teenaged children and elder citizens became partners, all in an effort to assist a ship in distress.

The townspeople worked so well together that they had earned a reputation on the Great Lakes for being a top-rate rescue station, an honor and a responsibility they took very seriously. Yet because of the serious nature of their rescue efforts, the citizens of New Clare also had a deep appreciation

of life and celebrated it to the fullest. At that moment, however, celebration of life was the last thing on Fiona's mind.

It was midmorning when she finally trudged up the stone
path to the lighthouse. At the sound of a whistle in the distance, Fiona paused at the top of the dune to shield her eyes
and look down on the town, where she could just make out
a train snaking its way along the southern edge of New Clare
heading west to Chicago.

From her vantage point she could also see St. Paul's
Church, the tall, white Catholic church that sat in the middle
of Kilkenny Street, one of two main thoroughfares in New
Clare. The other was Wexford, and the two streets together
formed the shape of the letter T, with Kilkenny being the top
bar of the T and Wexford being the stem.

Having started out as a Potawatomi Indian trail, Kilkenny
Street housed the oldest establishments in town—the general
store, the livery, the blacksmith's shop, the sheriff's office,
the hotel, the doctor's residence and the cemetery along one
side of the church. The park with its bandstand, on the other
side of the church, was a newer addition.

Along Wexford sat the red frame schoolhouse, the apoth-
ecary shop, the bank, the tannery and a law office. Wexford
ran north one-half mile, leading straight to the lake.

Fiona sighed wistfully. New Clare had been a good place
in which to grow up, a place filled with her many relatives
and close friends, yet the vast world beyond the town's shel-
tering arms beckoned to her, a world she had read of, dreamed
of and longed to experience firsthand. She had lived nearly
twenty-four years as the lighthouse keeper's daughter, and
though not all of them had been happy years, neither would
she have traded her life for any other. But it was time now
to break away, to find out who and what she was. It was time
to discover Fiona Cleary.

By dusk, Fiona was back at the lake, walking the sand
dunes in the cool evening air, as was her habit. She had always loved walking the hills of straw-colored sand, even
when they were covered with snow. There was a tranquillity

about the dunes that she had never found anywhere else and knew she would miss when she left. She sat at the top of one dune and shaded her eyes to stare out at the distant horizon.

Somewhere out there her future awaited her.

The lake was calm now, a deceptive, glassy calmness that belied its dangerous nature. She turned her gaze to the northwest, in the direction of Chicago Harbor, the largest and busiest harbor on the Great Lakes. She closed her eyes and pictured in her mind's eye what it must look like there—the large ships lying at anchor, a multitude of horse-drawn wagons being loaded with cargo, dockworkers shouting to each other, sailors streaming toward the saloons to while away the hours. She imagined the big stores of Chicago, too, and the streets filled with fancy carriages. Someday, she vowed, she would see the great city for herself.

Turning her gaze to the east, Fiona tried to picture Grand Traverse Bay, and at the far northeast, Mackinac and the passage to Lake Huron, all places she had read of in her travel books, but had never seen.

Though she had lived all her life in the tiny port town of New Clare, Indiana, Fiona had never sailed the Great Lakes, nor did she ever intend to. Storms on the lakes erupted with a vicious suddenness that too often caught mariners unprepared. Crew members of the smaller lake boats that called at their port warned that even seasoned sailors felt safer on the open seas than they did on any of the five lakes. The mountainous lake waves struck more fiercely and more frequently than any ocean wave. And all sailors, including her father, agreed that of the five, Lake Michigan was the most dangerous.

Indeed, in the quarter of a century her father had been keeper of the light, over two hundred wrecks had occurred at the southern end of the lake. Yet in all those years, only two accidents had been attributed to the beacon going out, and those had taken place just after her mother's untimely death, when her father had been distraught and unconsolable. From that time until the present, not one single ship had struck through the fault of the lighthouse keeper.

Fiona turned to look back at the lighthouse. Made of Mil-

waukee brick and Joliet stone, the two-story rectangular structure had been constructed by the U.S. government in 1857.
At the north end of the building sat the lantern, a tall, whitewashed tower that rose forty feet into the air and housed a
Fresnel lens of the fifth order, visible for fifteen miles. The
tower contained its own spiraling staircase, separate from the
house, yet connected through an arched doorway.

Fiona gazed up at the widow's walk that circled the top of
the tower just below the windows. Neither of her sisters had
ever set foot on the wooden walkway; Deirdre had a great
fear of heights and Ena had refused on principle. Thus it had
fallen to Fiona to clean the windows. She smiled, remembering how she had often stood at the railing in the early morning
hours staring at the horizon, dreaming of the day she could
visit the many places she had read about.

Now, at last, her dream was within reach. She had cut short
her career as schoolteacher and handed in her resignation at
the end of the school term in June. She would stay in New
Clare to see Deirdre safely delivered of her babe and then she
would be gone. By the end of September, she would begin a
new chapter of her life.

With a wistful sigh, Fiona rose from the sand, brushed off
the back of her skirt and began walking. She followed a path
down to the beach and strolled along, moving away from the
lighthouse and the dock until she stopped with a gasp and
pressed her hand to her mouth. Two sailors' bodies had
washed up onto the sand, each wearing a life vest. She
quickly turned her gaze from their bloated faces and continued on.

Farther down, a large piece of timber had washed ashore,
its lettering bearing the name of the ship, the *Thomas E.
Paine*. Another body lay a few feet away, the fingers of one
hand resting on the timber as if the man had used it as a life
raft.

Fiona glanced at the man and immediately wished she
hadn't. It was such a terrible waste of life. He'd been a rea-
sonably young man, in his early thirties by her estimation,
and extremely handsome. His hair was dark and wavy and in
back fell to his collar. His jaw was square and strong. A

confident face, she decided. One used to giving orders. He wore no captain's uniform, however. Possibly he'd been a first or second mate. She felt that all-too-familiar pang of grief for the wife and children waiting in some distant harbor for his safe return.

But as she looked at him, his fingers twitched and she jumped back with a gasp. *Saints in heaven, is he alive?* Fiona watched him closely, but he didn't move again. Had she imagined it?

She started to circle around him when she saw the man's fingers curl into the sand, as if trying to grab hold of it. A low, hoarse groan erupted from his throat as he slowly pulled one leg up under him and stretched it out again, as if attempting to crawl farther away from the lake waters.

Fiona hesitated only a second, then hurried to kneel beside him. "Save your strength, sir. I'll fetch help for you. It won't take long."

He groaned again and struggled to open his eyes. "Where am I?" he rasped.

"New Clare. Your ship struck a sandbar in the storm last night."

His eyes opened and fixed on her—dark, intelligent, questioning eyes. His throat muscles worked as he tried to speak again through lips coated with sand. Fiona gently brushed his long, damp hair away from his forehead, noticing a deep gash under the hair. "I'll bring help. You'll be all right." She jumped to her feet and started away at a fast stride.

"The light was out."

Fiona came to a stop and spun to stare at him, unable to believe what she had heard. But his eyes were shut and he seemed to be unconscious again. Surely, then, she had been mistaken. He hadn't spoken at all.

Her father would *never* let the light go out.

❖ 2 ❖

"*KEEP HER HEAD into the wind, Mr. Calloway. Give me full steam. I need full steam.*"

"*Mr. Paine, the engine room's flooding.*"

"*Then, by God, start the pumps.*" *A heavy crash behind the men caught both by surprise. Paine turned as a giant wave demolished the pilothouse, sweeping the pair off their feet and down the spar deck. Travis grabbed the corner of the deckhouse at the stern before he was swept overboard. Calloway, he was relieved to see, had done likewise. The ship plunged into a trough and began to roll heavily with the waves washing over her.*

"*Drop the anchors,*" *he yelled above the winds and crashing waves.* "*We've got to keep the ship from drifting any farther south, Mr. Calloway. We can weather the gale as long as we don't hit a sandshelf.*"

"*I'll give it my best, sir.*"

"*How far are we from land?*"

"*Can't say, sir. We can't be close, though, or we'd have seen a light.*"

Travis slowly opened his eyes and gazed in bewilderment at the unfamiliar whitewashed ceiling above him. A glance around showed that he was lying on a lumpy, narrow iron bedstead covered by a somewhat faded patchwork quilt in a small room with little to recommend it. Other than the bed, there was a pine chest of drawers, a small bedside table, a ladderback chair in one corner and a crucifix on the wall above the bed. Whose bedroom was he in?

By the light streaming through the gauzy curtains at the single window to his left, he guessed it to be midmorning. But of what day? He tried to sit up and gasped aloud as every muscle, every bone in his body screamed in agony. A deep breath brought him a sharp, knifelike pain on the left side of his rib cage. He lifted the quilt to examine his injuries and discovered he was wearing an unfamiliar white union suit.

What the hell was going on? And why wasn't he on board his ship?

And then he remembered. With a tormented groan Travis covered his eyes with the heels of his hands. The *Thomas E. Paine*, the pride of the Paine family's shipping fleet, was wrecked. And he was to blame.

Travis diligently searched his memory but could remember very little of what had happened after the summer storm had come upon them. Still, a steamer the size of the *Thomas E. Paine* should have been able to weather the squall. What had he done wrong?

With a disconsolate sigh, he dropped his hands to the bed. "Hell, it was only what they expected of me." His voice came out in a hoarse whisper. He winced from the burning in his throat and swallowed, but that only brought him more pain.

"What *who* expected of you?"

Travis glanced at the doorway. A comely young woman stood on the threshold, carrying a green wooden lap tray with a cup on it. He watched her move gracefully across the room toward him. She wore a plain black skirt and white shirtwaist with a silver watch pinned to the bodice. Her waist was trim and her neck slender. Her rich brown hair, pulled loosely on top of her head, held a reddish cast. She had a fair complexion, wide blue-green eyes and a generous mouth. She wasn't a beauty, yet she had a fresh, natural attractiveness he would have found quite appealing under different circumstances.

He remembered he had seen her somewhere before.

She placed the tray on the bedside table and turned to look at him with eyes full of sympathy and concern. Travis felt his temper shorten. Being the object of a woman's sympathy didn't sit well with him. His reputation with the ladies had hardly been earned by being a sympathetic figure.

"Is your head feeling better?" she asked, staring at a point above his right eyebrow.

Travis reached up and felt a thick pad of gauze covering one side of his forehead. *Damn it!* When had she bandaged him? "Fine," he muttered.

"I've brought you a cup of broth." Her voice was pleasant and smooth with just a trace of an Irish accent. "It should soothe your belly as well as your throat. You swallowed quite a lot of sandy water—and spewed it up, as well. There's a bucket on the side of the bed should you feel the need to use it."

He attempted to sit up, but the stabbing pain in his ribs stopped him.

"Let me help you," she quickly offered. She leaned over him, affording him a whiff of the clean, feminine scent of violets.

"I'm not an invalid." Travis slowly pushed to his elbows, grimacing from the agony of it, but determined to do it himself rather than have her think him a weakling. He held himself there as she propped pillows behind his back.

At that close a distance, he could see the creamy porcelain texture of her skin and the green flecks in the blue of her eyes. They were lovely eyes, memorable eyes. His head pounded from the effort to remember where he'd seen those eyes. "I've met you before, haven't I?"

She gave him a wary glance as she perched on the edge of the bed. "You don't remember?"

"I don't even know how I got here."

"It will come back."

"Where am I?"

"The lighthouse at New Clare."

New Clare? But that's at the southern end of Lake Michigan.

There was more he wanted to ask her, but his throat was

so sore he decided it could wait. Travis took the cup she offered and brought it to his lips. The strong smell of chicken nearly gagged him.

"Don't force yourself to drink it," the young woman told him. "If your stomach is still unsettled, it's best to wait."

Travis thrust the cup at her and eased down into the bed.

"I'll put it here on the table where you can reach it," she said. "Why don't you try to get some rest?" It was more of an order than a question. Travis wasn't used to taking orders from a female, but he didn't feel well enough to argue the matter. He turned his head and closed his eyes. The soft click of the door closing was the last sound he heard before falling into a heavy slumber.

Fiona quietly closed the door and stood for a moment in the hallway outside the spare bedroom, thinking about the stranger within. "He's a handsome devil, to be sure," she said aloud as she started downstairs. Of course, she always had been particular to men with strong, lean jaws and dark hair.

Fiona imagined that his wife would be overjoyed to learn of his rescue. If she were ever to marry, Fiona decided, she'd want a man as handsome as that one, as long as he wasn't a sailor. She only regretted that he still had to face such devastating news about the rest of the crew. But that was part of the risk of his occupation.

When Travis next awoke, the light was fading. It took him a few moments to remember where he was and what had happened, and then he wished he hadn't. His hands curled into fists at his sides and his jaw clenched. "Damn it to hell!" he croaked.

How could he have erred so greatly? How was he to tell his father he had failed again? He lay there brooding until finally the growling of his stomach distracted him. With considerable effort he eased himself to a semi-reclining position, reached for the cup on the bedside table and took a tentative sip of the chicken broth. It was cool now and soothing to his throat.

Travis waited until the first sip settled in his stomach, then took another sip. A third and fourth went down before his stomach rebelled. He barely got the cup to the table before heaving the meager contents of his stomach into the bucket. His ribs hurt so badly from the effort that tears sprang to his eyes. With a curse, he sank back to the bed. If he wasn't in hell, he was surely damn close.

A quick knock preceded the return of his earlier visitor. She opened the door and smiled. "I thought I heard you shifting about. The bed squeaks, you see." She glanced into the bucket as she approached the bed and shook her head. "I feared it was too soon for broth, but my father insisted." She shrugged her shoulders. "We'll just try again in the morning."

"Forget the damn broth," Travis managed between clenched teeth. "I think my ribs are broken."

She frowned in concern. "The doctor was here earlier, but you were sound asleep. I'll go to town and fetch him straightaway. Is there anything I can do for you before I leave?"

Shoot me and put me out of my misery, Travis wanted to snarl. But he only frowned and shook his head.

"Is there anyone you'd like me to wire? Your wife, perhaps, or your family?"

"No."

She stared at him for a moment as if she were trying to figure him out, then she picked up the bucket and walked away.

Travis closed his eyes and leaned back against the pillows. *You're absolutely right. I'm not worth the bother.*

Fiona stopped rolling out her piecrust long enough to glance at the clock on the cupboard shelf. The doctor had been upstairs with their houseguest for nearly half an hour, making her fear that the man's injuries were much worse than she had thought.

She still puzzled over the sailor's reply to her offer to send a wire. She could not imagine why he did not want to contact his wife or family. What was it he had said earlier?

"Hell, it was only what they expected of me."

Fiona pursed her lips. Was it his family he was referring to? Did he feel he had somehow let them down? It really made no sense to her at all. She would have liked to know more about him, such as what his name was, where he was from, and who it was he thought he had disappointed—but she sensed by his sharp answers that it would not have been wise to pester him. She would just wait until he was ready to talk. She had learned from experience that after the initial shock had worn off, he would need to talk.

"Is the rhubarb filling ready, Dee?" she asked, wiping her brow with the back of her hand. The evening had turned muggy and warm, with no breeze to stir the air.

"Ready," her sister replied with a weary little sigh.

At the sound of the doctor's heavy tread on the stairs, Fiona and Deirdre both turned expectantly. Finn and Carvey came in just as Dr. Carnahan stepped into the kitchen. "How is he?" Fiona asked, wiping her hands on her apron.

The doctor settled his bulk in a kitchen chair. "A few broken ribs, numerous contusions and bruises. Nothing that time and care won't heal. Fiona, you'll need to keep that gash on his forehead clean and freshly bandaged and apply salve to his bruises."

"How long would you say it'll be until he can get up, Doc?" she asked as her father took a seat on the opposite side of the table. She glanced at him and her brow wrinkled. She had never seen him look as old as he did at that moment.

The doctor scratched a broad muttonchop sideburn. "I'd say it will be a good six weeks before he can do any hard physical labor, but he should be up and about within the week."

Fiona handed the doctor a glass of cool lemonade and returned to her piecrust. "You didn't say anything to him about the rest of the crew, did you?"

The doctor finished the drink and let out a sigh of contentment. "This weather is draining on a body, eh, Finn? To answer your question, Fiona, no, I didn't. I agree with you that it can wait until he's on the mend. He has enough to deal with at the moment."

"He's bound to ask about the others, Fiona," her father said in a weary voice. "It's only natural."

Fiona opened the oven door and slid the pie inside. "If he asks, then we've no choice." She straightened and glanced around at the people gathered in the room. "If he doesn't, no one is to say a word until he's better."

Travis woke up the next morning stiff, sore and famished— and totally at the mercy of strangers, a situation he found irritating at best.

"Come in," he snapped at a knock on the door, and was immediately angry that his voice was still hoarse. He was used to booming orders, not whispering them.

"Feeling better this morning?" the young woman with the lovely eyes asked him brightly. She had on a dress in cranberry and gray plaid and carried the same wooden lap tray as before.

"Do I *look* better?"

She gave him a chiding glance as if he were nothing but a spoiled child. "You'll mend soon enough."

"Soon enough for whom?" The child in him couldn't help snapping back.

She ignored his churlish behavior and studied him with intense concentration. "I believe a shave would do wonders for your temper, if you think you're up to it."

Travis ran a hand along his jaw and gave a grunt of displeasure. Her unflappable attitude was getting on his nerves. He was beginning to think having her sympathy was preferable. "I hope you've brought something more substantial than broth."

She gave him a sidelong glance as she placed the cup on the table beside him. "Broth is all you're getting today. Doctor's orders."

"The doctor can go to hell."

"I'll thank you to watch your tongue in this house, sir," she said firmly. "I know you've had a bad time of it and are feeling poorly, but you've no reason to be rude to me. I'm only trying to help."

She was right, but Travis didn't want to admit it. He frowned and looked away.

"Now then," she said, returning to her former cheerful self, "here's your broth. I'll come back in a bit with the salve the doctor sent for your bruises. You can let me know then about that shave."

He accepted the cup and cautiously sniffed the contents, wishing to avoid a repeat peformance of his last attempt at the broth. "Are there any men in the house?"

"There's Carvey Gannon, my brother-in-law, and there's my father, Finn Cl—"

"I'd prefer one of the them to see to the shaving."

Her delicately arched eyebrows drew together in bewilderment. "Don't you trust me?"

"Let's just say I trust my own gender *more*."

She planted her hands at her waist and gave him a decidedly icy glare. "Is that so?"

Travis took heart in the fact he had finally succeeded in getting under her cheerful skin, but the unfortunate truth was that he was in no mood for a battle, either. He retaliated by putting the cup to his mouth and ignoring her. When she kept glaring at him, he paused to say, "That will be all."

She opened her mouth in indignation, shut it again, spun around and stormed out of the room. Travis felt vindicated as he sipped the broth. That would teach her to be so cheerful.

Carvey was sitting at the kitchen table drinking coffee when Fiona returned from the second floor. At her stormy entrance he glanced nervously at her. "Did you find out anything from the sailor?"

"Only that he's arrogant and rude." She walked to the stove and poured herself a cup of the strong brew. "And to think I thought he was handsome," she muttered to herself. She took a sip of coffee and turned to her brother-in-law. "He'd like you to shave him, Carvey."

Carvey swallowed hard. His prominent ears turned bright red. "He wants me to shave him?"

"He doesn't trust me," Fiona explained angrily. "It seems a female can't do the job as well as a male. It took all my will not to give him a piece of my mind." She huffed in exasperation.

"Have pity on the man, Fiona. He's the sole survivor of a shipwreck."

Fiona let out a heavy sigh, staring bleakly into the dark, steaming coffee. "That's the *only* reason he didn't get a thorough tongue-lashing."

Carvey quickly scraped back the chair and unfolded his tall, thin form to its full height. "I'll go get my shaving kit."

"I'll be up directly. I still have to tend to his injuries." Fiona paused to take another sip of coffee, then added in an undertone, "If he'll trust me."

Fiona entered the bedroom with her basket of medical supplies just as Carvey was finishing the sailor's shave. If it had done nothing to improve his disposition, the shave had at least made their guest look less like a sea wolf.

"Thanks," the man said in a gruff voice, running a hand over his smooth, lean jaw. Except for the towel around his neck, his chest was bare down to the bandages around his ribs.

"No bother at all," Carvey mumbled, his ears turning red as they always did when he was embarrassed. "Glad to be of help."

Fiona waited until her brother-in-law had collected his shaving implements and left the room; then she sat down on the edge of the bed, put her basket on the bedside table and removed the jar of salve.

"Will you lean forward a bit, please, so I can reach your back?" She kept her tone businesslike and brisk. After he had given her a surly look and reluctantly complied with her request she felt compelled to admonish, "Rest assured I don't like doing this any more than you like having it done."

His answering grunt rankled her even more. She dipped her fingers into the jar and began to apply the salve to the cuts and bruises on his back and shoulders, sparing little thought to his discomfort. But he bore her administrations stoically, and that, together with the battered condition of his body, quickly tempered her ire. Her movements gentled. It was a wonder the poor man had survived the storm at all.

As she worked her way around to the collarbone and down each arm, she couldn't help but admire the man's physique. His shoulders and chest were well defined. His tanned, muscular arms were covered with a sprinkling of coarse, dark hair, as were his strong, broad hands. Below the bandages, his belly was trim with not an ounce too much of fat, and his facial features were inarguably good-looking. It was a shame his temperament wasn't as handsome as he was. She recapped the jar, put it in the basket and took out her scissors and gauze.

He gave her a wary look. "You're not going to wrap my ribs again, are you?"

Fiona cut a piece of gauze and set it aside. "The bandage around your ribs is fine. It's the gash on your forehead that must be cleaned so it doesn't become infected." She gently removed the adhesive strips from his head, fully expecting him to stop her at any moment and demand that Carvey do it instead.

But he remained silent until she had nearly finished, and then he asked almost grudgingly, "What's your name?"

"Fiona Cleary." She glanced at him curiously, wondering if he were at last making an attempt to be sociable. "And yours?"

"Travis Paine."

Fiona looked at him with surprise. "Is the *Thomas E. Paine* your ship, then?"

Travis gave a derisive laugh. "Hardly."

She waited for him to elaborate as she finished taping the fresh gauze in place. Instead, he glanced at the half-empty cup of broth on the table as if he wanted it. "Would you like me to get it for you?" she asked.

"I can manage," he grumbled.

So much for his being sociable. "Suit yourself." Fiona rose abruptly, picked up her basket and started for the door. "I'll leave you to rest."

"I'd rather you stayed. I have some questions I'd like answered."

She paused with her back to him, hoping he would not ask

about his crew. She didn't think she had the heart to tell him. *Courage, Fiona,* she told herself. She squared her shoulders and turned to face him. "Ask them, then."

Travis took a sip of the broth and swallowed. "How did I get to New Clare?"

"You floated here on a timber."

For a moment, he studied her quizzically, then his face cleared. "You found me on the beach, didn't you?"

"I did."

He seemed relieved to have remembered. He put the cup aside and leaned forward anxiously. "Can you tell me how the rest of my crew fared and where they're being housed?"

It was the moment she had dreaded. Fiona dropped her gaze and smoothed her palms down the white apron she wore over her skirt. Drawing a steadying breath, she said quietly, "None but yourself survived, Mr. Paine."

❖ 3 ❖

TRAVIS STARED AT the top of Fiona's bent head, trying to make sense of her words. How could he be the only one to have survived the shipwreck? The men of the *Thomas E. Paine* were experienced sailors. It was true none knew how to swim—most sailors didn't—but surely they'd managed to make it to shore somehow. After all, they had crossed the lakes in all kinds of weather.

"It's not possible." He placed the cup on the table and sank back against the pillow. "It's *not possible*."

"I'm very sorry."

Her words didn't register. He stared blankly at the ceiling. "Then it was my error that sent them to their graves. I was acting captain." He slammed both fists down on the bed, the pain in his ribs nothing compared to the agony in his heart. "God damn it! I should have died with them!" Travis dug his fists into his eyes and clenched his teeth to keep from shouting curses to the heavens.

When Captain Martin had taken ill during the voyage, Travis had believed he'd been given his golden opportunity to prove to his family at last that he was capable of being master of his own ship. He'd paid his dues, working his way from seaman up to second mate and then to first, hoping his father would finally recognize his ability and give him his own ship to command, as he had Travis's brothers.

And what had Travis done with his golden opportunity? He'd wrecked the biggest, newest, fastest ship in the fleet. The irony suddenly struck him as preposterous. He began to laugh, releasing his pent-up frustrations, his agony, his bitterness, until he was limp from laughter and his face was wet with tears.

But Travis sobered quickly when he thought of all the good men who had been lost, the friends he would never see again. His eyes teared up and his throat began to ache. He suddenly remembered Fiona and glanced toward the door, but she was gone. He turned his face to the pillow, but he could not weep.

.

When Fiona returned to the kitchen, Deirdre was giving Jamie a bath in the galvanized tub and Carvey was putting on his gray tweed cap, getting ready to leave. Fiona wiped a tear from her cheek. "I told him, Carvey."

"Told who what?" Deirdre asked, lifting Jamie from the tub.

"Our guest, Dee." Fiona sank wearily onto one of the kitchen chairs and rested her forehead in her hand. "I had to tell him about his crew being drowned."

Carvey looked down at the floor and shoved his hands deep into his pockets. "What did he say?"

"His name is Travis Paine, and the ship belongs to his family. He's not the captain, but he was in charge when it struck." Fiona paused to let out a heavy sigh. "He's taking full responsibility for the wreck."

"That's a relief," Carvey said with a sigh.

Fiona glanced up in surprise. "Why is that?"

Carvey's ears turned red and he ducked his head. "You know how it could be, Fiona. He could claim the light wasn't on."

Fiona tensed. "Why would he do that? The light *was* on."

"He could try to lay false blame, is what I meant," Carvey said quickly.

With a worried frown, Deirdre pulled Jamie's shirt over his head. "What will we do if he *does* claim the light was out?"

"What we'll do is not borrow trouble," Fiona replied firmly. "The light was *on*, and that's that."

Jamie ran over to Fiona and wrapped his chubby arms around her legs. "Feena hold?"

Fiona gave the child a smile and swept him up into her arms. "Yes, Jamie boy. Aunt Fiona will gladly hold you."

He gestured upward with a pudgy hand. "Go up!"

"You want to visit Grandpa in the tower?" At his enthusiastic nod, she laughed. "Okay, Jamie boy, it's up to the top we go."

As she stood up with the child, Carvey opened the front door and mumbled, "I'm off, Dee. I'll be back in a bit."

"If you'll wait a moment I'll give you a list of supplies I need," Deirdre told him.

Carvey cast a quick, sheepish glance at Fiona before saying quietly, "I hadn't meant to go into town, Dee."

"I'll go," Fiona offered from the other side of the room. "I want to check on Aunt Tullia anyway."

"Hello, Da."

Finn Cleary stopped in the midst of polishing the lens of the big beacon and turned. His face looked haggard and his eyes distant, but at the sight of his grandson, he seemed to brighten. "Will you look who's come to visit!"

"Gampa!" Jamie called happily and stretched out his arms. Finn tucked his polishing cloth in his back pocket and took the boy from Fiona.

"Another storm coming in, Da?" Fiona asked, peering at the sky from one of the large windows. She knew her father would light the beacon on a summer day only in the case of a storm. In the early spring and fall, prime squall weather on Lake Michigan, the beacon was maintained twenty-four hours a day. The rest of the year it was lit only at night until the lake froze over in the winter, when the big light was shut down until the shipping season resumed in March.

"No, Fiona. I just came up to clean the prisms."

Finn stood Jamie on the floor and watched the boy run to the window. "How is the sailor?" he asked.

"Suffering mightily," Fiona replied. "He wanted to know about his crew."

Finn shook his head and let out a heavy sigh. "Poor lad," he muttered.

"His name is Travis Paine, of the Paine Shipping Company." Fiona paused. "He was acting captain."

"And a captain is supposed to go down with his ship," Finn said sadly as he eased himself into his chair.

"I couldn't understand at first why he refused my offer to wire his family," Fiona said, "but perhaps he's ashamed."

"He has nothing to be ashamed of!" Finn said sharply, fixing his gaze on Fiona. "It was the storm that did it, nothing else."

Fiona stared at her father, bewildered by his fierce reaction. Finn averted his gaze and said in a flat tone, "He should wire his family. They'll be fair sick with worry."

"He's a stubborn one, Da. Maybe you should talk to him."

"Maybe I should." Finn was silent for a moment, then said quietly, "I'm thinkin' of retiring next season, Fiona."

Fiona turned in surprise. "But you need five more years of service to get a decent pension, Da!"

"I'm just thinkin' about it, Fiona, that's all."

Fiona started to argue, but thought better of it. Her father was merely upset about the shipwreck. In a day or two he'd change his mind again. "I'm going to town to pick up supplies for Dee. Shall I leave Jamie up here with you?"

"I think I'll take him round to the sailor's room to introduce the boy and myself. Maybe I can help the sailor get his mind off his troubles. Let Dee know or she'll be beside herself thinking Jamie has fallen into the lake."

Fiona smiled. "I'll be back in time to cook dinner. We wouldn't want our guest to suffer at Dee's hands."

"There's truth in that, Fiona."

Brody's General Store was a beehive of activity when Fiona stepped from bright sunlight into the dim interior later that day. The town was gearing up for the Festival of Lughnasa, the annual August celebration of the first fruits of the harvest, and the mood was bright. Long green-and-white banners were draped across one end of the counter and a pile of green shamrocks sat nearby, waiting to be hung in store windows and on lampposts throughout the town.

A group of children ran past her on their way outdoors, holding peppermint sticks and laughing at each other's silliness. Several ladies stood at the counter on the right side of the long, narrow store, selecting material from the colorful bolts on the shelves against the wall for their festival costumes. At the far end, a customer waited at the grilled window of the small post office to collect her mail.

Fiona was relieved to see her Aunt Tullia's smiling, gamin face on the opposite side of the window, which meant her "episode" had been short lived. Tullia had been postmistress of New Clare for as long as Fiona could remember and hadn't missed a day of work in fifteen years.

"Good day, Auntie," she called gaily. "Glad you've recovered."

"Thanks to you, dear girl," Tullia called back. "You still haven't given me your answer about directing the play for the festival, Fiona."

"But I have, Auntie. You must have forgotten."

Tullia turned back to her customer and said coyly, "Emily, don't you agree we simply can't put on a production unless Fiona directs it?"

"Now, Auntie," Fiona scolded good-naturedly as she walked up to the women, "you've been putting on your productions for ten years. I've only directed the last one. And for me, it *was* the last one, as I told you the other day."

"We'll talk more about it on Sunday," Tullia said, giving her a little wave of dismissal. Fiona shook her head as the two women resumed their conversation.

"Afternoon, gentlemen," she said to the men sipping glasses of ginger beer around the cold potbellied stove. She received nods and smiles in return. In the winter, the old stove was such a favorite gathering place for the men that there was practically no room to maneuver around them. In the summer, they continued to gather there even though there was no reason for it.

She stopped at the counter that ran the length of the left side of the store and waited until Pegeen Brody was free.

"Afternoon, Fiona." Pegeen greeted her with a dimpled smile. "Did I hear Tullia say that you'll be directing her production for the festival?"

Fiona laughed. "It's wishful thinking on Tullia's part. I told her I wouldn't do it and I don't intend to change my mind."

Pegeen gave her a knowing look. "We'll see. I hear you have a guest at home."

"That we do, Peg. The only survivor of the shipwreck, poor man."

"That's what Carvey told us just a bit ago." Pegeen gestured toward the rear of the store. "He's in the back with Dev."

"Carvey is here?" Fiona asked, casting a puzzled glance at the doorway at the back of the store. "How odd. I'm sure he said he wasn't coming to town."

"What's all this talk I hear about a sailor staying at the lighthouse?"

Fiona turned as Bridget Riley, one of Deirdre's friends, came strolling up to the counter, her frilly white parasol poised delicately over one shoulder, her pale blond hair swept back at the sides to hang down in long banana curls.

Fiona had little patience with Bridget, who had been spoiled silly by her doting parents and still acted as though she were a blushing sixteen-year-old schoolgirl. Bridget was unmarried, though not from a lack of offers. Her comely face and hourglass figure made her quite popular with the bachelors in town, including Fiona's cousin Devlin Brody, owner of the general store. And Bridget somehow managed to keep them all dangling while she made up her mind as to which one would be the best choice for a husband. Fiona pitied the man she selected. He would be doomed to a life of pure misery.

She forced a polite smile. "Afternoon, Bridget. Yes, it's true we have a guest."

"He's the only one to survive the shipwreck," Pegeen explained. "Fiona discovered him half dead on the beach and took him back to the lighthouse to recover."

Bridget gave Fiona an innocent, wide-eyed look. "However did you manage that by yourself, Fiona?''

It was on the tip of Fiona's tongue to tell Bridget she knew very well she couldn't have managed it by herself. Instead, she decided to tweak Bridget's uppity little nose. ''Why,'twas nothing at all, Bridget. I'm much stronger than I look.''

Bridget blinked four times, opened her mouth to speak and closed it again. Fiona made a mental note to tell her father she'd rendered Bridget Riley speechless. He'd enjoy that greatly.

Bridget shifted the closed parasol to the other shoulder and patted her banana curls. ''Perhaps I'll pay Deirdre a visit tomorrow. I haven't seen her for nigh on three weeks. She must be nearly as big as a house by now. Good day, Fiona, Pegeen.''

''Good day, Bridget,'' both women called in unison.

''My, but isn't she the nosy one,'' Pegeen commented, watching the girl stroll away, ''suddenly deciding to visit Dee. She wants a look at the sailor is all, so she can make another conquest.''

Fiona laughed. ''I doubt she'll have any luck with this one. He's hardly in a state to carry on a flirtation, though I must admit he's a handsome devil.''

She suddenly recalled her last conversation with Travis Paine, and the piercing sadness of his remarks. *It was my error that sent them to their graves. I was acting captain. I should have died with them!* Fiona sighed, feeling again his pain.

''Handsome, you say, Fiona?''

Fiona shot her cousin a warning glance. ''Now don't get that gleam in your eye, Peg. He's probably married. And you know very well I'd *never* marry a sailin' man and spend the rest of my life worrying I'd lose him to the lakes.''

''But you've always longed to see the world. What better way than from a ship?''

''I'll sail the ocean, Peg, but I'd as soon walk as sail any of the Great Lakes. I'll go see what Carvey and Devlin are up to while you're filling my list.''

Pegeen glanced down the list of supplies. ''We're all out

of tea for the time being, Fiona, and we have no cornmeal, either.''

Fiona was surprised. "No cornmeal?"

"And you'll have to wait a month or longer for the muslin." She leaned closer to whisper, "Dev's having a hard time of it right now, Fiona. I can't say any more than that."

With a worried frown, Fiona walked toward the curtained doorway at the rear of the building. Devlin Brody was a known gambler, but his gambling had never before affected his business. She couldn't imagine that he would let it now. He was too proud of his reputation as a successful businessman.

When she stepped through the curtain to the storeroom beyond, Devlin was sitting at a small pine table across from Carvey talking in a low, hushed voice. A pitcher half full of beer stood between them.

"What are you two conspiring about?" Fiona asked goodnaturedly. Both men looked around in surprise.

Carvey's ears reddened and he jumped to his feet. "I only stopped to see how Tullia was feeling."

Devlin half rose from his chair and in a harsh voice said, "Sit down, Carvey. There's no need to rush away." Devlin turned an angry glare on Fiona. "The divil take you, Fiona! Announce yourself before bustin' through like that!"

"St. Christopher's eyeballs. Devlin! You're acting as if you've something to hide." Fiona said it teasingly, yet at the same time it struck her that there might be "truth in it," as her father would say. "You haven't answered my question. What are you two conspiring about?"

"How best to rid the town of nosy schoolteachers," Devlin replied. He glared at her for a moment, then burst into laughter, his sudden show of temper now hidden behind an engaging mask of pleasantry, a mask Fiona knew better than to trust.

As a child, Devlin had been a bully and played more than his share of cruel tricks on her. As owner of Brody's General Store, he had earned a reputation as an authority on everything from the state of the Union to the best way to get rid of leaf mold. Even the circuit judge consulted with him, which Fiona thought was more likely due to Devlin's intimidating nature than to any inherent wisdom he was blessed with.

Devlin had curly brown hair, small brown eyes, a ruddy complexion, a bulbous nose and a wide, open smile that camouflaged a greedy nature and calculating mind. Devlin had never married and swore to one and all that he preferred it that way. Fiona knew he was all bluster on that matter, however, for he had proposed and been rejected several times. *Wise women, all of them,* she thought to herself. Of course, he had yet to propose to Bridget Riley, who was his current favorite.

Devlin was four years older than his brother, Tom, and ten years older than Fiona. Tullia, his mother, and Fiona's mother had been sisters, but any similarity between the cousins ended there.

His bantering tone didn't fool Fiona now, but she only smiled cagily. "You'd best call in sharper minds than yourselves then, boys. *You* certainly aren't up to the task of ridding the town of Fiona Cleary." She turned her back on them and sailed through the curtain with a satisfied grin.

But as she carried her basket of supplies home, Fiona frowned in contemplation. She had always relied on her instincts to guide her, and her instincts were telling her now that something was afoot. She prayed that whatever it was did not involve Carvey.

❖ 4 ❖

FIONA TAPPED ON the bedroom door and peered around it. Travis was staring broodingly at the ceiling and she knew he was mourning the wreck and his lost crew. Her father had spoken with him the day before, but he'd had little success in cheering him up and none whatsoever in convincing him to wire his family.

"Feeling hungry this evening, Mr. Paine?" she asked. When he didn't respond she said, "I've brought you a bowl of potato leek soup. It's mild and quite delicious; it was my mother's recipe." She eyed him as she set the tray on the bedside table. "I thought it would be easy on your stomach."

He turned his head toward her. Fiona was troubled by the tortured look in his eyes.

"How many bodies have been found?"

She said quietly, "Fourteen at the last count."

Travis turned away from her and in a voice thick with emotion said, "What will they do with them?"

"They've been buried in the cemetery beside the church. We'll hold a memorial service for them soon."

There was a long moment of silence, then in a barely audible voice he said, "I want to be there."

"I'll have to check with the doctor."

Travis's head jerked around. His eyes were cold and determined. "I *will* be there."

Fiona met his gaze evenly, knowing his anger stemmed from the pain of his loss. "I'll let you know when it will be."

Some of the coldness left his eyes and he seemed to relax a bit.

"If it will help ease your mind," she told him, "the cargo has been unloaded from your ship. It's being stored at the warehouse at the end of the pier."

Travis's face registered his surprise. "The cargo wasn't damaged?"

"I've not seen it myself, but if it were in ruins Tommy wouldn't have bothered to unload it."

"Who's Tommy?"

"Tom Brody is my cousin. He's in charge of the rescue crew. He handles all the details whenever there's a shipwreck."

Travis closed his eyes and turned his head away. His hand slowly tightened around the edge of the quilt until his knuckles turned white. "I need to send a wire to the Paine Shipping Company."

Fiona was relieved he had changed his mind. "I'll be glad to do it for you. What would you like to say?"

"*Thomas E. Paine* struck at New Clare Harbor, stop. Cargo intact, stop." He glanced over at Fiona. "Shouldn't you be writing this down?"

"I'll remember it exactly as you said it."

He gave her a skeptical look and continued, "Crew drowned, stop. Signed, Acting Captain Paine."

Fiona gave him a puzzled look. "Is that all?"

"That's all."

"Nothing about your own condition?"

"I said that's all."

"But your family will want to know—"

"That's *all*," he snapped.

Fiona bristled. "I realize it's difficult for you to accept the deaths of your crew, Mr. Paine, but—"

"*Difficult?*" His fists clenched and unclenched at his sides. "Why don't you try profound? Or unthinkable? Or absurdly unfair? Or just plain incomprehensible?"

Fiona recognized the hurt and frustration behind his angry

words and her heart went out to him, but she was at a loss
as to how to help. In his present mood anything she said
would only make matters worse. She decided silence was her
best alternative and turned to go.

"Wait."

Fiona halted at the door and glanced back at him. Travis
met her gaze briefly, then looked away, yet it was long
enough for her to see the remorse in his eyes. She waited
while he hauled himself to a sitting position.

"I'll try some of your soup."

Fiona hid a smile as she hurried to place pillows behind
his back and position the tray across his lap. In his own way
he was trying to apologize for being short with her. "There
you go," she said kindly. "Is there anything else I can do
for you?"

"No." He scowled down at the bowl. "Yes, damn it. Stay
a while longer. It gets lonely up here."

Fiona opened her mouth to tell him she had duties to attend
to and that frankly she'd rather scrub floors than put up with
any more of his rudeness. Instead, she decided perhaps it
would be better for him to have someone to talk to, to keep
his mind off his troubles. But first she had to set him straight
about a few matters.

"I'll stay *if* you ask me politely and *if* you'll stop ordering
me about."

Travis considered her request for a moment, picked up a
spoon and dipped it in the soup. "Agreed," he grumbled.

Fiona folded her arms and tapped her foot on the floor as
he took a spoonful, and then a second. He glanced up at her
with a puzzled expression. "What is it?"

"What did you just agree to do?"

"To stop ordering you about."

"And what else?"

He scowled at her. "And nothing else."

Fiona leaned forward and glared at him. "You also agreed
to ask me politely to stay."

He swallowed a third mouthful, then gave her a perturbed
look. "How many times did you hear me say 'Agreed'?"

"Once."

"How many requests did you make of me?"

Fiona did a slow simmer as he finished the soup. She was sorely tempted to push his face into the bowl. "I made *two* requests, but since you agreed to only *one*, I'm under no obligation to comply with yours." She turned sharply and walked to the door.

"Ouch! Damn it!"

Fiona glanced back to find Travis holding a fingertip to his mouth.

"What have you done?"

"This tray," he said with a glare, "is full of splinters."

Fiona walked back to the bed, felt beneath the tray and shook her head. "That wood is as smooth as a baby's backside."

He held his index finger out. "What would you call that, Miss Cleary?"

She leaned closer to study his finger. "Divine retribution, *Mr. Paine.*"

For a long moment their gazes locked, Fiona's determined glare meeting Travis's hard, assessing one. She refused to look away, refused to be intimidated by him. Indeed, she was even beginning to enjoy pitting her will against his.

Travis looked away first, though she knew it cost him a measure of pride to do so. "Understand something, Miss Cleary," he said, setting the tray aside, "I'm used to giving orders. There's no time on board a ship for politeness."

"You're not on a ship now, Mr. Paine. You're a guest in my father's house. And by the very floor I'm standing on, if it weren't for the ordeal you've gone through, I'd tell you exactly what I think of your poor manners."

Travis leaned back against the headboard and crossed his arms over his chest. "Spoken like a true Irishman."

She raised her chin defiantly. "And proud of it."

He studied her for a long moment, then with one hand he indicated the ladderback chair in the corner. "Would you stay and keep me company, Miss Cleary?"

His quick change of heart surprised her. Fiona frowned at him, debating whether she wanted to subject herself to any more of his insulting behavior. Though she wasn't sure why, she finally decided to give him the benefit of the doubt and stay for a while. She, at least, would behave in a civilized fashion even if he did not. Fiona pulled up the chair, sat, and arranged her skirts around her.

"How many in your clan?" he asked her.

"My *clan?* We live in the United States, Mr. Paine, not Ireland."

"Your family, then."

Fiona counted them off. "From the Cleary side, there's my father, who you've met, my sister Deirdre, her husband Carvey Gannon and her son Jamie, my sister Ena and her husband Boyne Murphy, and me. My mother is deceased. And then there's the Brody 'clan,' which is my mother's side of the family. I won't name them, however. The town is full of Brodys and I'm certain you'd be bored silly if I were to try."

"I'm certain you're right."

Fiona ignored his sarcasm. "And what of the Paines? Where do you hail from?"

"Pennsylvania since Revolutionary times. England before that." He gave her a long, critical look. "Ever heard of *Common Sense*?"

Fiona planted her hands on her waist and gave him a steely look. "And how is your coming from Pennsylvania common sense when I've only just met you?"

Travis's burst of laughter was cut short by a grimace. He let his breath out slowly as though to avoid straining his rib cage. "*Common Sense* was a pamphlet written by an ancestor of mine," he explained, pressing a hand against his ribs. "I thought perhaps you'd read about him in school. Thomas Paine." He cast her a skeptical glance. "You did go to school, didn't you?"

Fiona seethed. Just because she was Irish didn't mean she was stupid. She was about to tell him so, too, when an idea occurred to her. "No, sir," she replied with a purposefully heavy brogue. "Niver attended school. We Irish don't believe in formal book learnin'. Everything we need to know we learn from the land and the sea, as the good Lord intended."

Travis gave her a skeptical look. "You're jesting, aren't you?"

"Sure and didn't the merciful Lord plant our people on the richest, greenest piece of land on this earth and surround us with a sea just burstin' with his fine, finned creatures?"

He looked stunned. "How can you communicate if you don't read and write?"

Fiona raised her chin another notch. "What would you say we're doing now, Mr. Paine?"

Travis scratched his head. "Is the whole town—" He paused as if to search for just the right way to phrase his next thought. "—of your belief?"

Fiona could hardly keep a straight face. "Stupid, do you mean, Mr. Paine? New Clare is an Irish community. What would you think our beliefs would be?"

He looked flustered. "I didn't say you were stupid. That wasn't what I meant at all."

"You'll have to forgive me, then, Mr. Paine. I don't always grasp the meanin' of you educated folks' words. Was the soup all right?"

"Delicious," he was quick to reply. "This was your mother's recipe?"

"That's right." Fiona smiled dulcetly. "Cooking is one of our few enjoyments, you know, along with farming, fishing—" She walked to the doorway and threw Travis a coy glance over her shoulder, "—and tweaking people's noses." She quickly closed the door behind her and clapped a hand over her mouth so he wouldn't hear her laughter. *That* would give him something to think about.

Dr. Carnahan was sitting in the kitchen talking with her father when Fiona returned from Travis's room.

"Good day, Fiona," the doctor called pleasantly. "How's our patient faring?"

"On the mend."

"He ask about his men yet, did he?"

"Yes, and he'd like to attend the memorial service."

"He should be able to get around in a few days." The doctor smiled. "Tell him he has my permission to go."

"Oh, he'll go all right, permission or not, as he's already informed me." Fiona ignored their raised eyebrows, took her straw hat from one of the pegs behind the door and addressed her father. "Mr. Paine has asked me—in his endearing fashion—to send a wire to his shipping company, Da, so I'm off to town to do his bidding, though why I agreed to do anything for that blackguard is beyond me."

"St. Patrick protect us," the doctor quipped. "Fiona's dander is up."

Fiona frowned thoughtfully as she pinned the hat in place. "Do you know he refuses to say anything in the wire about his own condition? And it's his family who owns the company."

"He's a proud man, Fiona," the doctor interjected. "I sensed that the first time I spoke with him."

"I'll agree that he's proud, Doctor, too proud for his own good, in fact. Yet it seems not so much a matter of pride as of guilt." Fiona paused to pull on her gloves. "Think of it; under his command his ship struck a sandbar and his men drowned, yet he survived. It's a terrible burden for a man to carry. And I can think of no way to ease his mind other than to convince him he's not to blame, which I cannot do. He *is* the one who was in command of the ship."

Her father rose suddenly and went to stand at the window, his hands deep in his pockets. At first, Fiona thought he had spied someone coming up the path, but he seemed to be merely staring out at the lake, a somber expression on his face. She watched him curiously. "Da? Is something wrong?"

He let out a long sigh. "Nothin' to concern yourself with, Fiona."

Dr. Carnahan eased his bulk from the chair. "Well, I'd best go see my patient and be on my way. Fiona, if you wait until I'm done, you can ride back to town with me."

"Thank you, but I'll probably be home before you've finished." With a puzzled frown, Fiona glanced back at her father, then closed the door and started down the stone path to Wexford Street.

The sun was setting as she turned east onto Kilkenny and

headed for the train station, which housed the telegraph office. She passed Brody's General Store, but stopped in front of the cabinet shop belonging to her sister, Ena, and brother-in-law, Murph. There she cupped her hands around her eyes to peer inside. Murph was at the rear of the shop sanding a hoopback chair. Her sister was nowhere in sight. Fiona tapped on the glass, waved, and continued on.

Edwin O'Banyon had his feet propped up on his desk and was reading the evening newspaper when Fiona opened the door to the telegraph office. Edwin was five feet five inches tall, the same height as Fiona, and only a bit heavier. His small stature and slender frame gave him the appearance of being no more than eighteen years of age, though he was actually thirty-four. To distract from his thin, pointed nose and weak chin, Edwin wore a handlebar moustache, which he kept tightly curled and waxed. His dark brown hair was parted in the middle and slicked back with hair oil.

Ena had always maintained that Edwin had a serious crush on Fiona, and though she didn't like to admit it, Fiona suspected her sister was right. At mass each Sunday, Edwin always had a tiny gift for her—a flower he had picked along the way, a bonbon he had spied the day before in the bakery window or a poem he had written, most often about birds. Unfortunately for Edwin, Fiona politely but firmly ignored his romantic overtures, though he never ceased trying.

When he saw who his caller was that evening, Edwin quickly swung his legs to the ground and jumped up, his face flushing with excitement. "Evening, Fiona. What brings you to town so late?"

"I need to send a wire to Erie, Pennsylvania."

With a flourish, Edwin took a pencil from behind his ear, sat down again and pulled a writing tablet toward himself. "Go ahead. I'm ready."

Fiona repeated the message just as Travis had dictated it, then waited while the telegraph operator positioned himself at his transmitter and tapped out the wire.

"Did you want to wait for a reply?" he asked.

"Thank you, no, Edwin. If anything comes in for Mr. Paine, have it sent out to the lighthouse."

As she turned to leave, Edwin remarked, "I hear he's a handsome fellow."

"You know what they say, Edwin," Fiona replied with purposeful ambiguity. "Handsome is as handsome does."

"But don't you think it's unusual," Edwin persisted before she could make her escape, "that Mr. Paine has nothing of a more personal nature to say to his employer, seeing as how his employer is his father?"

Fiona wasn't surprised that Edwin knew about Travis's connections with the shipping company. Nothing remained a secret for long in New Clare. "Mr. Paine is greatly troubled by the loss of his men, Edwin. Perhaps he will contact his family again once he's come to terms with it." She walked to the door.

Edwin nearly fell over his chair trying to get to the door to open it for her. "It's awfully dark tonight, Fiona," he said, peering outside. "Would you like me to see you home?"

"Thank you, but I had planned to pay a visit to Ena."

"Then I'll see you at church," he called as she hurried down the street.

"I can hardly wait," Fiona muttered under her breath.

Travis was leaning against the pillow with his eyes closed when there was a hard rap on the bedroom door and Dr. Carnahan ambled in.

"Evening, lad. Fiona tells me your stomach is better. How are the ribs?"

"They hurt like hell."

"There's no getting around the pain, lad. Takes time and care, is all, and you'll not find a better nurse than Fiona to help you with it." He situated his ample form on the bed and leaned over to scrutinize the gauze bandage on Travis's forehead.

"It's hard to believe she doesn't know how to read or write," Travis remarked.

The doctor's bushy black eyebrows lowered. "Who? Fiona?" He laughed heartily. "Did she tell you that? Ah, she would, that one. Full of mischief as a child. It's good to see her at it again. Been too long. She's been the glue that keeps this family together, you know. I see that often in middle children.'' The doctor leaned back, humor sparkling in his brown eyes. ''Fiona knows how to read and write all right. She's a schoolteacher.''

A muscle twitched in Travis's jaw. So the schoolteacher had tweaked his nose, had she? He let out a gasp of pain as the doctor probed his injured ribs.

''Take a deep breath.'' Dr. Carnahan rested his head against Travis's chest and listened intently.

''When can I get up?'' Travis asked.

The doctor straightened. ''You'll have to stay put another day or two. And of course it will be four to six weeks before you'll be able to do any heavy lifting or carrying.''

''I'm going to the memorial service.''

The doctor looked at him kindly. ''I wouldn't try to stop you, lad.'' He rose with a groan and lumbered toward the door. ''Don't be too put out with Fiona for pulling your leg. She's a good woman, our Fiona.''

When the doctor had gone, Travis slumped back against his pillow with a dejected sigh. Four to six weeks for his ribs to heal. He glanced at the window and wondered how badly the *Thomas E. Paine* was injured and whether she was salvageable. If he could have her repaired before sailing home, there was still a chance he could save face with his father. He needed to get out to see her, to assess her damages. Damn his ribs anyhow!

He raked his fingers through his hair, trying, as he had done each day since the wreck, to remember those last minutes before all hell broke loose on the ship. What had he done wrong? What order could he have given that would have prevented the wreck?

He finally drifted off to sleep only to be awakened by a familiar voice. Travis's head lifted off the pillow and his eyes searched the darkened room for his second mate, sure he had heard Calloway talking to him. When Travis realized it was only a dream, he slumped back against the pillow and closed his eyes, but he couldn't get the vision out of his mind. Calloway had been trying to tell him something about the ship's position. Travis slammed his fist against the bed in frustration. What the hell had it been?

A few faint strands of a song sung in a high soprano drifted through the open window. Travis cocked his head and listened. The voice was clear and melodious, though the tune was unfamiliar to him. Growing ever more curious, he eased his legs over the side of the bed and stood, wincing at the pain his efforts cost him. Slowly he moved to the window and looked down.

Sitting on a sand dune near the lighthouse was a woman of slender build and long dark hair. As he watched, she rose, shook out her skirt and began to meander down the shoreline. Was it Fiona? He wasn't sure. She had mentioned something about having two sisters, but he couldn't remember any more about her conversation.

He saw the woman stop to pick up a stone from the sand and skip it far out across the water. She gave a quick glance over her shoulder, as if afraid of being caught in such a childish act, then shrugged and continued on. Travis smiled. That quick glance had been enough to see her face. It was Fiona.

Her unbound dark hair gleamed with silver highlights in the moonlight and blew about her face in wild abandon. Her white dress billowed in the evening breeze and revealed slender ankles and bare feet. She moved with a grace that was as natural as it was enticing. He found he couldn't stop watching her.

Travis stood by the window until she was far down the shoreline, then he waited impatiently for her return, wanting to catch another glimpse of her, wondering what she was doing out on the beach at that time of night. Was it her habit to walk the dunes?

He was suddenly curious to know more about her and wished he had paid more attention when she'd talked. But all he could remember was the trick she had played on him.

He was still smiling when he eased himself back into the bed, but it took only a sharp pain in his ribs to remind him of his own sorry plight. His smile disappeared and for the hundredth time he reviewed in his mind the sketchy details of the last minutes of the *Thomas E. Paine*.

Perhaps the clue was to be found in his dream, if he could only remember it. His mother had always held great stock in dreams. Travis frowned at the thought. His mother was also half mad.

A door closed in the hallway outside his room and he suspected Fiona had returned from her stroll. He imagined her sparkling eyes, her cheerful smile and her pleasant, lilting voice and he suddenly had the strongest urge to talk to her. But what would he say? What reason would he have to bother her at that time of the evening?

With a scowl of frustration, Travis turned over and went to sleep.

•5•

WHEN FIONA QUIETLY opened the door the next morning and looked in, Travis was sitting up in bed, his usual frown missing. "I've brought you breakfast, Mr. Paine."

He said nothing to her as she crossed the room, placed the tray on his lap and shook out the napkin, but his dark eyes followed her every movement, making her feel as though he were scrutinizing her. When she stepped back, he glanced down at the food before him. "Another of your mother's recipes?" He leaned over to cautiously sniff the bowl.

"Yes, and there's no poison in it, just oatmeal made with fresh milk and a sprinkling of brown sugar." Fiona walked to the door, hesitated and looked back. "We're off to mass now. When I return, I'll put more salve on your bruises."

"Thanks, but you needn't bother. I'll manage."

Fiona gave him a skeptical glance as she took the small glass jar from her skirt pocket and walked back to place it on the bedside table. He was being polite, which was quite out of character.

"When you return," he said, "I'd appreciate it if you would bring me some writing paper and a pen."

Curious, she tilted her head. "Have you decided to write a letter home?"

"No. I'm going to teach you the alphabet. Since it appears that I'll have time on my hands while my ribs are mending,

I can't think of a better use for it than to help you learn to read and write.''

Mother Mary, what have I begun? Fiona thought in a moment of panic. "I've no desire to learn, Mr. Paine. I'm happy the way I am."

"Just think of the benefits, Miss Cleary. You'll be able to read the words to the songs in church."

Fiona was growing more flustered by the second. "But I've memorized them all. I don't need—"

"And you'll be able to read bills of sale. You won't have to worry about being cheated."

"Oh, but I never worry about being cheated. My cousin Devlin owns the general store and Tommy's wife Pegeen—"

"I won't take no for an answer, Miss Cleary. It's the least I can do after what you've done for me."

"I've done nothing but bring up your meals, Mr. Paine," Fiona insisted.

"You also saved my life. It may take a long time to repay you, but I will. I'm known for my tenacity. Do you understand the word *tenacity*, Miss Cleary? To put it in simple terms, tenacity is sowing an apple seed so that eventually you can serve up freshly baked apple pie."

Travis's condescending attitude was nearly her undoing. Fiona's blue-green eyes glittered with indignation as she lifted her chin. "I thank you for the explanation, Mr. Paine, but I see no sense in sowing the apple seed in the first place when my neighbor has an orchard full of apple trees."

"But if your neighbor puts a fence around his orchard to keep out the—uh—trespassers, what then, Miss Cleary?"

Fiona crossed her arms defiantly. "I'd wait until dark and climb his fence."

"Ah, but your neighbor has just turned his bull loose in the orchard."

Fiona narrowed her eyes to angry slits. "Then I'd bring along a cow. Now as for the pen and paper—"

Travis held up one hand. "Wait a minute. If I understand you correctly, you would wait until dark, lead your cow down to your neighbor's orchard to keep his bull occupied, climb his fence and pick his apples—and you would repeat this procedure every time you want to make a pie, rather than grow your own apple tree?''

Fiona's mouth curved up at the corners and her eyes sparkled in triumph. ''*That*, Mr. Paine, is tenacity.'' She spun around and marched to the door.

''About the paper and pen, Miss Cleary . . .''

Fiona winced. There was no way out of it, nothing to do but confess her lie and be done with it. She squared her shoulders and turned to face him. ''The truth is, Mr. Paine—''

''The truth is, Miss Cleary,'' Travis countered with a mocking grin, ''that schoolteachers aren't the only ones who know how to tweak noses.''

''The nerve of that man,'' Fiona fumed as she and Deirdre prepared the roasted chicken and potatoes for their Sunday dinner, ''leading me on that way.''

''You *did* tell him you didn't know how to read and write,'' Deirdre reminded her.

Fiona waved the paring knife in the air. ''Only because he called me a stupid Irishman.''

Deirdre's pale blue eyes widened in shock. ''He did?''

''Well, not in so many words, but he did imply it by questioning me about whether I had attended school.'' Fiona peeled the last potato and placed it in the roasting pan. ''The arrogant, muleheaded oaf!''

''But, Fiona, remember the tragedy he's lived through.''

''Tragedy or not, Dee, there's no call for his constant rudeness. If adversity is the true test of a man's character, then Mr. Paine has failed the test.''

''Yoo-hoo!'' a high voice called from outside.

Fiona and Deirdre both looked around as Bridget Riley sashayed through the door into the kitchen in a bright yellow and white striped dress with a wide black sash at the waist and a full bustle.

''Bridie!'' Deirdre called happily. She dropped the carrots she had been scrubbing and waddled across the room as fast as her cumbersome belly would allow. The two young women kissed cheeks, then leaned back to look at one another.

"You look wonderful, Dee!" Bridget cooed.

As big as a house was how you put it yesterday, Fiona thought, angrily slicing through a potato.

"And you look as beautiful as always," Deirdre returned. "Will you have coffee and cookies with me? Fiona baked sugar cookies just yesterday. I know they're your favorite."

"I'd love some," Bridget replied absently, looking around the room as if she were missing something.

Fiona knew exactly what it was. Her audience. Bridget had been hoping to find Travis up and about, and for some reason Fiona found that notion annoying. With a loud clatter, she set the plate of cookies on the table in front of Bridget.

The girl eyed her warily. "Hello, Fiona."

"Afternoon, Bridget." Fiona began to chop the chicken into pieces, her cleaver making a heavy *thwack, thwack* on the wooden cutting board beneath it.

"I hear you have a visitor," Bridget said to Deirdre, munching daintily on the sugary confection. "Mr. Paine, I believe?"

"Yes, the poor man," Deirdre said with a melodramatic sigh. "Broken ribs and a crushed spirit. He's taking the drowning of his crew very hard."

Forming her mouth into a sad pout in a show of sympathy, Bridget leaned closer to her friend. "Do you think he'd mind if I offered my condolences, Dee?"

Fiona split the chicken breast in two with a vicious chop.

"I'm sure he'd appreciate it greatly." Deirdre glanced at her sister. "Mr. Paine is awake, isn't he, Fiona?"

Fiona whacked the meat again. "Sit and rest, Dee. I'll take Bridget myself."

Fiona took the stairs at a fast pace, leaving Bridget trailing breathlessly behind her. Instead of tapping on the door and proceeding in as she usually did, Fiona merely gave one quick, light rap, then waited for Travis to respond, hoping he was fast asleep.

"Come in," she heard him call.

"You have a visitor," she stated as she opened the door. Bridget pushed past her and sailed straight across the room as Travis hurriedly attempted to sit up.

"Mr. Paine, it is a pleasure to meet you at last," Bridget cooed, daintily holding out a black-gloved hand. "I'm Bridget Riley, a friend of Dee's."

At Travis's puzzled look, Fiona interjected in a flat voice, "*Dee* is Deirdre, my younger sister."

Travis took the proffered hand, his cool, assessing gaze quickly sweeping over Bridget's comely form. "The pleasure is all mine, Miss Riley."

Bridget smiled down at him and he up at her until Fiona could stand it no longer. With a huff of exasperation, she stalked to the corner, lifted the pine chair and set it down behind Bridget so hard that the girl jumped. Bridget turned and gave Fiona a hard glare.

"You must tell me where you come from, Mr. Paine," Bridget said as she made herself comfortable on the chair.

"I come from Erie, Pennsylvania, Miss Riley."

"Erie! How exciting!" she exclaimed, pressing her hands together. Fiona made a choking sound.

Travis peered around Bridget. "Miss Cleary, wouldn't you be more comfortable sitting down?"

"There are no more chairs, Mr. Paine."

He smiled.

Fiona narrowed her eyes at Travis. He was trying to get her out of the room. She leaned one hip against the chest of drawers and folded her arms across her chest. "I'm perfectly comfortable, thank you."

Bridget glanced over her shoulder. "Weren't you in the midst of preparing dinner, Fiona?"

"Dee's cooking today, Bridget, and you know how she feels about preparing dinner. I wouldn't dream of getting in her way." Fiona smiled sweetly. Bridget knew exactly how Deirdre felt about cooking, but she would never be so gauche as to argue with Fiona in front of a man. It would ruin her image.

Bridget gave her another sharp look, then turned with a smile. "Perhaps we could take a short stroll along the beach, Mr. Paine. Fresh air would do you a world of good."

"I would love nothing better," Travis told her, "once my physical condition has improved."

"Oh, how silly of me. You're such a strong, handsome man that I've forgotten you've just survived a shipwreck. And now I've gone and reminded you of it." She sniffed tearfully. "I feel just dreadful. You must hate me."

Fiona could stand it no longer. Rolling her eyes in disgust, she pushed away from the chest and headed for the door. "I'll be downstairs if you need anything, Mr. Paine. And should your stomach turn, the bucket is under the bed."

I'm going to throttle Fiona for this.

Travis covered his mouth to hide a yawn. Bridget Riley had been chattering on for the better part of an hour about heaven only knew what, and it was all Fiona's fault. She had deserted him, left him with the empty-headed twit, and now Travis had no idea how to get rid of her short of ordering her out.

The only reason he had encouraged Bridget in the first place was to see Fiona's reaction, hoping he could kindle a little green-eyed jealousy. He had certainly inspired his share of that emotion from other women. Instead, he had seen Fiona's back as she left the room. Obviously, his interest in Bridget was of no concern to Fiona Cleary.

Perhaps Fiona had a beau. It was a possibility Travis hadn't considered and wasn't sure he cared to. Yet why shouldn't she have someone special? She was attractive, intelligent, capable, and not too far into spinsterhood to be molded to fit a man's needs. Yes, he decided, she must have a beau. That would explain her lack of interest. But who was this man? Captain of one of the small boats that docked in New Clare?

"And what is *his* name, Mr. Paine?"

Travis rubbed his jaw. "I wish I knew."

Bridget tilted her head to the side. "You don't know your father's *name*?"

Travis reddened with embarrassment. "I beg your pardon, Miss Riley. I didn't hear your question."

"I asked you about your father's name. Are you named after him?"

Travis frowned. What on earth did she want to know that for? "My father's name is Jefferson Paine. I was named after my mother's brother."

"How fascinating!" she cooed.

"No, Miss Riley, what is *fascinating* is that my father chose both of my brothers' names but couldn't be bothered to choose mine."

Bridget stared at him in wide-eyed bewilderment. Travis drummed his fingers on the bed and plotted his revenge against Fiona.

The savory aroma of roasted chicken wafted across the room, making his stomach growl. He imagined the family gathered at their table downstairs, stuffing themselves with food while he died of tedium a floor above. He doubted Bridget would even notice.

At the creaking of the stairs, Travis shifted his gaze to the doorway, hoping Fiona had come to save him. It was her father instead, a no less welcome relief. "Come in, Mr. Cleary," he fairly boomed.

"Afternoon, Bridget," Finn said with a nod. "Mr. Paine, we thought you might like to join us for our Sunday dinner if you're feeling up to it."

Travis could have kissed him. "I'd like to try."

"Bridget, you're always welcome," Finn added, "as you know."

Bridget chewed on her full lower lip and glanced from Travis to Finn, obviously in a dilemma. After some deliberation, she said, "Thank you for the offer, but I truly must get home. Mama is away today and Papa would be disappointed if I weren't home to have dinner with him. But I'll be back to visit again soon, Mr. Paine. Never fear." She rose and stood gazing down at him, her mouth in a wistful pout. "Perhaps you'll be sufficiently recovered so that we can take a walk together next time."

"I'll look forward to it, Miss Riley."

With a smug little smile, Bridget sashayed out of the room, stopping just long enough to throw a flirtatious glance back his way. Travis waited until he heard her footsteps on the stairs, then he pushed back the sheet and eased his feet over the side of the bed. "I'll look forward to it about as much as I'd look forward to catching the pox. Would you hand me my pants, Mr. Cleary?"

Finn did as asked. "You were taken with our Bridget, I see."

"I was tempted to smother her with my pillow. It's no wonder she's unmarried. Unless she finds a deaf man, I'd say she's going to have a hard time of it, too."

"Actually, she has a string of suitors, Mr. Paine."

With a wince, Travis stepped into his pants and fastened them at his waist. "Fiona's castoffs?"

Finn sighed wearily. "Fiona has no castoffs. She refuses to be courted. She's intent on leaving New Clare once the babe is born."

Travis stared at Finn dumbfounded. "Fiona is—with child?"

"Saints preserve us, Mr. Paine. I'm speakin' of my youngest daughter, Dee. You met her son, Jamie, and her man, Carvey."

"I didn't mean to—" Travis searched for a way to extricate himself from the situation, "—to insinuate that Fiona—"

Finn shook his head. "No harm done, Mr. Paine. I should have made myself clear."

Travis sat on the edge of the bed and struggled to pull on his socks. "Fiona wants to leave New Clare?"

"That's the truth of it. Her heart's desire is to see the world, and when Fiona makes up her mind to something, there's no deterring her."

Travis mulled over Finn's revelation as they proceeded downstairs to the kitchen. He was surprised Fiona wanted to leave New Clare, especially since she seemed very close to her family, something he'd never experienced in his own life. What was she looking for? Adventure? Love? Did she have a deep thirst for knowledge?

His curiosity about Fiona perplexed him. After all, she had shown no interest in him, and he was just a stranger passing through. What did it matter to him why she wanted to leave?

Or, for that matter, *that* she wanted to leave? It was her life. He had his own problems to worry about.

And then he met her warm, open gaze across the kitchen and knew that it did matter.

❖ 6 ❖

THE LIGHTHOUSE KITCHEN was a rectangular room with a black iron cookstove at one end, a sink and counter along the side and a fireplace at the other end. In between sat a long pine table surrounded by eight ladderback chairs. Cheerful red-and-white gingham curtains dressed the window over the sink and a short clay pot filled with white daisies and black-eyed susans graced the table. As simple as it was, Travis nevertheless found the room cozy and welcoming.

As he took the seat Finn indicated at the foot of the table, Travis became aware not only of Fiona's eyes on him, but also of six other pairs watching him. He glanced quickly at Fiona, saw her fold her hands and bow her head, and followed her example as Finn said a prayer from his chair at the head of the table.

"Well now," Finn said when he'd finished, "it's time you met the rest of my family, Mr. Paine. Of course you know Fiona to your right, and Carvey past her. Ena, my eldest, is next, and that's her husband, Boyne Murphy, across from her."

"Call me Murph," the thin, balding man said with a grin. "Everyone does. I own the only furniture shop within sixty miles. Make it all myself, I do." He gave a nod of his head and looked at his wife Ena, who beamed proudly at him.

Finn continued. "Tullia Brody, my sister-in-law, is next,

and that's my youngest daughter, Dee, to your left, with little Jamie in his high chair beside her.''

Travis nodded and murmured a greeting to each one.

"Welcome to our table, Mr. Paine," Finn announced. "Ena, pass the food."

Travis watched each dish pass from one person to the next, traveling around the table to the right. The family conversed pleasantly and without interruption while the food made a complete circuit and was placed back in the middle. Even little Jamie, sitting in his tall, wooden chair, seemed happy to be there.

How different they were from his family. On those rare occasions when he and his brothers had been allowed to eat with their parents, servants in starched white aprons had served food from silver bowls. And, of course, no one had ever spoken, not even their mother, unless first spoken to by Jefferson Paine. Silence, cold and severe, had ruled the table.

"More potatoes, Mr. Paine?" Fiona asked him.

Travis glanced down at his plate, unaware that he had made a clean sweep of it. "Thank you."

She handed him the bowl and Travis took another helping. The food was simple yet delicious, and he soon found himself asking for more chicken. He tried to pay attention to the conversations swirling around him, but watching Fiona interact with her family was much more interesting. She was arguing with her aunt, whose name Travis had completely forgotten, about taking charge of some kind of production. Neither woman was giving an inch, yet there seemed to be no animosity between them. He'd never seen anyone argue without getting angry.

The aunt suddenly turned her head to include Travis in the conversation. "Have you ever heard of the Festival of Lughnasa, Mr. Paine?"

Damn it, what was her name? Twyla? Tilly? He decided not to risk it. "No, ma'am. I've never heard of it."

"It's our harvest festival," the lady replied. "An old Irish tradition."

Fiona explained further. "It's a celebration of the first fruits of the season. We hold it every August. And *Aunt Tullia* is in charge of the entertainment.''

Tullia! That was it. Travis gave Fiona a sidelong glance, wondering if she had emphasized *Aunt Tullia* for his benefit.

''Fiona directed *The Legend of Sleepy Hollow* last year,'' Tullia explained, ''and did such a splendid job that everyone is counting on her to do it again this year.''

''*Everyone* is only yourself, Auntie,'' Fiona replied firmly.

''But someone must take charge,'' Tullia insisted. ''You've a strong voice and solid constitution, Fiona. You're the best of the lot.''

''Ask Devlin to do it,'' Fiona countered. ''No one will argue with him.''

Tullia waved away her idea. ''Devlin is much too busy these days. He's been traveling into Chicago to conduct his business. Why, the poor boy says he has no time for his *own* leisure activities, let alone for the festival.''

Finn's gray eyebrows drew together. ''What kind of business does Devlin have in Chicago?''

''I don't pry, Finn,'' Tullia snapped. ''If Devlin wants me to know, he'll tell me.''

Travis could see angry sparks fly between Tullia and Finn as the two glared at each other. He felt a light touch on his arm and turned his head. Fiona leaned toward him and said quietly, ''They're always at it, those two. You'd never know that they actually have a great respect for one another.''

As she spoke, Travis stared at her, thinking he'd never tire of looking into her eyes. They held such vibrance and warmth, such openness and honesty. He wondered what it would feel like to have those eyes look at him with love.

His nostrils flared. The violet scent Fiona wore stirred his blood and made him want to touch her, to stroke her creamy skin. A blush suddenly colored her cheeks, letting him know she was as aware of him as he was of her. Travis looked away, knowing he had embarrassed her.

''You'll have to come to our festival, Mr. Paine,'' Tullia continued, as though there had been no pause in the conversation. ''It's a little over three weeks away.''

''It's ever so much fun,'' Deirdre added, her light blue eyes shining with excitement. "We have contests and games, dancing, food, plays, races and—"

"Ponies!" Jamie shouted, clapping his hands in glee, which brought laughter from everyone, including Travis. But he immediately sobered, remembering the reason he was sitting in their kitchen in the first place.

"I doubt that I'll still be here. I have to get back to Erie." His stomach knotted at the thought of having to face his father.

"Is that where the shipping company is located?" Murph asked.

Travis pushed the last piece of chicken around on his plate, his appetite suddenly gone. "Yes, it is."

"Jamie, hold still a minute." Deirdre held her son's chin while she wiped it clean. "You must be eager to see your family, Mr. Paine."

Sparing him an untruthful reply to Deirdre's statement, Ena asked, "Are you going to the memorial service?"

"Of course he is," Fiona replied sharply, and turned the subject to something else, but not before Travis witnessed the annoyed look she shot her sister.

In his room that evening, Travis stood at the window staring at the deserted beach below, thinking about Fiona's sharp reply. He wanted to believe she had been trying to spare him further discomfort, but it was also possible that he was reading too much into her actions, that she'd had her own reasons for turning the subject away from the shipwreck, though he couldn't imagine what they could be.

A figure dressed in white suddenly stepped from the shadows below and moved down the dune toward the water. He recognized Fiona immediately by her graceful movements and long flowing hair, and realized that he had been standing at the window in the hopes of catching a glimpse of her.

"What a fool I am," he muttered and turned away. He couldn't understand his sudden interest in her. Was it the thrill of the hunt? The novelty of discovering a woman who didn't want to be courted? Or was it merely a matter of manly pride that she hadn't seemed the least bit interested in him?

He sat down on the bed, took off his shoes and scowled at his feet. He had to stop thinking about Fiona and start thinking about his ship. He knew he should have contacted his father to let him know the full extent of it, but he couldn't give Jefferson an accurate report until he'd been out to see the damage himself.

With muttered curses, Travis eased himself onto the bed and lay back on the pillow. After the memorial service, he would borrow a boat and get out to the ship to assess the damage. He would not think any more about Fiona Cleary.

Fiona wrapped her arms around her legs, rested her chin on her bent knees and gazed out at the horizon. The sun was little more than a red glow in the west. A gentle breeze stirred her hair and the cool sand felt good under her feet.

In one more day it would be the first of August, bringing her another month closer to leaving New Clare. She wished she had someone with whom she could share her excitement, but none of her family wanted to think about her leaving, let alone hear her plans.

And what plans she had! Fiona sighed contentedly, imagining herself on a train chugging eastward. She'd get off where she felt like it, explore cities at her whim, until she reached the coast. From there she would decide where to go next. The only flaw in her plan was that eventually she would run out of money. At that point she would have to make a choice—either find work wherever she happened to be, or go back to New Clare.

Unless. . . .

Fiona sighed again, indulging herself in her private fantasy where a handsome stranger traveling east falls madly in love with her and sweeps her off to all the faraway places she's always wanted to see. She closed her eyes and smiled, picturing herself and her fantasy lover strolling arm-in-arm through the streets of Paris, stopping in a little out-of-the-way cafe to drink French coffee together, staring across the table into each other's eyes.

All at once Fiona's eyes opened wide and she sat up

straight. Her handsome stranger had somehow acquired a face. The face was Travis Paine's.

"Fiona, you're a dreamer," she said angrily. "Imagine falling for the likes of Travis Paine! He's a sailin' man—it's in his blood—and you'll be wise not to get any foolish notions about him!" She rose, brushed off her skirt and started back toward the lighthouse.

From the beach she could see a light in the window of the room where Travis was staying. It brought to mind the conversation around the dinner table and she remembered how Travis seemed to pull inside himself at any mention of his family. Clearly there was discord among his family members, but she could not imagine a family turning on one of its own. It was unthinkable.

Ena *would* have to bring up the shipwreck. Fiona shook her head. Sometimes it seemed she was the only one of her sisters who had any sense at all. In truth, the thought of leaving her father in their hands often made her uneasy. Deirdre would soon have two youngsters to care for. Would she be able to manage if her father fell ill? In case of an emergency, could Ena be counted on to help?

"If I think like that I'll never leave New Clare," Fiona chided herself. Once she was gone, it would be their concern, not hers.

When she climbed the stairs to the second floor, Fiona saw light shining from beneath the door to Travis's room and she couldn't help but take pity on him. Travis Paine was a man used to action. Forced confinement would not sit easily with him. She took a book from her room and tapped lightly on his door.

"Come in."

Fiona opened the door and peeked inside. Travis was lying with his hands behind his head, still fully dressed, staring at the ceiling. He seemed surprised to see her and pushed himself to a sitting position.

"I brought you something to read, Mr. Paine. I know it must be frustrating for you to sit up here twiddling your thumbs." She walked to the bed and handed him the book.

Travis turned it over and read the cover, then looked up at

her curiously. "It's a travel book. Do you like to travel, Miss Cleary?"

"I surely hope so."

How warm his gaze has become of late, she remarked to herself, *so different from his first days at the lighthouse.* He was, indeed, a handsome man. She stared at him a moment longer and suddenly realized she was picturing him sitting across from her in a little French cafe, gazing at her adoringly, holding her hand and murmuring words intended for her ears only. With a blush stinging her cheeks, she backed toward the door. "I—I have more books when you finish that one."

"How was your walk?"

"My walk?"

He glanced at the window. "I saw you on the beach this evening."

"Fine. It was a fine walk." Fiona's whole face felt as if it were on fire. He had been watching her from his window. "Just fine," she muttered and quickly left his room, pulling his door shut behind her. She stood in the dark hallway with her hand over her heart, wondering why it should be racing. She felt her cheeks; they were hot to the touch. Mother Mary, what was happening to her?

"God bless you, my son."

Somberly, Travis shook the priest's hand and walked down the church steps to the surrey waiting a short distance up the road. Finn was sitting in the front with Jamie and Deirdre beside him. Carvey and Fiona sat on the back bench. Fiona had made room for Travis next to her.

Travis stopped on the wooden sidewalk beside the surrey and gazed up the road ahead of him. "I'd like to walk back, if you don't mind."

"I understand, Mr. Paine," Finn said somberly.

Travis walked away, unable to say more. The memorial service had been moving to the point of being unendurable. And though the townspeople had taken him to their bosoms and consoled him with words born of their own tragedies, he still ached with grief and bitter rage. He wanted to shout curses to the heavens and cry like a baby, but he could do neither. Long years of suppressing his emotions had taken their toll.

The surrey creaked as it passed him. Travis watched it start north up Wexford toward the lake. He sighed wearily, remembering that he had intended to get out to the ship. In truth, he didn't think he could stomach seeing the deserted, ruined vessel.

Travis crossed the street to the bank. Ahead, Fiona stood in front of one of the buildings along Wexford, her face partially hidden by the shadow of her black straw hat. Her charcoal-gray dress with its ecru collar and cuffed, elbow-length sleeves was appropriately subdued.

"Would you mind if I walked with you, Mr. Paine?" she asked solemnly as he came up to her.

Travis knew she had given up her ride because she was feeling sorry for him and that only made him angrier. "Do I have a choice?" he grumbled.

Fiona came to a sudden stop, but Travis continued on. He knew he had no call to take his anger out on her. She had only followed her conscience. He looked back at her and remorse ate at him. She was walking ten feet behind him. Her back was straight, her hands in their ecru gloves were curled tightly at her sides, her chin was tilted at a defiant angle and her eyes stared past him. She was hurt, but she wasn't about to let him know it.

Guiltily, Travis stopped and waited for her, his hands deep in his pockets, his head bent. He fell into step beside her and they walked in silence. In truth, he was in no mood for conversation and hated to even try, for fear of saying something again that would hurt her. He wished she had gone on with her family; it would have spared them both this discomfort.

Yet, after a time, he had to admit that her quiet presence was somehow soothing to his raw emotions.

That thought made him pause. Travis had never before viewed a woman as a soothing presence. His past dalliances with the opposite sex had been just that—dalliances, pleasant diversions, an outlet for normal male needs. As for his mother, he and his brothers were never sure how she would react from one moment to the next. Most of the time she simply locked herself away in her room—hardly a soothing presence. Hardly a presence at all.

He glanced covertly at Fiona and couldn't help but admire her. She radiated determination and a quiet, inner strength rare for someone her age. *The glue that keeps this family together* was how the doctor had described her. It seemed a fitting portrayal. And she had given up her ride because she felt sorry for him.

A part of him wished it were for more of a reason than that. Nevertheless, he felt like a heel for the way he had snapped at her. He rubbed the back of his neck. "Miss Cleary—"

"You needn't say anything, Mr. Paine," Fiona cut in, her voice brisk and businesslike. "I know it's been a trying day for you."

"Miss Cleary, I owe you an apology."

"I should have left you alone. It seems I'm always butting in where I shouldn't."

"Even so, *I* shouldn't have—"

"You have every right to be angry with me."

Travis grabbed Fiona by the arm and pulled her to a stop. "Would you stop making excuses for my behavior and let me apologize? I was wrong to snap at you, damn it, and I'm sorry!" Travis clenched his jaw and swore silently. He had done it again.

But rather than getting angry and pulling away from him, Fiona dipped her head and covered her mouth to hide a grin, as though she found the situation humorous, which, in fact, it was in a perverse way.

Travis couldn't stop a grin from spreading across his own face. He released his hold on her arm and they began to walk once again. And for some reason he felt some of the grayness lift from around him.

A buggy passed by. "Our condolences, Mr. Paine," the gentleman inside called to him.

"That's Brian Kelly, our newspaper editor," Fiona whispered. "He's a member of the rescue team, as well."

Travis nodded politely to the man. "Thank you, Mr. Kelly."

''Yoo-hoo, Mr. Paine!''

Travis winced at the high singsong voice. He glanced around to see a brown and yellow carriage pull up even with them. Bridget Riley leaned out one of the windows and waved her handkerchief. ''Yoo-hoo!''

Travis gave her a nod. ''Hello, Miss Riley.''

Fiona leaned around Travis and smiled sweetly. ''Morning, Bridget.''

The handkerchief drooped. ''Oh, hello, Fiona. Wasn't the service just lovely, Mr. Paine?''

''Very moving.''

Bridget ducked her head inside and Travis could see her having a discussion with the carriage's occupants, whom he assumed to be her parents.

''She's about to ask you to dinner,'' Fiona warned him.

''How do I get out of it?'' he asked *sotto voce*.

Fiona glanced at him curiously. ''You don't want to have dinner with Bridget?''

''I'm not very good company at the moment.''

''Really? I hadn't noticed.''

Travis shot her a disgruntled look.

Fiona blithely ignored it. ''I suppose you'll have to make up something then.''

''Yoo-hoo, Mr. Paine!''

Travis winced again, but forced a smile when he turned toward the carriage.

''Would you care to join us for dinner, Mr. Paine?'' Bridget called.

''I would love to, Miss Riley.''

Travis glanced at Fiona to see that her mouth had dropped open. He smiled to himself. Maybe she was a little jealous after all.

❖ 7 ❖

"YOU'LL COME TO dinner?" Bridget clapped her hands in glee. "Oh, that's wonderful!"

"I'd love to, Miss Riley," Travis continued, "but we'll have to make it for some other time. I'd already planned to inspect my ship this afternoon. It was kind of you to invite me."

For an instant Bridget's face fell, then she forced her practiced smile. "I'll hold you to it, Mr. Paine." She leaned back inside, her mouth drawn up petulantly as the carriage pulled ahead of them.

"Quick thinking," Fiona remarked.

Travis glanced at her, but couldn't decide if she was relieved or not. He rubbed the back of his neck. "The truth is, I *do* need to get out to the ship. I wasn't in the mood for it, but there's no sense putting it off. I'll need to get her repaired, if possible, and get back to Erie. Is there a rowboat I can borrow?"

She gave him a skeptical glance. "Are you sure you're up to it?"

"I feel fine."

Fiona didn't look convinced. "We can take one of the rescue gigs."

"*We*?"

"Yes, Mr. Paine. You and I," Fiona replied, "unless you

fear I'll push you over the side. Knowing that you trust your own gender more, I can understand your reluctance.''

Travis sighed. She was never going to forgive him for the shaving incident. ''You misunderstood me, Miss Cleary. I meant only that men are more experienced in shaving since they do it every day.''

''And how would you know whether or not a woman shaved her husband or father every day?''

Travis realized it was useless to argue. He gave a resigned shrug. ''I wouldn't.''

''Then tell me about Erie.''

Her quick switch of subjects momentarily flustered him. ''It's just a city like any other city, I suppose.''

''Is it anything like New Clare?''

''It's nothing like New Clare. Of course, New Clare is nothing like any city I've ever visited.''

''You don't like New Clare?''

''You know, Miss Cleary, I find your habit of turning my words around particularly annoying.''

Fiona's eyes sparkled with mischievous intent. ''I see. Then you like New Clare. It's just me you find annoying.''

A muscle twitched in his jaw. ''Why don't I tell you about Erie?''

Travis began to describe his hometown in as much detail as possible, trying to paint a picture in her mind. Despite his earlier annoyance, he found he enjoyed the way Fiona listened so attentively, as though each word he uttered were of the utmost importance.

When he finished, she questioned him at some length and then in a resolute voice said, ''I'm going to see Pennsylvania, you know, and many other places as well, just as soon as I can get away from New Clare.''

They halted at the bottom of the stone path that led up to the lighthouse, and Travis studied her determined profile. ''Why are you so set on leaving?''

''There's nothing for me here. But out there,'' Fiona said, gesturing toward the east with a wide sweep of her arm, ''the whole world is waiting to be experienced.''

''What of marriage, a family of your own? Surely you have

a beau in town, or a sailor who comes into port.'' He watched her closely.

"Marry a sailor and you marry the seas.'' She shook her head. "That's not the life for me. I've got my plans made.'' She turned her head to look at him and he could see the excitement dancing in her eyes. "I'm going to see it all, you know—Dublin, London, Paris, Rome, Athens—by all the shamrocks in Ireland, I swear I will.''

She was so achingly beautiful in her determination that his heart swelled with envy. How he yearned to feel so passionate about life, to have such fervent desires. Surely at one time he had felt that way. What had happened to him?

Fiona sighed. "I haven't the money to travel to Europe just yet, so I'll start here first—Chicago, Boston, New York—''

"You'll have to see Niagara Falls.''

"Have you been there?'' she asked excitedly.

"Many times. It's not far from Erie.''

Her eyes deepened in color and her mouth curved up in a wistful smile. "Tell me what it's like.''

"Well, it's like—'' Travis paused, searching for a way to describe the falls to her. He closed his eyes, and in his mind's eye, pictured it as he had first seen it, as a child of eight. "It's like nothing you've ever seen before, or could even imagine. It's a whole river pouring over a high, rocky, U-shaped ledge—for all of eternity—with mist from all that falling water rising over a hundred feet in the air and the noise so loud you have to shout to be heard above it. And when the sun shines through the mist just right, you can see a rainbow arching so far out over the falls you think it must surely reach halfway around the world.''

Fiona pressed her hands to her cheeks and stared straight ahead, as if awed by the very thought of such a fantastic sight. "It must be wondrous to behold,'' she whispered. Travis wished suddenly that he could be the one to show her the falls, that he could experience the excitement of seeing it through her eyes.

By the lighthouse, Fiona paused once again to gaze out at the lake, still caught up in her dreams. He heard her sigh, and then she turned to look up at him. "Thank you, Mr. Paine,'' she said sincerely, as though he had done her a tremendous favor.

Travis gazed down into Fiona's eyes and thought again how lovely they were, so warm and vibrant, so full of expectations. His gaze traveled over the smooth contours of her face, with its delicate cheekbones and creamy skin, to her lips, so soft and supple—and innocent. With any other woman he would have pulled her against him and tasted those sweet lips. With Fiona, he jammed his hands into his pockets to keep from touching her. It seemed criminal to do otherwise.

With great reluctance he tore his gaze away and turned to look down on the town. "You said you could get me a boat."

"I'll change my clothing and meet you down at the docks in a quarter of an hour," she told him.

Travis heard the door open and close. He watched the tiny figure of a horse and buggy move slowly up Wexford to Kilkenny and stop before the steepled white church. He thought of the warm reception the townspeople had given him that morning and the family meal he had attended with the Clearys the day before. For a second he imagined himself living in New Clare, with a family to come home to each night and a wife to greet him at the door. But it wasn't just any wife he pictured. It was Fiona.

Travis shook the image out of his mind and headed down to the water. Fiona had no time for sailors and he had no time for fanciful daydreams. If he ever hoped to earn command of his own ship, he had work to do.

And Jefferson Paine to face.

Fiona sat on the bench in front of Travis and watched him struggle to row the boat. By the set of his face she could tell he had strained his mending ribs.

"St. Christopher's stockings! Your pride will be the death of you yet." Fiona rose, arms akimbo. "Up with you now. If you snap those ribs again you'll be abed a month or longer."

Travis clenched his teeth and continued to row. Beads of sweat dotted his forehead and the front of his white shirt was plastered to his chest. "I can manage."

His stubbornness infuriated her. "And so can I, or don't you believe a female can pull a set of oars?"

Throwing Fiona an irritated look, Travis dropped the oars and traded places with her, turning away from her so he faced the *Thomas E. Paine* in the distance. She studied him curiously as she rolled up the sleeves of her light blue cotton dress, wondering what it was that made him so fiercely prideful that he couldn't admit he needed help.

"May I ask you a question, Mr. Paine?"

"Do I have a choice?" he grumbled.

"Is it your father you despise?"

Travis's head jerked around and his eyes turned cold. "I've never said anything to you about my feelings for my father."

Undaunted, Fiona continued to row. "It wasn't what you said, but what you didn't say."

He gave her a disgruntled look. "And what was that?"

"All I know is that if I were in a shipwreck, the first thing I would do would be to let my father know I was all right or not all right, depending on my condition."

"He got my telegram. He knew I was all right."

Fiona slanted him a disbelieving glance from beneath the wide brim of her straw hat. "Did he now?"

"Let me put your mind at ease, Miss Cleary. My father's only concern will be whether the ship can be repaired and how much we've lost in damaged cargo. My mother won't even be aware of the wreck, or, if she is, she won't give a damn. My two brothers will heave sighs of frustration and shake their heads in regret while secretly reveling in my disgrace."

Fiona paused in her rowing to glare at him. "That's a terrible thing to say about the people who love you!"

Travis chuckled dryly. "You've led a sheltered life, Miss Cleary. Being part of a family doesn't guarantee you love—or acceptance."

She started rowing again in long, furious strokes. "No one's family can be that hard-hearted."

"Don't get me wrong. My brothers aren't bad fellows. They've merely become adept at doing whatever it takes to please my father. If that includes shunning me, then so be it."

"And you? Do you try to please your father?"

"No, in fact, I've always managed to displease him. No matter what I did, it was never good enough." Travis picked up a smooth, flat, black stone lying in the bottom of the boat and rubbed it slowly between his thumb and fingers. "For a time I convinced myself that it didn't matter, that I could enjoy life, live it to the fullest, without his approval. But every time I went home for a visit, there were my brothers, prosperous ship captains, doing everything right and basking in it. And there I was, a profligate, a rakehell, the black sheep of the family, disgracing the fine, upstanding name of Paine."

With a flick of his wrist, Travis tossed the stone over the side of the boat. "So here I am right where I started, vying for my father's approval and never quite getting it right."

For a while, the gentle swoosh of the oars and the shrill cries of the gulls overhead were the only sounds to be heard. Lost in thought, Fiona barely noticed the slow trickle of perspiration between her breasts. *How sad for them all—for the father who cannot love his sons just for themselves, for the mother who cannot see beyond her own selfish needs, and for the three sons who have never known the warmth and acceptance of family.* Her heart went out to Travis. The anger that was always so close to the surface was, in fact, self-loathing. She recalled the words he'd said aloud when he thought no one was listening and wondered if he really believed them.

"It was only what they expected of me."

"Do you truly believe your family expected you to wreck the ship?" she asked suddenly.

Travis cocked an eyebrow. "You have a good memory."

"You could be wrong, you know."

"About your memory?"

She gave him a piqued look. "About your family."

Travis smiled, but the smile didn't reach his eyes. "I could be. But I'm not."

The lake was smooth and it didn't take long for Fiona to cover the distance from the pier to the big steamer. She rowed alongside the damaged vessel and dropped anchor. Though he was still in some pain, Travis managed to climb the rope ladder thrown over the side of the ship and hold out a hand at the top to help Fiona on board.

The ship was listing to the starboard side, making it impossible for Fiona to walk without bracing herself against something. Determinedly, she followed Travis around the deck while he inspected the damage, but he stopped her when she started down into the main hold after him.

"Wait here," he commanded.

"Why?"

"It might be flooded."

Fiona watched with a frown as he disappeared into the darkness below. "Then you shouldn't go down either," she called.

Silence was her only answer. Disregarding his mandate, Fiona proceeded down the steep steps, holding the walls on either side to keep her balance. "And who will have to bring you meals on a tray if you hurt yourself again?"

"Stay up there!" Travis barked from somewhere below. "That's an order, Miss Cleary!"

"You're not my captain, Mr.—"

The vessel suddenly rolled slightly, throwing Fiona off balance. She pitched forward, only to be caught by a pair of strong arms and set on her feet. She looked up at Travis, her heart still racing from the scare. In the dim light she could barely make out his rugged features, but she could feel his dark gaze searching her face. Then she saw a flash of white teeth and knew he was smiling. Or was he gloating?

"Now you see why I said to wait up on deck." He turned her around and pushed her to the narrow wooden steps. "Up you go."

A quarter of an hour later, Fiona was sitting at the top of the opening waiting impatiently, her chin propped on her palm, her toe tapping a rapid staccato. What if Travis slipped and fell and reinjured his ribs so badly he couldn't call for help? How would she know?

She wouldn't. That was the whole problem. With a determined huff, Fiona stood up and began to move quietly down the steps.

"I thought I told you to stay above!"

Fiona gasped. She had been so intent on watching her footing she hadn't heard Travis start up the steps toward her.

She lifted her chin defiantly. "I thought you might need my help."

"Don't think so much, Miss Cleary."

Fiona shot him an icy look. She turned and was starting back up the steps when the vessel shifted again, causing her to teeter precariously. Travis's arms slipped around her waist to steady her, and for just a moment, he held her tightly against him. "Are you all right?" he asked, his voice husky in her ear.

Feeling the iron hardness of his torso through the thin cotton material of her dress and the strong arms that bound her against him, Fiona's pulse leaped wildly and she found herself suddenly breathless. "Fine," she squeaked.

Travis helped her up onto the main deck, then stood with his hands on his hips and his legs braced for balance, looking around the ship. "She's taken a beating, but she's salvageable. I'll have to hire a crew to tow her off the sandbar first thing tomorrow."

Fiona couldn't seem to concentrate on what he was saying. The memory of his arms around her, of his deep, husky voice in her ear, even of his scent, left her feeling weak-kneed and confused. She gave him a surreptitious glance to see if he had been similarly affected, but he seemed more intent on the particulars of his vessel.

Travis made his way to the side of the ship, then turned to look back at her. "Ready to go?"

Fiona nodded, trying to maintain a casual air. Travis helped her over the side, then waited until she was in the rowboat before following her down. He gave her no argument when she took up the oars, so she knew his ribs were still hurting. She rowed with all her might, wanting to get back to shore quickly to distance herself from him, praying he would think the flush of her cheeks was merely due to her exertion.

Why had his touch affected her so? It certainly wasn't because she liked him, for she didn't. Not at all. She couldn't abide men who were arrogant and rude, even if there was some reason to pity them.

And why in the name of St. Peter hadn't *Travis* been affected by their encounter?

She wouldn't let it happen to her again, no matter how sorry she felt for him.

Fiona was not to escape Travis's presence as quickly as she had hoped. Once they reached land, Travis asked to inspect the cargo stored in the warehouse. After returning home for the key, Fiona pushed back one of the huge double doors and led him inside the massive structure. Windows cut high in the two-story walls illuminated tall columns of wooden crates stacked in neat rows that filled one-fourth of the interior.

Travis walked between the rows of crates, stopping here and there to read the lettering on the sides. For a time he was lost from sight, then he came walking toward her, an angry, mistrustful look on his face. "Where's the rest of my cargo?"

Fiona gave him a puzzled look. "The rest? Isn't it all here?"

"Does this," he replied, gesturing toward the stacks of crates, "look like it would fill the hold of my ship?"

Fiona bristled. "I'm hardly the one to judge since I wasn't allowed down in your silly hold in the first place."

"What's here is less than a third of what was on the ship, and most of this is damaged." He faced her once again, and she could see the unspoken accusation in his eyes. "Who was responsible for unloading my cargo, Miss Cleary?"

"My cousin, Tom Brody, but he wouldn't—"

Travis spun around and walked out.

❖ 8 ❖

"WHAT DO YOU intend to do, Mr. Paine?"

Travis's stride was brisk and furious as they headed back up the pier toward the lighthouse. Fiona had to hurry to stay even with him.

"I intend to see your cousin Tom Brody."

"Do you now? And just how do you think you'll find him?"

"You're going to take me to him, Miss Cleary."

"Not by your orders, Mr. Paine. By request or not at all."

A muscle twitched in Travis's jaw and when he finally spoke, Fiona could see that it was with great reluctance. "Will you take me to see your cousin, Miss Cleary?"

"I'll let you know."

Travis took hold of her arm as she turned to go up the stone path to the lighthouse. "I *have* to find the missing cargo," he stated. "Do you understand?"

How dare he treat her as if she were simpleminded! Fiona's eyes narrowed into icy slits. "I'm not stupid, Mr. Paine. Before I tell you I can go this moment, I'll first see if I'm needed here or if anyone needs anything from town. Do *you* understand, Mr. Paine?"

Travis searched her face for a moment; then his expression changed, as if he realized he had gone too far. He released his hold on her arm. Without a word, Fiona marched up to the lighthouse and slipped inside, muttering under her breath about his lack of manners. In truth, however, it wasn't Travis's rudeness that concerned her, but the missing cargo. She prayed Tommy would have an answer.

But Tom Brody was just as puzzled as she was.

"I'm sorry, Mr. Paine, we unloaded what we found in the hold and that was what you saw in the warehouse."

Travis frowned as Tom stopped his work over the anvil to mop his glistening brow with a big red handkerchief. His curly brown hair was damp from his labor and his arms had a sheen of perspiration on them.

Tom's smithy shop had an open front to let in the breeze, yet the temperature inside was nearly unbearable. Fiona felt a trickle of sweat run down her spine and pulled her own handkerchief from her sleeve to pat her neck dry.

"What's in the warehouse is barely a third of the cargo we were carrying," Travis told him. "I checked the ship myself. Other than water damage, the hold was secure. The cargo could not have floated away. Either it never made it to the warehouse or someone removed it."

Tom thumped his barrel-shaped chest. "*I* supervised the unloading of your cargo myself. Everything that was in the hold went straight to the warehouse and I'll swear it on the Holy Bible if you like."

Fiona knew by Travis's expression that he thought Tommy was lying, and that infuriated her. "There has to be an explanation," she insisted. "Perhaps you've forgotten how much was being transported, Mr. Paine, or perhaps you unloaded some in another port."

"Or perhaps," Travis said in a steely voice, gazing steadily at Tom, "it was stolen."

Tom turned an angry red and balled his meaty, work-roughened hands into fists. Fiona knew her cousin well enough to guess what he had in mind and decided she should intervene before someone got hurt. "Mr. Paine, my cousin is the only one who has access to the key to the warehouse, other than Carvey and my father, and you'll not find a more honest fellow alive than our Tom Brody."

"Thank you, Fiona," Tom muttered grudgingly.

"You're welcome, Tommy."

Travis threw her an exasperated glance. "I can see I won't get any answers here."

Fiona stared at Travis's back as he strode out of the black-smith's shop. "What do you think, Tommy?"

Tom Brody scratched his head. "It's a puzzle to me, Fiona. Most likely he hit his head harder than he thought."

"Yes," Fiona mused, "that has to be it. He just doesn't remember."

"We've got to keep the ship from drifting any farther south, Mr. Calloway. We can weather the gale as long as we don't hit a sandshelf."

"I'll give it my best, sir."

Travis tossed restlessly in his sleep, twisting the sheet around his body as he relived the nightmare of the storm. The night air was humid and still. He kicked away the cloying cover and slipped deeper into his dream.

"How far are we from land?"

"Can't say, sir. We can't be close, though, or we'd have seen a light."

Travis's eyes snapped open and he sat up in bed, his heart pounding, his body drenched in sweat. Now he understood why Calloway had been wrong.

There had been no light.

For the third morning in a row, Travis joined the Clearys for breakfast. But that morning there was a subtle difference. Fiona sensed the change the minute Travis sat down at the table. His expression was remote and his dark eyes seemed to scrutinize each person at the table, as if trying to uncover their secrets.

Carvey and her father were already digging into their fried eggs, sopping up the creamy yolk with freshly baked and toasted oat bread. Fiona set a platter of ham on the table and turned back to the stove, where she had more eggs cooking. Travis reached for a slice of the succulent meat as Deirdre set out cups of coffee for everyone.

"Sleep well, Mr. Paine?" Finn Cleary asked.

"Adequately, thanks," Fiona heard him reply. "I want you to know I've wired home for money. I'd like to pay you for my room and board."

Her father seemed both embarrassed and upset by the offer. "You're a guest here, Mr. Paine, not a boarder."

"Still, I can't continue to accept your hospitality without compensating you."

There was a moment of silence, then her father said in a solemn voice, "You owe us nothing, lad. Your gratitude is all the compensation we'll accept."

Fiona glanced around at Travis to see his reaction and decided he didn't look at all convinced. She saw Carvey give her father a furtive look, then quickly drop his gaze, his ears turning a bright red. Puzzled by his odd behavior, Fiona dished the eggs onto a serving platter and sat down beside Deirdre, who was cutting Jamie's meat.

"Is something bothering Carvey?" she asked quietly.

"He seemed fine earlier," Deirdre responded with an unconcerned shrug. "Eat your ham, Jamie. Oh, Fiona, we're getting low on coffee."

"I'll pick some up in town today."

Travis finished his food, leaned back in his chair and turned toward Finn. "It must be rough being on duty all night up in the tower."

Finn shook his graying head. " 'Tisn't easy, that's true, which is why I don't do it anymore. I'm too old. Carvey tends the beacon at night nowadays, and before him, our Fiona helped me with it."

"So Carvey was on duty the night of the shipwreck?"

Carvey's fork halted in midair, then slowly he lowered it to his plate, as though he had lost his appetite. Finn answered in a somber voice, "In truth, Mr. Paine, that would have been me. Carvey came down with a stomach ailment during the night. I took over for him."

Deirdre hiccuped loudly, then burst into tears, which started Jamie howling in his high chair. Carvey scraped back his chair and went to comfort his wife while Finn tended to the little boy. For a second, Fiona's gaze clashed with Travis's, then she looked away. Why was he questioning them? What was it he was after?

A shiver ran up her spine as she suddenly remembered the words he'd murmured on the beach. *"The light was out."*

Travis couldn't possibly believe that. He was just searching for someone to blame for his misfortune. Her father would not have let the light go out.

Moments later calm descended once again upon the kitchen and everyone resumed eating. To Fiona's immense relief, Travis made no further mention of the shipwreck.

Travis stood in the shadows on the west side of the lighthouse watching Fiona as she hung freshly laundered bedding out to dry. As she worked, the light summer breeze snapped the corners of the white sheets and molded her pale green dress to her long legs. The sleeves of her dress were elbow length, revealing creamy forearms. Her auburn hair had been swept up loosely and tied with a ribbon, leaving long curling wisps to hang down her neck. She held two wooden clothespins between her lips and she was humming softly.

Travis took pleasure in watching her and could have stood there longer if he hadn't had more pressing concerns. He had just come from the warehouse where he had inspected the remainder of his cargo. Of the one hundred cases of spirits he had been transporting, not one was left. Only seventeen of the seventy-five crates of silk remained, and they were water damaged. Of the woolens, he found only twenty out of two hundred crates, and of the fifty crates of china, ten remained, filled with nothing but broken plates and cups.

Thousands of dollars of merchandise gone and a ship wrecked, and he was accountable. Travis rubbed the back of his neck, imagining the ugly scene when he finally had to face his father. He rolled his head to one side and then the other to relieve the tension in his neck muscles. If he could prove that the wreck hadn't been his fault and track down the missing goods, there was still a chance he could redeem himself.

But that was a big *if.*

His eyes narrowed as he watched Fiona. If it was true that

everything from the hold had made it to the warehouse, then only three people would have had access to it: Tom Brody, Carvey and Finn. Make that four, Travis reminded himself. Fiona herself had been the one to take him inside the building. Each had the opportunity to remove the goods, but which one had the motivation?

That question led to another that had been pushing its way to the forefront of his mind. Was it merely a coincidence that the light was out the night of the storm, or had someone engineered the wreck in order to make a tidy profit on the cargo?

The idea certainly wasn't a new one. Travis had often heard stories of the plundering of wrecked ships. By law, any cargo on an abandoned ship became the property of those who claimed it. However, since Travis had survived, the ship had not been abandoned. Whoever had taken the cargo had also broken the law.

Because of that, Travis knew he should report the theft to the authorities so they could take proper action. But in a town where half the population was related to the Clearys, he realized he had little chance of seeing justice served. He was better off investigating it himself. Once he had proof, the authorities would have no choice but to uphold the law.

So which one of the four suspects was the most likely culprit?

Carvey was a meek, almost timid soul, and new to the job of lighthouse keeper. It seemed unlikely he would do anything to jeopardize his new position.

As head of the rescue team, Tom Brody appeared to be nothing more than an honest, hardworking smithy, but how could Travis know for certain? Greed could do terrible things to a person's integrity.

And then there was Finn Cleary, who, on the surface, was a warmhearted, harmless old man. Yet Finn had been on duty the night of the wreck and could have put out the light on purpose. The only flaw in Travis's logic was that at Finn's age he would have needed help removing all those heavy crates from the warehouse. He'd have needed men with the strength to lift a case full of whiskey.

Or pull a set of oars through the water.

Travis saw Fiona glance at him over her shoulder and he knew she'd caught him staring. He pushed away from the wall and ambled toward her. Fiona was the last person on his list. He might as well start with her.

He took a wet sheet from the basket near Fiona's feet and handed one corner to her, stretching the other end out so she could more easily hang it. Fiona mumbled her thanks through the clothespins in her mouth, shooting him a wary glance.

"I was just down at the warehouse," he told her, watching her closely, "taking inventory. When I left Erie, I had one hundred cases of whiskey on board, yet now there's not one to be found. Interesting, isn't it, that not one single case survived the wreck?"

"Are you certain you were carrying spirits this trip?" she asked without looking at him.

"As certain as I'll ever be with no proof. The bill of lading was destroyed in the storm." He paused to pick up another sheet. "By the way, does the lighthouse keeper stay in the tower all night?"

Fiona plucked a clothespin from her lips and fastened the sheet to the line. "Not all night. The oil needs to be filled at midnight and checked again before dawn, usually around four in the morning. Only during bad weather would he stay in the tower all night."

"So it's possible that the light could go out after midnight and not be discovered until much later."

Fiona turned slowly to face him. "What are you saying, Mr. Paine?"

"There was no light the night of the shipwreck, Miss Cleary. I want to know why."

Her features seemed to freeze into place. "You're wrong, Mr. Paine. My father would never let the light go out. In fact, the light was *on* when I came down to the lake early that morning. I saw it with my own eyes. If you don't believe me, ask anyone who came in answer to the harbor bell's summons and they'll tell you the same."

"I'm sure they would, considering New Clare seems to be composed mainly of your relatives. I'd be a fool to think anyone in this town would admit it if your father were to blame for the wreck.''

Fiona snatched the empty basket from the grass and balanced it on one hip. ''My father has opened his house to you, Mr. Paine. Is this how you repay his hospitality? By accusing him of causing your shipwreck? Or is it that you can't accept responsibility for your own actions?''

At her stinging rebuke, so like his own father's, Travis's eyes narrowed and his teeth clenched. ''That light was *not* on, Miss Cleary, or we'd have been warned of the sandshelf in time to take action.''

''I don't have the time or inclination to debate the issue with you, Mr. Paine. Believe what you will.'' Fiona marched across the lawn and stepped into the house, closing the door behind her with an angry slam.

Travis glared at the door for a moment, then raked his fingers through his hair, trying to control his temper. ''Damn it, I know what I saw. There was no light.''

But how was he to prove it?

''Yoo-hoo!''

Travis turned at the familiar sound and saw Bridget strolling up the path toward him, her hips swaying provocatively in her pink and white large-checked dress. A matching parasol shaded her face from the sun.

Travis forced a pleasant smile. ''Good morning.''

''Morning, Mr. Paine.'' Bridget dipped her head and slanted her bright blue eyes at him. ''Fancy catching you outside when it was you I was coming to see in the first place.''

''Fancy that.''

Bridget linked her hand through Travis's elbow and smiled up at him. ''You promised to have dinner with me. I'm here to take you up on your offer.''

Travis assessed her thoughtfully. If there were any helpful tidbits of information to be learned about Finn Cleary, Carvey Gannon or Tom Brody, featherheaded Bridget would be the one to tell him.

''I would very much like to have dinner with you, Miss Riley. What time shall I be there?''

❖ 9 ❖

FIONA STOOD JUST inside the door, one hand on her racing heart, her breath coming in short bursts. Travis was wrong! By the kerosene in every lamp in New Clare, that light was *on* the night of the wreck.

She pushed away from the door and set the laundry basket in the pantry. Somehow Travis had to be convinced of her father's innocence. Fiona glanced around the kitchen as if it might hold an idea, then paced to the front door and back, her brow furrowed, the tip of her thumbnail between her teeth.

As she passed the window, a spot of bright pink caught her eye and she paused to peer through the glass. On the stone path leading up to the lighthouse stood Bridget, her face alight with joy, her hand resting familiarly on Travis's arm. Fiona's immediate reaction was anger at Bridget's bold pursuit of their guest, but then she reconsidered.

If there was one thing sure to get Travis's mind off the shipwreck, it was Bridget.

"Will you fancy that now?" Fiona said aloud. "I'm actually grateful to the likes of Bridget Riley."

Travis nodded and smiled at the passersby as he strolled through town with Bridget on his arm. He had been introduced to more people than he cared to remember and was beginning to feel like a freak in a sideshow. Bridget's preening and strutting annoyed him no end, and his temper was growing shorter by the minute. How did he ever think he could tolerate an entire meal with her?

They turned off Kilkenny onto Franklin Street and stopped before a two-story white frame house fronted by two giant maple trees. The house was surrounded by a white picket fence complete with a squeaking gate.

"Mama will be *so* pleased to see you," Bridget chirped.

Ye gods! Travis thought suddenly. An older version of Bridget. He could feel his neck muscles tightening.

Bridget's family didn't disappoint him. Not only was there Mama Riley to deal with, but also Papa Riley, who spent the whole dinner hour ingratiating himself with Travis. The poor couple seemed so desperate to marry Bridget off that Travis suspected they would gladly throw in a couple of head of cattle.

He rubbed his neck and smiled politely as Mama Riley sat beside him on a wine-red velvet sofa in the parlor after dinner and chattered on about her daughter's accomplishments. Papa Riley sat on the edge of a brown straight-backed chair pulled up so close he and Travis were nearly sitting knee to knee. In the background, Bridget played the piano and warbled "Bringing In the Sheaves."

Travis shook his head at the offer of a cigar, but accepted the whiskey with a grateful nod to Papa Riley. A glance through the parlor window showed it was nearly dusk and he still hadn't had a chance to question Bridget. As soon as she paused to turn the page, Travis jumped up.

"Miss Riley, it will be dark soon. Perhaps you'd like to take a short stroll in your garden before I have to leave."

Bridget twisted around on the stool and batted her eyes at him. "Oh, I'd simply love to, Mr. Paine!"

Her mother tittered behind her hand and Papa Riley clapped him on the back. "Come again soon, lad. We'd love to have you."

"Thank you for your hospitality. You've both been more than kind." Travis gave a short bow, then took Bridget's hand and placed it on his arm. "Shall we, Miss Riley?"

From the corner of his eye, Travis saw her parents clasp

each other's hands. He shuddered inwardly at the thought that was surely going through their minds: marriage.

The garden was a small square plot of rose bushes behind the house, with a flagstone path cut through the center and a stone bench situated in the middle. While Bridget arranged herself on the bench in an artful pose, Travis propped one booted foot on the corner, draped his arm across his knee and leaned toward her, flashing a smile guaranteed to charm the stinger from a bee, or so he'd been told.

"Have I told you how fetching you look tonight, Miss Riley?"

Bridget giggled and dipped her head. "No, but you certainly may, Mr. Paine."

"Surely you already know you're the prettiest flower in the garden."

She gazed up at him with her baby blues shining in adoration. "Oh, you say the sweetest things. Are all men from Erie so gentlemanly?"

"I guarantee at least one is." Travis was almost feeling sorry for Bridget. She was too easy a target. He sat down on the bench and swiveled to face her. "I'll wager your friends are green with envy."

"Why is that?" she asked, batting golden eyelashes at him.

"You surely outshine every one of them. Of course, to be fair, I haven't met any of your friends but Deirdre Gannon, and she's rather—encumbered right now."

"Yes, poor Dee. But you're right, Mr. Paine." Bridget heaved a melodramatic sigh. "It *is* hard to keep a friend. Females can be such jealous creatures."

"Then I suppose you're lucky to have a friend like Dee."

Bridget smiled fondly. "Deirdre doesn't have a jealous bone in her body—" She paused to mutter spitefully. "—unlike Fiona."

Travis pretended not to hear her little jibe. "I suppose coming from good parents helps."

Bridget pursed her lips and cast him a secretive glance. "Perhaps that's true on their mother's side. . . ."

Travis lifted one eyebrow. "But not on their father's side?"

Bridget leaned closer and dropped her voice. "In truth, Mr. Paine, the Brodys considered Finn Cleary common. Tullia never did get over Fiona's mother marrying him."

"He seems a decent man to me."

"Decent, yes . . . *now.*"

Travis smiled to himself. His instincts about Bridget had been correct. "I can't believe Finn Cleary would ever do anything indecent, Miss Riley."

Bridget drew a figure eight on the bench with one finger-nail, lightly, almost carelessly, brushing the side of Travis's pant leg. "And what about you, Mr. Paine? Would you ever do anything—indecent?"

The invitation in her eyes was so blatant that, had Travis been female, he would have blushed. Instead, he tried to lead her back to the subject. "That, I suppose, would depend on your definition of *indecent.* Now in Finn Cleary's case—"

Bridget crossed her arms over her chest with a frustrated huff. "I don't want to talk about Finn Cleary or Fiona Cleary or Dee or any of the Clearys. Next thing I know you'll be asking me all about the last shipwreck or—"

Travis sat up straighter. "Last shipwreck?"

Briget glared at him. "See what I mean?"

He laughed. "You're absolutely right. We should be talk-ing about those gorgeous blue eyes of yours." He picked up one of Bridget's white, short-fingered hands and gazed deep into her eyes. "I can't seem to decide. Are they the color of bluebells or a robin's egg?"

Bridget blushed prettily and giggled. "Oh, Mr. Paine, I do so enjoy your company!"

"And I yours. Unfortunately, I must leave you now. I have to be up early tomorrow to start on the ship repairs."

Bridget pursed her lips. Travis rose and gave her a gallant bow. "Until the next time, Miss Riley."

"Come again soon," he heard her call as he let himself out of the gate. "Mama and I shall play our duet for you."

A shiver rippled down Travis's spine. That was a scene he didn't want to contemplate. What he did want, however, was to find out more about the shipwreck Bridget had mentioned, such as when it had occurred and under what circumstances.

He stopped at the telegraph office to send two wires: one to his father to let him know the physical condition of the *Thomas E. Paine*; and a second wire to Bob Haskell, the shipping company's office manager. If anyone would be able to gather information about a shipwreck, it was Bob. He knew all the insurance companies' investigators.

Travis realized he was acting on a hunch, but his hunches had paid off in the past. In fact, if he'd listened to his gut feelings instead of to Calloway on the night of the storm, his ship might be intact today.

"Where have you been, Fiona? I'm hungry."

Fiona's nerves were strung tight and it was all she could do not to snap at her sister. "Out walking the dunes, Dee. If you're hungry, have a slice of bread to tide you over until supper." She glanced around the kitchen and saw that her sister hadn't even begun to prepare the evening meal. "Stars and garters, Dee, couldn't you have started peeling the potatoes?"

Deirdre pulled out a chair and lowered herself onto it. "I just dug them up, Fiona, and my back hurts."

"Why didn't you have Da or Carvey dig them?"

"Da took Jamie to town and Carvey is sleeping."

Fiona pumped water into the sink and began scrubbing the still-warm potatoes. "Is he ill again?"

Deirdre sighed. "I don't believe so. But he tosses and turns so much in his sleep of late that I don't think he's getting enough rest."

"When did this start, Dee?"

Deirdre pursed her lips. "A month or two ago. Yes, it was around Da's birthday, the beginning of June."

Fiona worked quietly, peeling the earthy-smelling vegetables. She had so many worries, and this was yet another. Something was bothering Carvey enough to cause him to lose sleep. Was it that her father was getting closer to retirement? Had his birthday triggered Carvey's unease? Was he fearful that he couldn't handle the job of lighthouse keeper?

"Is Mr. Paine eating with us this evening?" Deirdre asked, breaking into her thoughts.

"He was invited to the Rileys'," she replied sharply.

"How thoughtful of Bridget," her sister said with a sigh.

Fiona began to slice the peeled potatoes. She would never have used the words thoughtful and Bridget in the same sentence, but at least the dinner invitation had given her time to ponder the problem of the missing cargo without Travis around to distract her thoughts.

The only way to clear her family of blame, she decided, was to find out what had happened to Travis's goods herself. If someone in New Clare had taken them, there would be evidence of the theft. She just had to find it.

"May I accompany you to town this morning, Miss Cleary?"

Fiona paused in the middle of pinning on her straw hat and glanced over her shoulder. Travis was standing in the kitchen doorway wearing new, tan cotton trousers, a white shirt and a smile on his handsome, smoothly shaven face. For a moment she brightened at the thought of walking to town with him, but then she reconsidered. Travis had accused her father of letting the beacon go out and Tom Brody of thievery. Why was he suddenly being so congenial?

There was one sure way to find out. Fiona finished pinning on her hat and said with a shrug, "I wouldn't mind the company."

She stepped outside into bright sunshine. The day was early and sunlight sparkled like diamonds on the water's surface. Shading her eyes to gaze out at the sea of blue, Fiona drew in a deep breath and slowly let it out. She loved summer mornings, when everything was fresh and new and alive.

"Where are you off to so early?" Travis asked her as they started down the stone path, Fiona in the lead.

"I have errands to do." She hoped Travis would not ask her what they were. She hated to lie, yet neither did she want him to learn of her investigation until she had solid evidence.

At the bottom of the dune they began walking side by side. Fiona called a greeting to Mrs. Quinn, who sat knitting in her rocking chair on the front porch of her tiny wooden frame house. "She's eighty years old," Fiona explained. "Her house was one of the first built here."

"Eighty." Travis let out a low whistle. "Remarkable. What's her secret?"

"Too stubborn to give in to old age." Fiona glanced at him from beneath the brim of her straw hat. "Are you wanting to hire someone this morning to tow your ship?"

"Yes. Any idea where to start?"

"If ever you want to know what's going on in town or who's available to work, you need only spend a little time at the general store."

"I'll remember that."

He smiled at her, and against her will Fiona felt herself blushing. *Devil's knees, Fiona, it's only a smile. Is that any reason to blush like a schoolgirl?* She decided to proceed to a neutral subject.

"How was your dinner last night?"

"Informative," he replied.

Fiona glanced at him curiously. "Informative?"

"Miss Riley is a wealth of information."

Fiona nearly choked. "This is *Bridget* Riley we're speaking of now?"

"She was kind enough to fill me in on some of New Clare's history."

Fiona puzzled over his statement for a moment, then she laughed. "Well, why didn't you say so in the first place? You spent the evening listening to gossip."

"Gossip I don't give much credence to," he said. "Facts I do."

Fiona had the distinct feeling that the information Travis had gathered had to do with her family. She didn't appreciate Bridget casting aspersions on her loved ones and found herself snapping, "My mother taught me to give credence to facts only if I'm sure of their source."

Instead of firing back a retort, Travis said simply, "Your mother sounds like a very wise person. You must miss her."

His statement so discomfited her that Fiona could not respond to it, not that she would have anyway. She had spent years trying not to think of how much she missed her mother and she refused to do so now. She pressed her lips together and walked on in silence until they reached the corner of Wexford and Kilkenny, then she halted in front of the bank and said stiffly, "I have business here."

"Miss Cleary." Travis paused, rubbed his jaw, and looked contrite. "I seem to have spoken out of turn."

Fiona watched a horse and rider trot by. "It will take me a few minutes to conduct my business. You can go on if you'd like. The general store is around the corner."

"Damn it, I'm trying to apologize!" Travis sighed and shook his head. "Why do you always make it so difficult?"

"There's nothing to apologize for, Mr. Paine," she said with indifference.

"Look, I'm not sure exactly what it was I said—"

"Then there's nothing to discuss except whether you'll go on or wait."

Travis gave her an exasperated look. "I'll wait."

He held the door open, but stood on the sidewalk outside rather than accompany Fiona into the bank. Within minutes she regretted being short tempered with him. Travis didn't know the circumstances of her mother's death. It was unfair of her to treat him as if he had purposely brought it up.

Standing next to the teller's cage, Fiona turned to glance through one of the two large front windows. Travis had his back to the bank and was standing with his hands in his pockets, patiently waiting.

It was an odd feeling, she decided, to have a man waiting for her. Not an unpleasant one, just odd. She'd never been courted, so she had no idea what it would be like to have a beau. Her mother's accident and her father's subsequent lapse had forced her to take up adult responsibilities at a young age. And now that she had the time, a courtship would be pointless when she would be leaving soon.

When Fiona emerged from the bank, Travis was lounging against a lamppost casually observing a pair of young ladies in brightly hued, full-bustled dresses walk past him. Both turned to glance back at him and giggle. Fiona felt a momentary stab of jealousy at his reaction, but immediately scolded herself. Travis Paine was a handsome man, the kind most females would be attracted to. They had every right to flirt with him and he with them. *She* certainly had no business feeling jealous over a man on whom she had no claim.

As she approached, Travis straightened and smiled. "Ready?"

Fiona nodded and fell into step beside him. Yes, it most certainly felt odd to have a man waiting. And most certainly not unpleasant.

Early morning was a busy time for Brody's General Store, and that morning proved no exception. Buckboards and surreys parked outside gave evidence of the farmers and their wives who had come to town to stock up on supplies. The door had been propped open, partly to catch the breeze before it turned hot and partly to aid the steady stream of customers entering and leaving.

Fiona paused just outside the store when she caught sight of her cousin Devlin standing half a block down the street supervising the hanging of a wide white sign. "Will you look at that now?" she mused aloud.

"Another of your relatives?" Travis asked, standing just behind her.

"It's my cousin, Devlin. Looks like he bought himself a saloon."

❖ *10* ❖

Fiona STOOD IN the street to read the sign that proclaimed in bold black letters: BRODY'S SALOON.

"Your cousin owns the general store, too, doesn't he?" Travis asked, standing beside her.

"That he does." Fiona pursed her lips. Devlin not only owned it, but also was in some financial straits with it, according to Pegeen. Unless, perhaps, buying the saloon was the cause of his money problems.

She took Travis into the store and introduced him to the group of men sitting around the potbellied stove. "Mr. Paine needs someone to tow his ship to Trenton Harbor for repairs," she announced. "Any of you fellows know a person who can help?"

There was a moment of thoughtful silence, then all heads swiveled toward one man sitting apart. He was younger than the rest, a brawny, red-cheeked, curly-haired Irishman with eyes that spoke of incredible sadness and a somber expression that didn't fit the rest of him. He had been staring vacantly across the store, but at their sudden silence, he turned to stare at Travis.

"Go on, Kevin," one of the men urged gently.

"It'll be a good start, lad," another murmured.

After a moment's hesitation, Kevin rose slowly from his wooden folding chair, twisting his tweed cap in his large hands. He met Travis's direct gaze straight on. "I'll see to towing your ship."

Travis glanced at Fiona and she nodded her approval. "Kevin Malone is a fine worker, Mr. Paine. You'll do no better."

"I'll need two tug boats for a ship that size," Malone cautioned. "It'll take at least six men to do it right."

Travis hesitated a moment, then offered his hand. "You're hired, Malone."

Kevin reached out and clasped Travis's hand, smiling broadly. Fiona saw tears of gratitude in his eyes as he turned away, and she felt her own fill up.

"Kevin's wife and two young children died last winter of influenza," she said quietly to Travis. "He blames himself for their deaths because he was away on a ship when they took ill. He's vowed never to sail again, but the sad fact is that he hasn't been able to work on land either. His heart isn't in it. As a result he doesn't know what to do with himself. That's why your offer has come at the right time." She paused to wipe a tear off her cheek. "I know he'll do a fine job for you, Mr. Paine. He's had a lot of experience with tugs."

"Is he honest?"

"There's no question of it."

Travis raised an eyebrow. "As honest as your father?"

Fiona had the feeling that Travis was baiting her, but before she could respond, she heard her aunt calling. She turned as Tullia came bustling up from the back of the store, rubbing her hands together, her impish face alight with cheer.

"You've saved me a trip to the lighthouse, Fiona."

"Hello, Auntie. How are you?"

"Overjoyed to see you, and you, too, Mr. Paine."

"Mrs. Brody," Travis replied with a nod, "you're looking in the pink."

Tullia laughed. "You're a charmer, Mr. Paine, there's no doubt of it. We were just speaking about you, in fact." Tullia indicated a group of ladies standing at the rear of the store near her post office window. "You know Fiona agreed to direct the production for our festival and—"

Fiona's mouth dropped. "Now, Auntie, you know very well I didn't agree to any such thing."

Tullia waved away her objection. "You did, dear girl, you just didn't say it in so many words. Besides, there's no one else to do it. And don't say Devlin can, for he's gone and bought himself a saloon."

Tullia smiled at Travis. "Now, Mr. Paine, for our festival it's always been our custom to put on a play. This year we've chosen *Rip Van Winkle* and wondered if you'd accept a wee part in it."

Fiona noticed Pegeen Brody trying to catch her attention from the counter on the left side of the store. "Excuse me, please, Auntie, Mr. Paine. I'll leave you two to settle this."

She made her way to the counter and waited while Pegeen helped another customer. As soon as the lady had gone, Pegeen whispered, "What's Tullia up to now?"

"Trying to convince Mr. Paine to be in her play." Fiona glanced back to see that the women had formed a circle around Travis. He was busy frowning and shaking his head at her aunt, his hands up, palms forward, as if warding off an attack. "Looks like she's winning, too."

"Tullia always wins. You know that yourself, Fiona." Pegeen gave her a sly glance. "And how do you feel about your guest now?"

Fiona shot her a piqued look. "Don't start that, Peg. My feelings haven't changed a whit." She turned her head to look at Travis standing so handsome and confident among the women. Was she telling Pegeen the truth or was she fooling herself?

The sad truth was that she *did* feel a strong attraction to Travis, but what good would it do to acknowledge it? Fiona turned back around and saw Pegeen grinning at her. "Is it true Dev bought the old saloon down the street?"

"Don't try to change the subject, Fiona," Pegeen said, shaking a finger at her. "You wear your feelings on your sleeve. You're enamoured of Mr. Paine."

"It doesn't matter if I'm enamoured or not, Peg," Fiona insisted. "I'm leaving, and so is he when his ship is ready. Now will you tell me about Devlin?"

Pegeen laughed. "All right. It's true. Dev bought the saloon. It came as a surprise to all of us."

"But I thought he was having money problems."

Pegeen raised her eyebrows. "That's what we thought. But Tommy came home the other evening and said Dev had just come back from Chicago looking like the cat who swallowed the canary. Then first thing this morning he walks in as proud as a peacock and announces he's the new owner of the saloon and that the sign is going up today."

Fiona's forehead wrinkled as she pondered Devlin's actions. "I suppose the bright side is Dev hasn't gambled away his money. He's invested it instead."

"That's exactly what Tommy said. By the way, I have those supplies you were wanting last week. Dev stocked up on everything while he was in Chicago."

Fiona glanced around to find Travis surrounded by Tullia's cohorts, all of whom were talking at once. "Wrap everything up for me, Peg, and include some coffee, as well. From the looks of things, I'd better go rescue Mr. Paine."

"Hello, Fiona," apple-cheeked Mary Sheridan called cheerfully as Fiona edged her way into the circle of ladies.

"Mornin' to you, Mrs. Sheridan, and to the rest of you ladies. If you'll excuse us, Auntie, Mr. Paine has to leave now to get started on his ship." She glanced at Travis and he gave her a grateful look.

"Fiona, why don't you want to direct *Rip Van Winkle* for us this year?" Mary asked.

Fiona shook her head. "I vowed I would never do it again, not after last time. I nearly throttled my aunt for choosing the actors she did."

Mary made a chortling sound. "You didn't think it a stroke of genius for Tullia's castin' of Paddy O'Hara as the Headless Horseman?"

Tullia clapped her hands at the memory. "That jack-o-lantern Paddy carried for his head was the perfect place to hide his flask."

Fiona sniffed. "Perfect all right. So perfect he was corned by the end of the play."

Mary slapped her thigh and hooted with laughter. "You should have seen Paddy, Mr. Paine. The poor man dropped the jack-o-lantern onto the stage and splattered the first two rows of the audience with bits of wet pumpkin."

As the ladies whooped with laughter, Fiona glanced at Travis, wondering what he thought of their silliness. To her surprise, he seemed to be thoroughly enjoying himself.

"I wish I could have seen that, Mrs. Sheridan," he replied with a charming smile.

He fits in so well he seems one of us. For a second Fiona found herself wishing he were. But what difference would it make anyway? She would be leaving soon.

"Fiona, my Edwin is hoping to win your lunch basket at the festival," Katie O'Banyon announced with a sly gleam in her eye, nudging the woman beside her.

Fiona managed to maintain her smile, though inwardly she shuddered at the thought of sharing a lunch with Edwin. She patted Katie on her ample arm. "Tell Edwin he's in luck then. My sister Dee has offered to make my lunch this year."

Katie O'Banyon's reply was a pained smile. Fiona glanced at Tullia and found her trying not to laugh. Deirdre's cooking skills were legendary in New Clare.

"Follow me, Mr. Paine," Fiona said to Travis. "I'll lead you out of this maze of clucking hens."

"We'll be in touch soon, Mr. Paine," Tullia called.

Fiona glanced back at Travis as she lead the way to the front. "Still in one piece?"

"That's the second time you've left me stranded."

She turned to give him a puzzled look. "When was the first?"

Travis started to speak, then closed his mouth, as if he'd decided to keep it a secret. Instead he asked, "What is this about winning a lunch basket?"

"All unmarried ladies make a special lunch in a basket to be auctioned off at the festival and shared with the bachelor who bids highest for it. It's a lively affair, to be sure." She stopped at the counter to pick up her package. "By the way, what *wee* part did my aunt offer you?"

"Rip Van Winkle."

Fiona laughed as she walked out the door ahead of him. "I'm not surprised by anything Tullia does. What was your answer?"

"I turned her down," he said from behind. "I hope to be gone before your festival."

Fiona's smile dimmed. She knew Travis was anxious to leave, but hearing him say it aloud seemed to take the joy from her day. It was yet another sign of the effect he was having on her. "Are you sure the ship will be ready that soon?"

Travis rubbed the back of his neck. "We'll see."

Outside the store, Fiona and Travis found Kevin Malone waiting with a group of five men. "We're ready whenever you are, Mr. Paine," Kevin told him.

Travis smiled and rubbed his hands together. "Good. Let's get out to the ship now and see what we can do."

Fiona experienced a strange feeling of emptiness as he strode toward the men. *He's forgotten me already*, she thought, and was stunned by the very notion that it bothered her. Why shouldn't Travis forget her? She would certainly forget him soon enough.

As though he had suddenly remembered something, Travis stopped and turned around. Quite unexplainably, Fiona found herself holding her breath, hoping she was the reason for his about-face. *St. Nick's bunions, Fiona! He probably has to go back to the store for something.*

But Travis didn't go back to the store. He walked back to Fiona instead. Her heart was thumping so hard against her ribs she was sure he could hear it. Shyly, she glanced at him from beneath the brim of her straw hat. Her pulse beat faster at the intensity of his gaze. "Did you forget something, Mr. Paine?"

Travis looked down at his shoes and cleared his throat, as though embarrassed by what he was about to say. "I forgot to thank you for your help."

Fiona quickly looked down herself. "It was no matter," she offered. "I'd have done the same for anyone."

She glanced up to see an odd, almost offended expression

cross his face. "Nevertheless, I would have been remiss not to thank you," he said stiffly.

Puzzled, Fiona watched Travis stride briskly off to rejoin the men. What had she said to offend him? With an exasperated sigh, she turned away.

"Fiona, hello!" Edwin O'Banyon came trotting up the sidewalk toward her, his hair oil shining in the morning sun, his black moustache in perfect twin curls.

"Hello, Edwin," Fiona replied tonelessly.

He twisted the tip of his moustache and rocked back on his heels. "You're looking as lovely as ever, Fiona."

"That's very kind of you, Edwin. If you'll excuse me, I must get home with my supplies."

"I suppose you know Mr. Paine is making inquiries about the June shipwreck," Edwin called as she started away.

Fiona turned around. "The *June* shipwreck?"

Edwin suddenly became coy. "I'd tell you all about it but I'm on my way to the restaurant for a piece of pie and coffee." He paused and then added, "I might have time to talk to you if you'd like to accompany me."

Fiona quickly weighed his offer. She didn't relish Edwin's company, but her curiosity was too great to pass up the opportunity. She smiled and took his arm. "A cup of coffee is just what I need."

But Fiona wasn't smiling as she sat across from Edwin in the hotel restaurant. Travis had wired someone in the Paine Shipping Company to find out the cause of the shipwreck that occurred the month before his own ship struck. She scowled into her empty coffee cup. What was Travis trying to prove?

Travis trudged up the stone path to the lighthouse, sweaty and tired, yet with a feeling of accomplishment. Kevin Malone and his crew turned out to be skilled men who weren't afraid to tackle a hard job. Through their efforts the ship had been safely towed up the shore some twenty miles to the shipyard at Trenton Harbor in Michigan. With his vessel in good hands, Travis could to turn his attention to finding his missing cargo.

He stepped into the lighthouse and was greeted with the

delightful aroma of meat roasting in the oven, the yeasty smell of freshly baked bread and the tangy scent of cinnamon, cloves and apples. The Clearys had already gathered in the kitchen and were preparing to eat. No one noticed his arrival.

Deirdre was fastening a bib around Jamie's neck as the child squirmed in his high chair. Finn sat at the boy's left, trying to entertain him with funny faces. Carvey was lifting a heavy roasting pan from the oven and Fiona was in the midst of placing a dish full of steaming potatoes on the table. Her cheeks were flushed from the heat of the stove and damp tendrils of dark hair clung to her forehead and neck. She wore a white bib apron over a dress of soldier blue that accented the creaminess of her complexion and the red highlights in her hair.

Travis had never seen her look lovelier and that made it all the more difficult for him. The attraction he felt for her, he knew now, was not reciprocated. Her remark that morning in front of the general store had only underscored it. She felt no differently toward him than toward any of her acquaintances.

And yet when Fiona glanced up at him, Travis's heart turned over. Was it his imagination or did her eyes grow brighter at the sight of him? Was her welcoming smile the same one she gave to any guest or was it given especially to him?

As though suddenly self-conscious, Fiona used the back of her hand to brush stray wisps of hair from her forehead. ''Come in and sit down, Mr. Paine. We were hoping you'd get back in time for supper.''

Travis went to the sink and pumped water over his hands and forearms, feeling inordinately happy to be a part of her family, if only temporarily. After splashing cold water on his face, he glanced around and found Fiona waiting with a linen towel. He dried his face with it and began to rub his hands vigorously. Their eyes met and he smiled at her. It seemed natural that she would be there holding a towel for him.

But as Travis continued to gaze at her and Fiona at him, his movements slowed and his smile turned serious. The moment was somehow so intimate that he was overwhelmed by a powerful need to touch her, to hold her in his arms, to feel her body against his.

Travis, you're a fool, he told himself. Even if Fiona did share his feelings, the fact was that someone in New Clare had robbed him blind, and as much as he wished it was not possible, it very well could have been one of the people in that kitchen, including Fiona. He could not forget that, nor could he let his growing attraction to her interfere with his mission.

Travis turned away, expecting to find that the whole family had been witness to their unguarded moment. He was surprised when no one seemed to be paying them any mind. He took a seat at the end of the table with Fiona at his right and tried not to think about what had passed between them, though with her next to him it was nearly impossible. Instead he focused his thoughts on the possibility that the beacon had been purposefully extinguished on the night of the June storm as well as on the night of the storm that had caused his own shipwreck.

Yet as Travis watched the Clearys over the course of the meal, he found it difficult to believe them capable of treachery. Especially Fiona. He kept remembering the look on her face that morning when Kevin Malone had volunteered his services. She had been as proud of Malone as if he were her own son and not a man older than she. Could that same woman have been part of a scheme that caused the deaths of innocent sailors?

From experience, Travis knew of three reasons why seemingly good people did bad things: greed, desperation and loyalty. Fiona was not a greedy person, nor did she seem desperate. But would she protect those she loved if they had done something wrong?

To that his answer was yes. He had witnessed several times how defensive she became when one of her family was threatened, even in some small way. Fiona was, without a doubt, fiercely loyal. No matter how else he felt about her, it was a point to keep firmly in mind.

As for the others, he could not answer to their greed or desperation without knowing them better. Their loyalty, however, probably ran as deeply as Fiona's. Travis asked himself again: Could any one of the Clearys have participated in a plan to wreck his ship? And again he had no definite answer. But he would be a bigger fool to discount them.

When the meal was over, Travis left the house and walked down to the lake to think, away from the distraction of Fiona and her family. The waves lapped softly onto the beach and a light breeze stirred the long-stemmed grass growing in the sand. He stood on the pier with his hands in his pockets, staring out at the expanse of water.

Whoever took his cargo would have had to make numerous trips into town with a dray. Surely someone had noticed a large quantity of merchandise being moved. He remembered the elderly lady knitting on her front porch and made a mental note to speak to her.

As the sun dipped lower in the evening sky, Travis walked back toward the lighthouse. He spotted a small stable on the east side and decided to take a look. The wide door opened quietly on well-oiled hinges, and the small row of windows down the west side gave him enough light that he didn't need a lantern. Inside stood the surrey with its fringed canvas top.

Travis stood with his hands at his waist, looking around the interior. On one wall were rows of shelves stocked with containers of kerosene. At the far end were three stalls. Other than the horse that occupied the first stall, there didn't seem to be anything inside. To be sure, he looked over the top of each stall door.

Against the far wall in the last stall, Travis noticed a large, square mound of hay that looked as if it had been recently put there. On his haunches, he poked a finger through the straw and felt wood beneath. He brushed away the straw and uncovered a crate with lettering stamped on the side. Travis's heart began to race as he traced the black letters with his index finger: THOMAS E. PAINE.

His adrenalin was pumping as he pried off the top of the crate and reached inside. He pulled out a bottle and read the label, then quickly pulled out another.

"Old Grand-Dad," Travis whispered.

He had found one of the missing crates of whiskey. In Finn Cleary's stable.

❖ *11* ❖

THAVIS CAREFULLY REPLACED the lid and covered the crate with straw. As he closed the stable door and walked toward the lighthouse, he turned over various possibilities of his discovery. It seemed more certain than ever that the Clearys were involved in the theft. But which one of them? Or were all three involved?

He heard his name and looked up to find Fiona coming toward him. She was dressed just as he had seen her from his window on other evenings. Her dark hair was unbound and her lightweight white dress molded itself to her long, shapely legs as she walked. He couldn't tear his eyes away from her.

She held out a sealed envelope. "This wire came for you."

Travis opened the envelope and read the telegram as Fiona started toward the beach. The reply was short and concise. The wreck of the *Reginald Fitzpatrick* had occurred in weather conditions identical to his own. In that incident, however, none of the crew had survived and the steamer had broken up. Travis's eyes narrowed. If the beacon had been out, there were no witnesses to tell about it.

It was the last line, however, that proved to be the most interesting. The *Fitzpatrick*'s cargo had never been recovered, but insurance investigators were satisfied that it had met the same fate as the ship. Frowning, Travis folded the telegram and slid it into his pocket. The investigators may have been satisfied, but he wasn't.

Fiona was some distance down the shoreline when she heard Travis call to her. "Going for a walk?"

Her pulse leaped at the sound of his voice, but she purposefully maintained a casual air. "It's my usual habit," she answered without looking around.

"Mind if I walk with you?"

Fiona slowed her pace to allow him to catch up to her. "Do I have a choice?" she asked, using the very words he had used after the memorial service. She gave him a sidelong glance to see if he caught it.

Travis rubbed his jaw and grinned sheepishly. "I suppose I deserve that."

Fiona couldn't help but laugh. As they walked down the beach together she gave Travis a coy glance, remembering the look he'd given her when she had handed him a towel to dry his hands. She'd never seen such a look in a man's eyes before—deep, bold and seductive. It had made her heart gallop and her limbs weak. It had made her think shocking thoughts that even now brought a stinging blush to her cheeks.

It had also made her realize that the attraction she felt for him was mutual. Was that why he had wanted to walk with her? she wondered. Fiona stopped to pluck an oblong pink and gray stone from the sand. Clearly something was on Travis's mind. He didn't do anything without good reason.

She held the stone out on her open palm. "Isn't it lovely? You wouldn't think an ordinary stone could have such color."

Travis took the small stone from her hand and gave it only a cursory glance. "Tell me about the shipwreck that happened this past June."

He certainly didn't waste any time getting to the point, Fiona thought with a disappointed sigh. But why was he asking *her* about the wreck? Hadn't he wired for that information? She began to walk again. "The ship was a steamer, like yours, but not as large. She struck a sandbar during a squall, not far from where yours struck." Fiona shuddered, remembering the horrors of the wreck, the broken bodies, the bereaved families. She let out her breath. "None of the crew survived."

"And the cargo?"

Fiona guessed where he was leading and her temper flared. "Why are you asking me, Mr. Paine?"

"You were here when it happened."

"I don't know what happened to the cargo from that ship, nor even what the ship had been carrying. Whatever it was, it never surfaced here. Whether it floated ashore in some other port I don't know either. I also don't like the way you're questioning me as if I had something to do with the missing goods. I'm not a thief, nor is anyone in my family."

A moment passed as Travis's brown eyes searched her face, then he looked down at the stone in his hand and slowly closed his fingers around it. *He thinks I'm lying!* Shaking with fury, Fiona began walking rapidly away from him, cutting across the sand through the high marram grass to the wooded area beyond.

"Miss Cleary!"

Fiona didn't turn around. She had seen the doubt in Travis's eyes and that was all she needed to know. She chided herself for foolishly thinking something extraordinary had passed between them in the kitchen.

"Damn it, wait up!" Travis caught up with her just as she reached a stand of cottonwood trees and took hold of her arm to stop her.

Fiona jerked free and glared at him. "Go back, Mr. Paine, and do your investigating if you must, but you won't find anything to point a finger at my family."

Travis looked at her as if he were about to say something; then he pressed his lips together in a hard line and looked away.

"You don't seem to understand the seriousness of your accusations," she continued angrily. "Any hint of misconduct and my father could lose his position, and Carvey with him. What do you suppose would become of them *then*, Mr. Paine?"

When they met hers, Travis's eyes were cold, his expression stony. "They're not my worry."

"You're right, they're mine, and I'll do all I can to protect them from the likes of you!"

Fiona stamped off through the cottonwoods and didn't return to the lighthouse until after dark. She was angered and hurt by Travis's seeming indifference and lack of trust. The hurt cut deeper than she cared to admit, for it meant that her feelings for him were very strong.

She suddenly couldn't wait for Travis to leave New Clare.

Two days later, in the middle of the night, Fiona was awakened by the faint sound of off-key singing. Curious, she slid out of bed and padded silently across the room to kneel at her open window. Even in the dim moonlight, the shock of red hair on a man's form slumped against the side of the stable told her who it was. Fiona shoved her feet into house slippers, grabbed her dark blue robe and hurried down the stairs.

"Carvey!"

Propped up against the side of the stable, Carvey had fallen asleep and was snoring softly, a bottle beside him on the ground. Fiona bent over her brother-in-law and shook his thin shoulders, wrinkling her nose at the strong odor of liquor. At her firm insistence, he opened bleary eyes and attempted to focus on her, then shut them again.

Fiona picked up the bottle and read the label. "Whiskey!" She shook him again. "Carvey, where did you find this?"

Carvey frowned and tried to push her hands away. "In th' stall. Go 'way!" He dropped his head onto his chest and began to snore again.

After groping her way around the stable, Fiona found an open crate in the corner of the last stall, partially hidden by straw, its lid lying beside it. "Mother Mary!" she whispered, lifting up one of the three bottles inside. She brushed away the straw and read the telltale black lettering on the side of the container.

Saints preserve us, where could this have come from?

Nearly ill with fear, Fiona covered the crate as best she

could and ran to the house for water. She poured a bucketful over Carvey's head, and as he spluttered and coughed and wiped water from his eyes, she knelt beside him and asked in a low, furious voice, "How did that whiskey get in the stable?"

"God's teeth, Fiona, are you tryin' t' drown me?"

"Shhh!" Fiona looked over her shoulder to be sure no light had come on in the house. "I'll do worse if you don't answer me truthfully."

"I dunno, Fiona," Carvey whined. "I just found it."

"Did you have to sample it, as well? Don't you know what it is, Carvey? It's part of the cargo that's missing from Mr. Paine's ship. He was carrying woolens, silks and *whiskey!*"

Carvey blinked at her in confusion. "What time is it?"

"Nearly three in the morning."

With a groan, he staggered to his feet. "Gotta go back."

Fiona jumped up and caught his arm. "You can't go back like that. I'll have to finish your shift. Go in the stable and sleep off your drunkenness. And don't say a word to a soul about the whiskey!"

"All right, Fiona, now let me be. If I don't sit down I'll fall down."

Fiona chewed her thumbnail as Carvey stumbled into the stable and made a bed on the straw. How had Travis's whiskey come to be in their stable? She glanced at one of the upstairs bedroom windows then adamantly shook her head. She would not believe her father had anything to do with it. There had to be another explanation.

In the meantime, she had to get rid of the whiskey.

Fiona slipped back into the house and stood at the bottom of the staircase, listening for sounds of anyone moving about. She dared not take the risk of Travis coming out to investigate. One glimpse of the whiskey and he would be sure to think Carvey and her father had stolen his cargo. And to think she had just told Travis he would find nothing to point a finger at her family.

Satisfied that they were all sound asleep, Fiona returned to the stable, gathered up the three bottles and carried them down to the lake. When she had emptied the last bottle of its contents, she took a shovel into the woods and began to dig a hole deep in the sandy soil.

By five o'clock, Fiona had buried all traces of the whiskey bottles, broken up the crate for kindling and refilled the beacon's oil. Tired and gritty from digging in the sand, she heated water in the kitchen and made a bath in the galvanized tub in the pantry. By the time she emerged in a clean gown, it was after six o'clock and her father had come down to make coffee.

"Why are you taking a bath so early, Fiona?" he asked.

She took two cups from the cupboard and set them on the table. "I couldn't sleep, Da."

Fiona brooded silently as they sat at the table with their steaming coffee. Who had put the whiskey in their stable and how had Carvey stumbled upon it?

She raised her eyes and found her father studying her.

"What is it, Fiona? I know you well enough to see you're troubled."

What could she tell him without upsetting him? Fiona decided to keep the information to herself for the time being. She rubbed her eyes. It felt as if the sand had even gotten under her eyelids. "Da, the beacon was on during the night of Mr. Paine's shipwreck, wasn't it?"

Finn scraped back his chair and took his cup to the sink. "Why would you ask me that, Fiona?" he asked crossly.

She hated telling her father of Travis's accusation because it would seem that *she* didn't trust him either. Still she found herself needing her father's reassurance. "Mr. Paine says the light was out, Da."

His shoulders seemed to slump, as though beset by a heavy burden. There was a long pause, and then he replied, "You know I'd never let the light go out."

Of course she knew it, and Fiona felt bad for having asked. She pushed tiredly to her feet. "I'm sorry, Da. I'm going upstairs to rest now. Tell Dee I'll be down later."

It was after eight-thirty when Fiona finally dragged herself from bed and made her way down to the kitchen. There she found a haggard-looking Deirdre making Jamie his breakfast.

"Mornin', Fiona," her sister said dispiritedly.

"Feena!" the little boy cried happily.

Fiona kissed the top of her nephew's head before going to the stove for coffee. "Didn't you sleep well, Dee?"

"Strap a sack full of flour on your belly, Fiona, and tell me how you'd sleep." Deirdre set a dish of oatmeal in front of Jamie.

Fiona was not surprised that her sister hadn't noticed her own exhausted state, for Deirdre rarely noticed anyone's discomfort but her own. Fiona was surprised, however, that her sister hadn't mentioned Carvey's absence during the night. Surely she had noticed he hadn't come to bed. Fiona poured coffee from the pot. "Where is Carvey?"

Deirdre frowned at her son, who had stuck his fingers into the oatmeal and was loudly sucking each fingertip. "He hasn't come down yet. Stop that, Jamie. You're making a mess." She glanced at Fiona. "Carvey offered to sleep upstairs in the tower last night so I could have the bed to myself. He thought I'd be more comfortable that way."

Fiona sipped her coffee quietly. Had Carvey really intended to be considerate or had Deirdre's discomfort been a convenient excuse to seek out the whiskey? Fiona decided she would have to question Carvey further. "Has Mr. Paine come down yet?"

"He took an early train up to Trenton Harbor to begin repairs on his ship."

Fiona was relieved that Travis would be occupied with his ship all day. It would give her a better opportunity to investigate the missing cargo.

❖12❖

FIONA PAUSED IN front of one window of the general store and tapped on the glass. Pegeen stood on a stool hanging green bunting along the top edge of the window, and at Fiona's tap, she peered under the material and smiled. "Come help me," she called through the glass.

"Thank goodness you've come, Fiona." From atop her stool, Pegeen handed down an armful of the material. "The pins are in my pocket. Everyone is so busy today I foolishly thought I could manage alone." She gave a merry laugh. "I can't imagine how it looks from outside."

"It looks fine, Peg," Fiona replied.

Pegeen stretched over her head to pin up more gathers. "Your Mr. Paine caused quite a stir this morning, Fiona. Could you hand me another pin?"

"He's not *my* Mr. Paine, Peg. What kind of stir did he cause?"

"He agreed to be Rip Van Winkle in the play. He came in early to tell Tullia." Pegeen held out her hand. "A pin, Fiona?"

Fiona's forehead wrinkled in bewilderment. "I can't believe he agreed to do it. He was so determined to be gone before the festival." She realized Pegeen was still holding out her hand and quickly provided her with a straight pin.

"He said he'd be back in time for reheasal this evening,"

Pegeen explained. "Tullia gave him his lines so he could study them on the train." She dropped her voice to a whisper. "And speaking of Tullia, she's on her way over here this minute. She's probably going to badger you again about directing her production. You'd better think fast if you still want out of it."

Pegeen barely finished her sentence before Tullia entered. "Fiona, my dear niece, I'm so happy to see you. How are you?" She pinched Fiona's cheek and smiled.

"Fine, Auntie, and you seem to be doing very well yourself. No more episodes, I trust."

Tullia pressed her hands together. "I couldn't be better. Have you heard the wonderful news? But Peg has surely told you by now. Your Mr. Paine has agreed to star in my production. All I need now is for you to direct."

Fiona gave her a stern look. "He's not *my* Mr. Paine, and I've told you before how I feel about directing."

"Now, Fiona, can you imagine anyone else. . . ." Tullia began a long enumeration of her qualifications, but Fiona wasn't listening. She was mulling over Travis's sudden change of heart. Why would he want to be in the play even if he *were* going to be in town that long? It didn't fit with what she knew of his personality. He wasn't one to take direction.

Fiona handed Pegeen another pin. Travis's capitulation could mean only one thing: He was planning to stay in New Clare until he found his thief.

"So you see, Fiona—"

"All right, Auntie. I'll do it."

Both Tullia and Pegeen stared at her with open mouths. Tullia was the first to regain her composure. She threw her skinny arms around Fiona's neck and hugged her. "You always were a sweet child. I'll go get the script. We'll start at seven o'clock this evening." She turned and bustled off, calling over her shoulder, "Be prompt, Fiona!"

Pegeen climbed down from her stool and put her hand against Fiona's forehead. "No fever that I can detect."

"I'm not ill, Peg. Tullia wore me down."

Pegeen shook a finger at her. "None of that malarkey

Fiona. I saw the look on your face when I told you who the new star of Tullia's production was. You've changed your mind for one reason alone, and that's to work with your Mr. Paine.''

"He's *not my* Mr. Paine!" Fiona snapped. "Why do you keep calling him *my* Mr. Paine? I barely know the man."

Pegeen shrugged. "Everyone in town calls him that."

Fiona was about to protest when Mary Sheridan called from across the store, "Mornin', Peg. Mornin', Fiona. Tell your Mr. Paine, Fiona, that I'm bringing my famous apple betty to rehearsal tonight especially for him."

Fiona glanced at Pegeen, who shrugged and smiled. At that point, Fiona knew it was useless to protest. Once the people in New Clare fixed an idea in their minds, it would be there forever. Travis was now *her* Mr. Paine and nothing she could say or do would change that. She sighed in resignation. "Where's Devlin this morning?"

Pegeen shoved the pins in her pocket and picked up the stool to move it to the other window. "Down at his saloon, no doubt. He's remodeling it, wants to have it ready for a grand opening on festival day."

Fiona raised her eyebrows. "My, he's sure spending the money."

Pegeen leaned closer to whisper, "It has Tommy worried, Fiona, I don't mind telling you. I heard the two arguing last night. 'Where are you getting all the money for this saloon?' my Tommy asks him. 'It's my concern, not yours,' Dev answers back. 'Don't forget who owns the store, Tom, *and* the smithy shop. *I* do, that's who. *You* work for *me*, Tommy boy, and don't you ever forget it.' "

Where *was* Devlin finding the money? Fiona mused. Had he borrowed it or come by it through some other means? She hated to consider that her cousin might have purchased the stolen whiskey from whoever had pilfered the cargo, but it wouldn't be out of character for Devlin to do so if he could turn a good profit on it. She decided to check into the matter herself.

"Poor Tommy," she said to Pegeen. "That must have hurt him."

"You'd think he'd be used to it after all these years, but it still makes him fighting mad. I rue the day Tom Brody decides he's had enough of Dev's bullying. They'll fight to the death, those two." Pegeen sighed sadly.

Fiona put an arm around the young woman's plump shoulders. "Tommy has more sense than that, Peg. Someday he'll buy the shop from Dev and then he'll never have to answer to him again."

"We have so little saved that I fear it will never happen."

"Don't think like that, Peg," Fiona replied firmly. "If you do, it *won't* happen. Now let's get the other window decorated. I have a few errands to do before I go home."

Devlin Brody was standing in his new saloon in front of a gleaming mahogany counter, his large head tilted back to admire the fancy hand-carved woodwork above and behind the bar. A heavy beveled mirror sat in the frame of the handsome mahogany backing, and overhead were specially cut panels designed to hold glassware.

"Beautiful, isn't it, Fiona?"

Fiona didn't think he'd heard her come in. "It's that, Dev."

"Only the best for Devlin Brody." He turned to look at her, his small eyes studying her suspiciously. "What do you want?"

"Is that any greeting?" Fiona walked up to the counter and ran her fingers along it. "I came to see your new toy."

Devlin shot her a contemptuous look and walked away. "It's not done. Come back on festival day."

"Since I'm here, if you don't mind I'll have a look around now."

Standing with his arms folded across his chest, a suspicious glower on his ruddy-complexioned face, Devlin watched her wander around the long, narrow room. "Why are you interested in my saloon, Fiona?"

"Going to have sarsaparilla on hand for the ladies?"

"I said—"

"Ladies *will* be welcome here, won't they?"

"—why are you interested in my saloon?"

"We're family, Dev. Why shouldn't I be interested?"
Fiona reached the door to the back storeroom and peered inside, but all it contained were stacks of paneling and freshly
milled lumber. There were no crates in sight.

"Have you bought your supply of whiskey yet, Dev?"
Fiona turned and found her cousin standing directly in front
of her, blowing like an angry bull, his large hands clenching
and unclenching at his sides. He was an intimidating man,
but Fiona remained undaunted. Like an animal, he could
smell fear.

"Why do you want to know?" he asked.

"Because some of the cargo from Mr. Paine's ship is missing, including cases of whiskey. I thought you might have
heard something about it."

"Ask Tommy. He's the one who'd know about missing
cargo."

"I intend to," Fiona said, not wanting him to know she
had already done it.

Devlin gave her a sly grin. "If you can believe what he
says. Wouldn't it be lucky if Tommy suddenly came into
money so he could buy me out?"

"Lucky, perhaps, but Tommy would never steal, if that's
what you're implying."

Devlin took a step closer and his smile became malicious.
"You always took his side in matters, didn't you, *little*
Fiona?"

At the mention of the nickname he had used on her as a
child, Fiona's heart began to race and memories of the hurts
she had suffered at his hands rushed to the surface. She took
a step back, but raised her chin haughtily. "I'll thank you to
move out of the way, you big lummox, unless you'd like my
heel on your toes."

Fiona glared at him until he stepped aside; then, with a
swish of her skirts, she left the saloon, only to be followed
by his ridiculing laughter. Outside, she took deep breaths to
calm the quaking of her limbs. She would have bet her last
penny that some of that whiskey had ended up in Devlin's
saloon. He would feel no remorse whatsoever in buying stolen

goods. Now she was right back where she started. Where had the crate of whiskey come from and where did the rest go?

"Afternoon, Mrs. Quinn," Fiona called as she walked up the well-trodden path to the front porch of the old house on Wexford. The elderly lady peered at her from behind her wire spectacles, her knitting needles clicking furiously as she rocked back and forth in her rocking chair. "Oh, it's you, Fiona. Afternoon to you, too."

"My, that's a lovely scarf you're knitting."

"It's for Mrs. Kelly's eldest girl. The poor lass has the ague. Why don't you pull up the other chair and sit with me?"

"If I had the time I'd love nothing better." Fiona perched on the top step in the shade of the porch, took off her straw hat and fanned her face with it. "Do you remember seeing anyone come up from the lake in the last two weeks carrying a wagonload of wooden crates?"

The knitting needles kept clicking. "Isn't that odd now? A young man stopped by this mornin' to ask me the very same thing."

"Was it by any chance the man who was walking with me the other day when we passed by your house?"

Mrs. Quinn paused for a moment, then looked up in surprise. "Faith, Fiona, it was! I knew I'd seen him somewhere before. That was your Mr. Paine, wasn't it?"

There it was again. *Her* Mr. Paine. Fiona let out a sigh. "Yes, unfortunately it was."

"I'll tell you what I told him. The only wagon to pass by has been the milk wagon and that's the truth of it."

Fiona rose and put on her hat. "Thank you, Mrs. Quinn."

Another dead end. And Travis had been one step ahead of her. She wished she knew what he would do next.

Fiona found Carvey weeding in the long rows of vegetables behind the lighthouse. Jamie played with a wooden truck at the far end of the garden. When he saw her, the little boy jumped up and ran toward her. "Feena, Feena! Come see!"

Fiona swung him up in her arms with a smile. "What is it, Jamie boy?"

"A 'tato worm! Da found a 'tato worm!" He wiggled to get down, then ran to the potato patch and hunkered down. "See?"

Fiona knelt beside him. "He's a squashed potato worm, Jamie."

"*I* 'quashed him!" Jamie announced proudly, thumping his chest. "Da says we have to 'cause they're bad."

As Jamie started off on a hunt for more worms, Fiona rose and went to where Carvey was kneeling between two rows of carrots. "Feeling better this afternoon?"

He didn't glance up, but his ears turned as red as his hair. "Some."

"Where did the whiskey come from, Carvey?"

He tossed a handful of weeds on a pile nearby and gave her an imploring look. "I don't know, Fiona. I found it while I was looking for rope."

She knelt beside him. "That whiskey came from Mr. Paine's ship, Carvey. I have to find out how it got in our stable."

Carvey sat back on his haunches and wiped the sweat from his brow with the back of his arm. By his pale color, it was plain to see he hadn't fully recovered. "I don't know, Fiona. I don't know how it got there."

"Carvey, do you know what would have happened if Mr. Paine had discovered it instead of us? He's already suspicious. The whiskey would have only confirmed his suspicions."

"I was going to get rid of it," he said in a plaintive voice. "I just wanted to taste it first."

"It was a foolish thing you did, Carvey, and lucky for us that *I* found you out here last night and not Mr. Paine."

"I *am* a fool, Fiona. A big fool." Carvey covered his face with his sand-coated hands and groaned pitifully. "Lord save me from my foolishness."

Taken aback by his outburst of emotion, Fiona glanced around to see if Jamie had overheard. "All right, Carvey, there's no need to carry on so. I got rid of the whiskey."

"What have I done, Fiona?" he moaned into his hands. "What have I done?"

"Nearly got us into trouble is what you've done. Just remember what I told you last night. Not a word to a soul." Fiona rose and brushed off her skirt. Carvey was still keening pitifully, so she walked to where Jamie was hunkered down poking potato vines with a twig. "Come on, Jamie, let's take these beets your Da dug for us to the kitchen. You can wash them in the bucket for me."

Fiona glanced back at Carvey as they walked up to the lighthouse. His tormented outcry worried her. Carvey had always been a sensitive soul and rather weak-willed, but he was not one to behave in such an unsound manner. Instinct told her that something other than the whiskey was bothering him.

Travis stood off to one side of the stage in the musty-smelling church basement and watched Fiona position the other actors for scene one of *Rip Van Winkle*. In her unadorned light green summer dress with its white collar and cuffs and modest bustle, and her auburn hair pulled back in a simple twist, she had the appearance of a country girl, but her demeanor was that of a diplomat. She had the script in one hand and was pointing to a spot upstage with the other.

"Over more to the left, Mrs. Sheridan. That's it. Now Mr. Tucker, if you will proceed, please. Where is Dame Van Winkle? Has anyone seen her?"

Travis grinned as Tullia Brody put in her two cents' worth. "Fiona, shouldn't Mr. Tucker come in from the other side? It seems clear to me—"

"Auntie, if you'd like to direct instead of me I'd be grateful, but please tell me one way or the other. We both can't do it."

Tullia put her finger to her mouth. "Not another word will come from these lips, Fiona, I promise." She turned and tiptoed off stage toward Travis.

Fiona rolled her eyes heavenward. "All right, Mr. Tucker. Let's begin again."

Travis found it delightful to watch Fiona. She was firm and

tactful at the same time. And as much as she had protested, she *was* the perfect choice for director.

"She's quite a girl, isn't she, Mr. Paine?"

"Who's that, Mrs. Brody?"

"Don't play coy with me, sir." Tullia nudged him in the ribs. "I know you've got an eye for my niece and don't tell me otherwise for I'm smarter than I look."

"You look quite smart to me."

Tullia laughed. "I like you, young man. You know, you'd be a fine addition to our family. Why don't you give up sailing and settle down here?" She leaned closer and whispered, "I happen to know of a very available girl."

"Since your niece will soon be leaving, who do you have in mind?"

"Are you two going to stand there gabbing," Fiona called, "or do you think we'd all like to go home sometime this evening?"

Travis looked up and found the entire cast scowling at them. "Mrs. Brody," he said with a short bow, "I believe I'm being summoned."

"I haven't finished with you, young man," Tullia called as Travis sauntered onto the stage.

"I'm sure you haven't." He came to a stop before Fiona. "I'm at your disposal, Miss Cleary."

She gave him a disgruntled look. "Would you stand over there beside the door, please? Does anyone know where Dame Van Winkle is?"

"Yoo-hoo! I'm here!"

Travis and Fiona both turned to see Bridget sailing across the floor toward the stage, raising the hem of her sky-blue, full-bustled, lace-trimmed dress above her ankles so as not to trip on it. Travis saw Fiona turn toward her aunt and give her a deadly look, and he coughed to hide a laugh.

"I didn't know Miss Riley was in the play," he said quietly to Fiona.

"I didn't know either," she grumbled. "My aunt neglected to tell me."

Bridget came to a breathless halt in front of them and began to fan her face. "Gracious, it's warm tonight." From beneath the brim of her feather-bedecked blue hat, she slanted Travis a coquettish glance. "Why, good evening, Mr. Paine. What a pleasant surprise to find you here."

Travis caught Fiona's faint mutterings and he rubbed his jaw to hide a grin. "A surprise for us both, Miss Riley. What part do you have?"

"I'm Dame Van Winkle." Bridget showered him with her brightest smile, then turned to give Fiona a quick, haughty once-over. "I've read my lines, Fiona, and I don't like them, so I've made some changes."

Travis could see Fiona start to boil. "You can't make changes in the script, Bridget," she explained tersely. "All the other actors are playing their parts as written."

Bridget stuck out her full lower lip. "Well *my* lines are horrible. They made my character sound like a muddleheaded shrew."

Fiona's eyebrows lifted. "Do they now? And why is that, do you suppose?"

"It's clear to me that the fellow who wrote it didn't know women very well." Bridget gave her a smug smile.

Travis could see Fiona take a deep breath, struggling for control. "The fellow's name is Washington Irving," she said slowly.

Tullia had quietly come up behind the two women and now patted Bridget's shoulder. "Dame Van Winkle *is* a shrew, Bridget, because she married a ne'er-do-well husband."

Bridget put her palms to her pink cheeks. "But that's dreadful!"

"Of course it's dreadful," Tullia said. "That's what Mr. Irving intended."

"Oh, I don't care about the story!" Bridget exclaimed, turning her big blue eyes on Travis. "I mean it's dreadful that Mr. Paine should have to play such a lazy man when he's so—"

"Auntie," Fiona cut in firmly, giving Tullia a telling look, "why don't you take Bridget offstage to go over her lines?"

"Come, Bridget," Tullia crooned, leading the petulant

Dame Van Winkle across the wooden floor. "Let's go over your lines the way they're supposed to be."

Travis could hear Bridget's whines of protest as she was led away. He turned back toward Fiona, folded his arms and prepared himself for an entertaining evening.

·*13*·

AT NINE O'CLOCK that night, Travis waited outside the church while Fiona doused the last light and closed the heavy wooden door. She looked around and spotted him, but didn't seem at all surprised, or even very pleased, to find him there.

"Praise the saints that's over," she said with a shake of her head.

Travis could have echoed her sentiments. It had been a long day and an equally long evening, though watching Fiona and Bridget had given him several good laughs. Still, he was feeling frustrated. The prospect of learning something about his cargo from Mrs. Quinn had vanished, and his chances of getting the ship repaired quickly looked bleak. His hope now was that in working with the people of New Clare, he would uncover information as to the whereabouts of the missing goods.

Foremost on Travis's mind that evening was not the stolen cargo, however, but Fiona. Unfortunately, as was usually the case, it seemed he was the *last* thing on her mind. He glanced at her as they started up Wexford toward the lake. She was such an intriguing mixture of stamina and vulnerability, of earthiness and loftiness, that he never ceased to be fascinated by her. But he was beginning to realize that what he felt for her was not just simple attraction. He *wanted* her, in every way a man wants a woman.

Yet what could he do about his feelings other than deny them? Someone in Fiona's family had stolen his cargo, and he was duty bound to find and prosecute the culprit, though it meant sacrificing his own chances of having a relationship with her. And even without the issue of the stolen goods which was hindering his pursuit, Fiona didn't want to be pursued. But how difficult it was to deny his desire for her, especially when she was so near that he could smell her soft, violet scent, could see the glints of russet in her dark hair, could almost taste the sweetness of her lips.

It was Fiona's way of looking at him, however, of turning those lovely eyes on him in such a way as to combine mischievousness with innocent allure, that stirred his deepest passions. Travis stifled a groan of frustration and willed himself to normalcy.

"It will be a miracle if I survive the next ten days," Fiona said suddenly, cutting into his thoughts. "If Bridget doesn't do me in, Aunt Tullia surely will."

"Mmmm." With his hands in his pockets, Travis kept his eyes on the ground in front of him. It would be a miracle if he survived the next ten days, as well. He wished he could tell Fiona how he felt about her, but he had never expressed such feelings before and now feared he would sound foolish. He had learned from an early age to keep his thoughts to himself to avoid ridicule. It was a difficult habit to break. Travis felt his temper shorten and knew it was because of his frustration.

"Here I am thinking only of myself," Fiona said, glancing at him, "when you must be bone weary after your long day. How is the work going on your ship?"

Travis was grateful for the opportunity to talk on a impartial topic. "It's going well, but slowly. Much slower that I had hoped."

"That's why you decided to accept a part in *Rip Van Winkle*, then? To keep yourself occupied?"

"Mmm."

"Does that mean yes where you come from?"

Travis glanced at Fiona and found her smiling impishly, which only increased his frustration. Damn it, couldn't she see he was in a quandary over her? He rubbed his jaw and said tersely, "It means, 'Yes, that's *part* of the reason.' "

"I see."

Travis didn't bother to elaborate. They both knew his investigation of the missing cargo was the other part of the reason. The largest part of it, in fact. But he didn't want to think about that. His thoughts were too focused on Fiona. Somehow he had to make her understand how he felt about her.

"Why did you change your mind and agree to direct the play?" he asked.

Fiona shrugged. "How could I refuse? You saw how persistent my aunt was."

"Yes, but I also know how determined you can be."

She gave him a coy glance. "You've figured that out, have you?"

"Anyone who would dodge a bull to keep from planting an apple seed is determined."

Fiona laughed. "I thought I was being tenacious."

"Right now you're being evasive."

She slanted him that part-mischievous, part-flirtatious glance that drove Travis mad. "Am I now?"

"You know damn well you are."

She grew quiet, her brow wrinkling, as though deep in thought. Travis had a feeling that she was about to embark on a whole new subject and decided then that he might never learn the true reason why she had agreed to direct.

"I don't mean to sound like Bridget," Fiona said, "but it occurred to me this evening how truly opposite you are from the character of Rip Van Winkle."

"I appreciate the contrast," Travis replied dryly, "but my father would disagree with you."

"Your father must not know you very well," Fiona countered.

"He's never bothered to try."

"It's his loss, then," she said sharply.

Travis glanced at Fiona, but her expression revealed nothing more than irritation. What had she meant? That he was worth knowing? Or was he reading too much into her remark because that's what he wanted her to mean?

"Mr. Paine," Fiona said, then hesitated. After taking a breath she said, "There's something I've been meaning to explain to you. Do you remember the other morning when you mentioned my mother?"

How could he forget? Fiona had nearly taken his head off. "Yes," he said. "I remember."

"I shouldn't have been so short with you. There was no way of your knowing the circumstances." Fiona paused, chewed her lip, then spoke in a voice tinged with sadness. "My mother's death was an accident. She fell down the tower steps and broke her neck as she was on her way to refill the beacon. I don't like to speak of it, none of us do, because it's a painful subject. She was a good wife and a good mother and—" Fiona looked down and Travis could tell she was trying not to cry. "—I miss her very much."

Travis wanted nothing more than to pull her into his arms and hold her, but he didn't trust his own reaction to having her that close to him. Instead he searched for words to comfort her, though he felt completely inadequate doing so.

"You're fortunate to have fond memories of your mother," he offered. When that didn't seem to make her feel better, he tried to think of something else to say to cheer her. "My mother has a hard time even remembering my name."

Fiona looked at him in shock. "You're making that up."

Travis felt as though a weight had lifted from his shoulders. For the moment he had managed to take her mind off her sorrows. "It's true. My mother is not right up here," he said, tapping the side of his head. "Everyone in town knows it, but Jefferson would never admit a wife of his could possibly have any kind of problem, so we all carry on as if she were perfectly normal."

Fiona shook her head, her eyes wide with wonder. "How sad for all of you."

Travis shrugged. "We manage, though it does get amusing at times. Imagine sitting at the table in a formal dining room, quietly eating your soup, when suddenly your mother tosses aside her spoon and begins to lap the broth out of the bowl with her tongue.''

Fiona pressed her fingers to her lips and Travis knew she was trying not to smile. ''That's dreadful!'' she exclaimed.

''The dreadful part was pretending there was nothing out of the ordinary about our mother eating like a dog.''

''Didn't your father stop her?''

''Of course. Jefferson raised his hand in the air, summoned a servant and said, 'I believe Mrs. Paine is finished with her soup.' ''

Fiona burst out into a giggle. ''I don't mean to laugh, but it *is* odd.''

Travis looked at her and his heart swelled with unfamiliar feelings of tenderness. He was glad he'd been able to cheer her, but at that moment he also wanted badly to kiss her. The only thing that prevented him from doing so was that he wasn't sure how she would respond.

As they passed Mrs. Quinn's house, he saw Fiona glance up at the elderly woman's porch, and immediately, a frown marred her brow.

''What is it?'' he asked.

She shrugged. ''I was just thinking of something Mrs. Quinn told me.''

Fiona seemed preoccupied after that and made no further attempt at conversation. As they approached the lighthouse, Travis found himself wishing he could spend more time with her. An idea came to him as they crossed the street and started toward the stone path. ''Are you still going for your walk this evening?''

Fiona deliberated a moment, then nodded. ''Yes, I think I will. It will do me good.''

''Mind if I join you?''

''Do I have a choice?'' they said in unison, and laughed at their shared joke.

Fiona sat on the sand to slip off her shoes and stockings. Travis hesitated a moment, then sat down beside her and followed suit. With their shoes dangling from their fingers and the sand cool beneath their bare feet, they turned away from the lighthouse and walked down the beach together.

*   *   *

Fiona wasn't sure whether letting Travis walk with her was a sound idea. She had so much on her mind that she could have used the time alone to clear her thoughts. With Travis beside her, however, that was impossible.

In spite of that, Fiona rather liked him being there. Travis was a very masculine man. Being with him made her feel like a woman, an entirely new experience for her. With Travis she wasn't the lighthouse keeper's daughter or the middle sister or Aunt Fiona or the schoolteacher. She was simply Fiona, but a new and alive Fiona who was acutely aware of each nuance of Travis's behavior: his subtle glances, the change in his eyes when she smiled at him, even the timbre of his voice. The thought of being alone with him on the beach was suddenly dizzying.

"What is this tall weed called?" Travis asked, pointing to the spiked grass growing in the sand away from the water.

"Marram grass."

"I've never heard of it."

Fiona looked around and spotted a plant farther away from the water. "Come, I'll show you something else." She led him through the tall grass and stopped to kneel in the sand. "Do you know what this is?"

Travis knelt beside her. "It can't be a cactus. They only grow in the desert."

"It's a prickly pear cactus and they grow here, too. My mother used to make jelly with them." Warming to her subject, Fiona jumped up and started down the sand at a rapid pace, calling for Travis to follow. She came to a halt before a large horseshoe-shaped depression between two sand dunes. "Do you know what this is?" she asked him, standing in the center of the depression with her arms outstretched. "It's a blowout. It's made by the wind."

Travis was standing a short way off, smiling curiously. Fiona tilted her head. "What do you find so amusing?"

"You really love it here."

"Of course I do."

"Then why are you leaving?"

With that one short question Fiona's good mood evaporated. The decision to leave New Clare had been a difficult one. She had encountered resistance from every direction and didn't wish more of it. "I'm going back now," she said in a flat voice. "I'm weary."

"What is it you think you'll find out there?" Travis persisted, following behind her.

"My future," she replied firmly.

"What future? What do you want out of life that you can't find right here?"

Fiona walked faster, furious that he should feel the right to demand answers. "That's my business, Mr. Paine. I'll thank you to remember that."

"Would you stop a moment? It's difficult to talk to you when you're three feet ahead of me."

With a frustrated huff, Fiona stopped and turned to face him. "What more is there to say?"

"Just this: You don't have any idea what the world is like. You've lived a sheltered life here."

"I'll find out, then, won't I?"

Travis gripped both of her arms, his eyes intently searching hers. "You're too trusting. You'll be taken advantage of."

"By men like you?" Fiona countered, meeting his direct gaze with defiance.

"Yes," Travis said huskily, "by men like me."

At the sudden darkening of his eyes, the flaring of his nostrils, Fiona knew she had pushed him too far. Apprehension tinged with excitement rippled through her as Travis pulled her into his arms and covered her mouth with his, gently at first, then with great passion. It was an exciting experience, being kissed, and suddenly she wanted to see where it would take her, feeling confident that she could call a halt if it became dangerous.

But Travis's kisses were more potent than Fiona expected. She barely noticed her shoes and stockings slipping from her fingers, or her arms winding around his neck. One of his hands cupped her head as his kiss deepened, holding her still. The other hand slid down her back and up again, pressing her tightly against his hard torso, letting her feel the sinewy strength of him. His taste was intoxicating, his scent arousing, his touch stimulating to the point of being excruciating. She felt as though she were drowning in new sensations, losing herself to him. Where would it lead her?

Nowhere.

Fiona broke the kiss and leaned her forehead against his chin. The kiss could lead nowhere. Travis was leaving New Clare and so was she, each with their separate dreams. She could not lose her heart to a man she'd never see again. She pushed away from him and picked up her shoes and stockings.

Travis watched, baffled, as Fiona started back up the beach toward the lighthouse. He was still breathing hard, his thundering heartbeat matching the one he had felt beating beneath her breast. Surely she didn't mean to deny the attraction between them. He had tasted the passion in her kiss, felt the desire in her touch. She would be lying if she said it meant nothing. Yet why had she turned away from him? Why was she even now headed home?

"Fiona!"

The sound of his voice, angry and confused, gave Fiona pause for a moment. So it was to be *Fiona* from now on, she thought wryly. No longer were they strangers. With that one kiss they had crossed the invisible line between formality and familiarity. No man had ever gotten that close to her before. Why had she let this one, this man whose destiny was to captain a lake ship, this person who thought so little of her family as to accuse them of thievery?

Travis caught up with her in several long strides. "Fiona, you can't run away from me."

"I'm not running away, I'm going home."

"What about what happened back there?"

"It was a kiss, nothing more."

"*Nothing* more?"

"That's what I said."

He pulled her to a stop. "Look at me, Fiona. Look at me and say it meant nothing more."

Fiona would not look at him, but kept her gaze fixed on the sand instead. He cupped her chin and tilted her head up. "Tell me *this* means nothing, as well." He kissed her with passion, his mouth crushing hers, then turning tender and yielding. As his kiss lengthened his arm around her tightened, molding her to his body, until she was left breathless and weak-kneed.

When Travis broke their kiss, Fiona fought not to sag against him, not to let him see how much his kiss had affected her. She dared not let him see. She could not jeopardize her dreams.

"Tell me now, Fiona, that my kiss means nothing to you, that you feel nothing," he whispered against her ear.

Fiona closed her eyes to collect her thoughts, then forced herself to show no emotion as she stepped back. "We have our separate dreams, you and I. Why complicate them?"

Travis stared at her as if he couldn't comprehend her words. Then he bent his head, raked his fingers through his hair and let out his breath. When he looked at her again, his gaze was piercing, his voice angry. "You're right, of course. Why complicate them? Still, I meant what I said. You don't know what the world is like beyond New Clare."

"And I meant what I said, as well," Fiona replied sharply. "It's my business, not yours."

"So you'll turn your back on your family and on the town you love to seek some elusive dream?"

"I can't explain it to you any more than I already have."

"You can't even explain it to yourself."

Fiona started to protest, then changed her mind. She had no need to defend her dreams to Travis Paine. "I'm going back."

Hurt, rejected, Travis stood alone on the beach, watching Fiona walk away from him. He had offered her his love and she had turned it down. Now he felt like a fool for revealing his feelings to her, for believing she felt as strongly about him as he did about her. Hadn't he learned as a child to keep his feelings to himself?

Travis clenched his jaw and strode down the shoreline. He should have stuck to his original goals, to get the ship repaired and find the cargo. Instead, he had stupidly let his feelings for Fiona detract him. But they would detract him no longer.

It was time to get back to business. To do that, however, he needed some answers.

"Just a minute, Fiona," he called.

It was the cold, impersonal sound of his voice that stopped Fiona. She swung around and watched warily as he stalked across the sand toward her, his features grim, determined.

"I'd like an explanation of the whiskey I found in the stable."

Fiona's heart leaped to her throat. Travis had found the crate! A sudden nausea swept over her and she had to force herself to remain calm. If he had found the whiskey, then he had discovered it before she had. Why had he waited until now to tell her? What had he planned to do about it? How could she answer without either incriminating her family or telling an outright lie?

Fiona's fingers curled into her palms, her nails digging into tender flesh. "I know of no whiskey in the stable. You must be mistaken."

"No, Fiona, I'm not mistaken. In fact, I'll prove it to you."

Fiona had no choice but to follow. She couldn't very well tell him he would find nothing there.

Circling the lighthouse, Travis led her to the stable and pulled the door open. Inside he found a lantern, lit it and carried it to the last stall. Fiona stood by the open door, her head lowered, waiting.

"Son of a bitch!" she heard him mutter. She raised her eyes as Travis spun around and glared at her. "Where is it?"

Fiona swallowed, her throat suddenly dry. "Where is what?"

"The whiskey!" he snapped.

In her mind's eye Fiona saw the liquor spilling from the open bottles, mixing with the lake water to be carried to the farthest ports of Lake Michigan and beyond. Where the whiskey was at that moment was anyone's guess. She could only be grateful he hadn't asked the whereabouts of the bottles. She looked him straight in the eye and said defiantly, "If I knew where your whiskey was, I'd tell you."

He crossed the short distance between them and stood glaring down at her. "There were three bottles of whiskey in here the other day—whiskey from *my* ship—right back there in that stall. If you didn't move it, then someone else did.''

Fiona said nothing, just continued to stare at him.

Travis spun around and went to check the other stalls. ''There *was* whiskey in here!'' he said, slamming the last stall door. ''It was in a box with the ship's name on the side. Damn it, I knew I should have gone to the sheriff.''

At the mention of the sheriff, Fiona's stomach knotted. She could not let Travis file a complaint. If any hint of trouble made its way to the lighthouse board, her father would lose his job.

''Mr. Paine,'' she began, then thought better of it and started again. ''Travis, I know you think the Irish are stupid, but do you suppose we'd be so stupid as to hide stolen goods on our own property? If your whiskey had been hidden here, wouldn't it seem likely that someone did it to make us look guilty?''

Travis studied her through narrowed eyes. ''If the whiskey was put here to make you look guilty, then why has it been removed? And who the hell is behind it if not someone in your family?''

If only I knew, Fiona thought morosely. ''I have no answers for you,'' she said, ''but I would like to offer my help.''

Fiona saw the suspicion in Travis's dark eyes as he pondered her offer. ''You want to help me?''

''It's my family you're accusing of thievery. I've every reason to want to find the real thief.''

''Or make damn sure *I* don't find him.''

Fiona looked at him squarely. ''You'll have to trust me.''

''What if it turns out to be a family member?''

''It won't. I can promise you that.''

''All right, *Miss Cleary*,'' Travis said with a cynical smile. ''Let's see if the two of us can find the real thief.''

Fiona met his dubious gaze evenly. They were strangers once again.

·*14*·

FIONA PERFORMED HER chores the next day with little awareness of what she was doing. Her thoughts were tumultuous, spinning from one problem to the next. Not only did she have to keep Travis from reporting the missing cargo, but she also had to help him find the thief. She decided to start her search by questioning Carvey more thoroughly, and as soon as her chores were finished, she set off to find him.

She found her father perched on an old wooden chair at the end of the pier, attending to his fishing pole. He seemed distant, preoccupied, and it struck her again how much he had aged over the past few weeks. When she questioned him about Carvey, he responded in a weary voice that he hadn't seen Carvey since early that morning. Fiona left with the uncomfortable feeling that her father was keeping something from her.

She discovered Deirdre sitting in the shade of a cottonwood tree behind the house reading to Jamie.

"Feena!" her nephew called as she approached. He jumped up and ran to her with arms outstretched. Fiona obligingly swung Jamie up in her arms and pressed a kiss on his warm little cheek. "Is Mama reading you a story?"

Jamie nodded emphatically and squirmed to get down. "Feena read, too."

"Next time, Jamie boy. Aunt Fiona has chores. Dee, where's Carvey?"

Deirdre leaned back against the tree trunk and fanned herself, looking flushed from the heat. "He went to town to see how Devlin's saloon is coming along. Jamie, are you ready for a nap yet? Mama is tired."

Jamie scowled fiercely. "No, Mama. Read."

Fiona heard her sister's weary sigh and couldn't help but wonder how Deirdre would ever manage two youngsters. She started toward the lighthouse to fetch her straw hat. "I'm going to town, Dee. I'll be back soon."

But she had no sooner started down the stone path when she saw Carvey start up it. As she drew closer to him she could see that his face was sickly white and he looked shaken.

"Carvey, are you all right?"

He seemed not to see her. Fiona stepped out of his way as he hurried past. She followed him back to the lighthouse, where he threw his tall, gangly form into a kitchen chair and covered his face with his hands.

"What is it? Are you ill?"

"Yes," he groaned through his fingers.

Fiona wet a cloth with cool water and applied it to his forehead. "I'll make you a cup of strong tea and then I'll fetch the doctor."

"No! I don't need the doctor. I'll be all right soon." Holding the cloth to his head, Carvey rose with effort and made his way to the bedroom in the back, where he lay face up, holding the cloth over his eyes.

Fiona stood in the doorway, worriedly chewing the tip of her thumbnail. "Did something happen in town?"

Groaning as though in great pain, he turned on his side and pulled his knees to his chest. Alarmed, Fiona went to him and leaned over his shoulder. "Carvey, does this have anything to do with your visit to Devlin?"

"It's my belly, Fiona. It burns so. Oh, God, it burns!"

"Fiona?" she heard from the doorway.

Fiona turned and found her sister standing just inside the door, a terrified expression on her face. Jamie was standing beside her, his finger in his mouth, his eyes wide as Carvey continued to moan.

"Carvey has a bellyache, Dee," she said quietly, moving toward her. "I'm going to fetch the doctor."

"What will I do if he gets worse?" Deirdre asked, her voice rising in fright.

Fiona put her hands on her sister's shoulders and turned her around, guiding her through the door. "Go put Jamie down in my bed for his nap, then fill the water bottle with heated water to put on Carvey's stomach. It won't take me long to get back and you can always fetch Da if you need help."

Dr. Carnahan had just returned from a house call when Fiona burst into his office, breathing hard. "Carvey is ill, Doctor. It's his belly. He's doubled over in pain."

The doctor started for the coat rack. "I'll get my hat and meet you at the buggy."

Pegeen and Tullia were waiting outside the doctor's office, worried expressions on their faces. "What happened, Fiona?" Tullia asked. "We saw you run past the store."

"Carvey is ill. Something is wrong with his stomach."

"It must have come on quickly," Pegeen commented. "He was in town not two hours ago visiting Dev at the saloon. I saw them talking together."

The doctor came striding out, his medical bag in hand. "Let's go, Fiona."

"We'll come out later to see how Carvey's doing," Pegeen called as the buggy jerked into motion.

Fiona rubbed her temples, beginning to feeling overwhelmed by her problems. And she still had rehearsal to get through that evening for *Rip Van Winkle*.

What else could possibly go wrong?

When Travis stepped off the train late that afternoon, Edwin O'Banyon hailed him from across the depot. "Telegram for you, Mr. Paine."

"Thanks." Travis opened it and scanned the message, then, with a muttered curse, crumpled it into a ball. "Damn that old man!'' he swore as he strode through the depot and headed for the lighthouse.

Jefferson Paine was sending his eldest son, Jordan, to New Clare to see that the ship was repaired and brought safely back to Erie. For Travis it was another slap in the face. His father couldn't trust him to do the job properly.

What the hell was he going to tell Jordan about the missing cargo? His brother no doubt had explicit instructions as to what to do with the goods. Travis ground his teeth in frustration. No matter what he did, it was never good enough. Why did he keep trying?

When he opened the door and stepped into the lighthouse, the kitchen was full of people. Besides Fiona and her father, Tullia was there, along with the doctor, Pegeen and Tom Brody and Ena Murphy. They were sitting at the kitchen table talking in hushed voices and drinking coffee. Travis thought at first that Deirdre had delivered her baby, until Dee herself came into the kitchen from the back room, her small heart-shaped face drawn with worry. Everyone turned to look at her.

Deirdre sank into an empty chair and laid her head on her arms. ''He's sleeping now.''

Travis noticed then that Carvey was absent. He shut the door and all heads swiveled toward him.

''Come in, Mr. Paine,'' Finn Cleary said, putting on a smile for his benefit. ''Will you have some coffee? Supper is a bit late, I'm afraid.''

''Yes, of course. That's all right.''

Fiona rose to get him a cup of coffee.

''Carvey's been taken ill,'' Finn explained in a quiet voice as Travis took a seat at the long table. ''He may have an ulceration of the stomach.''

Dr. Carnahan put down his cup and hoisted his bulk out of the chair. ''Well, I'd best be on my way. There's nothing more I can do now. Just follow my instructions and I'll stop by tomorrow morning to check on him.''

While Finn saw the doctor to the door, Fiona placed a cup of coffee in front of Travis, then went back to the stove. He watched as she lifted the lid of an iron pot and stirred the steaming contents with a long, wooden spoon. Around him the family conferred in hushed tones.

"He's been sleeping poorly lately."

"It had to be something he ate."

"His mother always had a weak stomach. Nerves, of course."

"That sort of thing runs in the family."

"We need to let his family know."

Fiona went to the cupboard, took out plates and set them around the table. Travis's gaze followed her as she prepared for the meal. She seemed intent on her task, yet he knew she was listening to the conversation, as concerned as the rest of them.

Travis envied their closeness, their concern. Had he ever felt such close ties with his family? Would his brothers rally around if he were taken ill?

"How's the ship faring, Mr. Paine?"

Travis glanced at Finn. "Coming along."

"Your crew working out okay?"

"Fine."

He raised his eyes and caught Fiona studying him speculatively as she placed a deep bowl of stew in front of her father. She finished setting out the food, placed freshly baked bread in the center on a plate beside a bowl of creamy butter and sat down beside Travis. Heads bowed as Finn began his prayer.

Travis glanced at the worried faces around the table. Could one of them have stolen his cargo, or was Fiona correct, that someone had put the whiskey in their stable hoping he would discover it and accuse them of thievery? Since the whiskey was no longer there, her theory seemed unlikely.

What if he hadn't checked the stable in the first place? What if Finn or Carvey had found the whiskey and disposed of it? Why would someone go to such lengths on the flimsy chance he would find it first?

Was he dealing with a stupid thief or a very clever one?

"Will you have some bread, Mr. Paine?"

"Thanks." Travis took the plate from Fiona, removed a

slice of bread and sent the dish along. "When did Carvey become ill?"

Fiona took some butter for her bread and passed the bowl to Travis. "All I know is that he came home from town ill early this afternoon."

"Who will take his watch tonight?"

"I will," she answered quietly and without hesitation.

Travis couldn't help but admire the way Fiona took everything in stride. He found himself wondering how she'd handle his father and decided she'd take Jefferson Paine in stride, as well. Travis was tempted to tell her about his brother's impending visit, but decided she had enough concerns on her mind at that moment without him burdening her with his own. She'd learn of it soon enough.

Fiona rose as soon as she finished. "We'll have to hurry, Auntie, if we want to get to rehearsal on time."

"Peg will lend a hand with the dishes," Tullia ordered. "Tommy can stay to help Finn care for Carvey. Dee has her hands full with the lad."

"I'll help in any way I can," Travis offered.

Tullia turned on him with a mock scowl. "You'll do nothing of the kind, sir. You're a guest in this house. Sit."

No one challenged Tullia's edicts.

Travis and Tullia were waiting outside when Fiona prepared to leave for the church. She hung up her apron, took her hat from the hook by the door and pinned it in place as they started down the stone path. It had been a long day, it promised to be an equally long evening, and it appeared she would also be having a very long night taking Carvey's watch. She wanted to feel sorry for herself, but she didn't have time for it.

And who should be waiting in front of the church, frilly parasol in hand even though there was no sun?

"Yoo-hoo! Mr. Paine!"

Bridget! "Someday I hope to understand why you hate me so," Fiona whispered to her aunt.

Tullia laughed. "Don't be a goose, Fiona. I didn't cast that part on purpose. None of the other ladies wanted the role."

"Bridget probably browbeat them out of auditioning for it."

"Good evening, Mr. Paine," Bridget cooed, tilting her head to give him a coy smile. "Here I thought I'd be late and I beat the three of you! Hello, Mrs. Brody." She slanted Fiona a quick glance. "Fiona."

"Bridget."

Travis hurried ahead of them to open the church door. Fiona followed her aunt inside, then turned to see Bridget loop her hand through Travis's arm and sashay in beside him, chattering all the while about her appointment with the dressmaker to be fitted for a new silk dress. As she passed, Bridget turned her head to give Fiona a smug smile.

With narrowed eyes, Fiona watched Bridget and Travis walk down the stairs into the basement. "I should have put my foot out and tripped her," Fiona muttered. "That would have brought Bridget down a peg or two."

Tullia laid a restraining hand on Fiona's arm. "Jealousy can be a poisonous thing, Fiona."

"Me? Jealous of the likes of Bridget Riley?" Fiona gave a light laugh.

"Deny it all you like," Tullia said with a knowing smile. "I know how you feel about your Mr. Paine. You might be able to fool yourself but you've never been able to fool me."

I have no choice but to deny it, Fiona thought sadly. She knew she had hurt Travis, but she also knew in the long run they would both be better off. She only wished that that knowledge could ease her pain.

When Fiona joined the rest of the cast assembled on stage in the great hall, she had questions to answer about Carvey's illness, as well as numerous offers of assistance. As Fiona responded, she couldn't help but notice Bridget standing at the back of the stage flirting shamelessly with Travis.

Bridget was wearing another of her fancy dresses, this one in a pale apricot color. The girl's wardrobe was endless, Fiona thought with a scowl as she called for the cast members to take their places. And now Bridget was adding a new silk dress to her collection.

The rehearsal progressed smoothly through the first act until Bridget's part came up; and then she started, fumbled and stamped her tiny foot in frustration. "I can't say these lines. They're silly! No one speaks like that."

Fiona narrowed her eyes at Bridget. "People used to talk like that, Bridget."

Bridget turned toward Travis and batted her golden eyelashes. "Don't you agree, Mr. Paine, that it sounds silly?"

Travis gave Bridget a smile that made Fiona's heart ache. "I would agree, Miss Riley, but you make even the silly speech of yesteryear sound charming."

Watching their little parlay, Fiona wanted to choke them both. "Well now, Dame Van Winkle," she said sharply, "are you ready to continue?"

With a sharp huff, Bridget turned and stalked to her spot on the stage.

Halfway through the evening, Fiona called a much-needed break, as patience was in short supply. Tullia sliced the peach pies Mary Sheridan had provided and set them out on a table with lemonade.

As Fiona ate her pie, Bridget sidled up to the table and picked up a plate and fork. "I just can't wait until my new dress is finished."

"Can't you now?" Fiona remarked in a bland voice.

"I know Mr. Paine is eager to see it, too." Bridget toyed with her dessert. "He told me so."

Fiona tried to ignore her. It was just another of Bridget's shallow ploys to make her jealous. With an unhappy sigh, Fiona stuck her fork into a syrupy peach slice and slid it into her mouth. If only Bridget's ploy were not quite so successful.

Suddenly she swallowed hard. *Stars and garters!* Why hadn't she thought of it sooner? The dress was *silk*! And where would Bridget get silk in New Clare unless it had been a special order?

From Travis's missing cargo.

❖ *15* ❖

"THE DRESS WAS silk, you say?" Fiona asked, keeping her tone casual.

"Lime-green silk!" Bridget amended.

"That must have cost your father a pretty penny."

Bridget broke off a piece of flaky crust and popped it in her mouth. "It was a gift."

"Was it now?" Fiona replied, watching her closely. "Well, your father always was a generous fellow."

Bridget gave her a mysterious smile. "Oh, it's not from my father. But it *is* from someone you know." With that, she turned and sashayed over to where Travis was standing. Fiona watched as Bridget offered Travis a bite of her pie, then made a show of brushing the crumbs off his lips and giggling.

Certainly Bridget wanted her to think the silk was from Travis; she would never admit that it wasn't. But which one of Bridget's admirers could it actually have been from? The only clue Fiona had was that it was from someone she knew.

The problem was that she knew everyone.

"Yoo-hoo, Mr. Paine!"

Travis winced. He had slipped offstage as soon as rehearsal had ended, hoping to keep out of Bridget's sight until she had left the church. Obviously, he had underestimated his onstage spouse's perseverance.

"Have you been hiding from me, you naughty boy?"

No such luck, Travis thought grimly, fully sympathetic with Rip Van Winkle's plight. He squared his shoulders and turned to face the little bluebird of harpiness. "If I *were* a boy," he answered somewhat curtly, "especially a naughty one, I doubt you'd be looking for me right now."

Bridget held a blue-gloved hand to her mouth and giggled. "You do say the cleverest things, Mr. Paine. Papa even said so and Papa is quite a clever man himself."

Not too clever or he would have married his daughter off long before now. Travis rubbed the tight muscles in the back of his neck. "Is there something I can do for you, Miss Riley?"

With a coquettish smile, she dipped her head and glanced up at him through her lashes. "It's awfully late and Papa wasn't feeling well this evening. I thought perhaps I could prevail upon you to see me home."

Travis glanced over her blond head. Fiona was discussing Mr. Tucker's lines with him and didn't look ready to leave. If he hurried, he might be able to see Bridget to her house and get back before Fiona had left the church so he could walk home with her. He told himself it was only to discuss the business of finding the thief. "I'll meet you out front in five minutes."

Bridget smiled like a child just given a bright red lollipop. "Five minutes," she chirped and sailed blithely out of the wings, making straight for Fiona.

Standing behind the heavy maroon curtain, Travis watched as Bridget interrupted Fiona, no doubt to brag about her chaperon for the trip home. He watched Fiona's expression closely, hoping to see some sign of jealousy, but, as usual, she reacted with bland disinterest.

Travis left through the side door and walked to the street, wondering why he felt such disappointment in Fiona's reaction. Hadn't she already made it clear how she felt about him? Weren't his main objectives to find the thief and recover the missing cargo? Wasn't his most important concern to redeem himself in his father's eyes?

With a scowl, Travis folded his arms and leaned against

the lamppost, waiting impatiently for Bridget to appear. After all, Fiona had made it perfectly clear she had no intention of giving up her dream for him. Perhaps his disappointment stemmed from something more than her rejection. Perhaps it was just simple disappointment in life. Perhaps he grasped for the unreachable because he knew he was destined to be disappointed. Perhaps he was—

"Yoo-hoo! Here I am!"

—doomed.

Fiona was halfway home when she heard Travis call her name. She slowed her step to let him catch up to her, but didn't turn around to acknowledge him. Not only was she tired, but she was also miffed because he had walked Bridget home. Surely he could see what a ninny Bridget was.

"Mind if I join you?" he asked breathlessly as he fell into step beside her.

Fiona could not bring herself to respond in the teasing way they had developed. Instead she shrugged her shoulders. "Suit yourself."

She walked a few more paces, fuming in silence, then finally could stand it no longer. "Did Bridget make it home safely or did you have to fight off a multitude of carnivorous creatures in the two blocks between her house and the church?"

To her surprise, Travis threw back his head and laughed.

She shot him a cold look. "What's so amusing, Mr. Paine?"

"You never cease to amaze me. Why are you jealous of Bridget?"

Hot spots of red colored Fiona's cheeks. "Me? Jealous of the likes of Bridget Riley?"

"If that wasn't jealousy rearing its pretty little green head, then what was it?"

"Why, it was just—" Fiona cast about for some rational explanation, but her exhausted mind refused to cooperate. She resorted to a half-hearted denial. "It *wasn't* jealousy."

He wagged a finger at her as they came to the end of Wexford Street. "Look me in the eye and say that."

Fiona knew she couldn't look him in the eye and lie, but if she were clever and not too tired, she might be able to circle around the truth. She kept walking. "If I were you, I'd be more concerned about where Bridget came by the silk for that dress than about reading some hidden meaning into my words."

By a quick glance in his direction, she saw she had Travis's full attention and knew she had outwitted him.

"What have you heard?" he asked.

"Only that the silk was a gift from an admirer, which might not mean much to you, but you see, there's not much call for silk in New Clare. Wool, linen and cotton, yes, but not silk unless it's special-ordered for a wedding or the like. It's just not a practical material, and the people here are very practical."

Travis was quiet as they climbed the stone path to the top of the dune. "So we need to find out who Bridget's admirer is," he said at last.

"Not who, but which one." Fiona sat down on the edge of the stoop to remove her shoes and shake the sand from them. "She wanted me to think it was you."

Travis sat down beside her and followed suit. "Which you didn't, of course, since you're not at all jealous."

Perhaps she had been too hasty in thinking she had outwitted him. Fiona decided it was safer to ignore his remark than to take exception to it. "First thing tomorrow I'll pay a call on Mrs. McDonnell, the dressmaker. Bridget may have said something to her about where the silk came from." A yawn caught her by surprise. She covered her mouth, slipped into her shoes and rose wearily to her feet, feeling the effects of the long day. "It must be nearly time to take Carvey's watch."

Travis was silent as he stood and looked down at her. For a moment he searched her face, as though seeking answers to hard questions, then slowly his gaze dropped to her mouth. At once his eyes darkened to nearly black, just as they had before their heated kisses on the beach. As his head dipped toward her, Fiona suddenly remembered in vivid detail the feel of his mouth on hers, the taste of him, the powerful surges of desire he aroused within her.

St. Christopher's stockings! He wouldn't try it again, would he? She was suddenly wide awake and breathless. Backing up to the door, she turned around, fumbled with the doorknob and rushed inside.

"Good night, Miss Cleary," she heard him call, amusement in his voice.

With pounding heart, Fiona crossed the kitchen to the staircase, and only then did she pause to glance back, but the doorway was empty. She felt a twinge of conscience for leaving him so abruptly, yet she had only to remind herself of the damage he could do to her father to feel justified.

Travis stood on the porch grinning at the closed door. Fiona was jealous of Bridget! Her fancy speech about feeling nothing for him was a lie. She was simply afraid to admit her feelings. He felt renewed, revitalized. With a jaunty spring in his step, he strode down the path to the beach. He was too wound up to even think of sleeping.

Then Travis remembered that his brother was coming and his spirits plummeted. "Son of a bitch!" he muttered, shoving his hands in his pockets. Every damn time he felt he was on the verge of accomplishing something, life had a way of kicking his legs out from under him. He wondered why he even bothered to try.

Yet Travis knew he would keep trying. Whether it was to please his father or win Fiona's admiration, something deep inside refused to let him give up. It was possibly the only good trait he inherited from his father.

Fiona checked the clock in the tower room, then, with a yawn, snuggled deeper into her father's big upholstered brown chair. She had another hour to go before it was time to refill the light with kerosene. To keep herself awake, she tried to ponder the mystery of Bridget's silk dress, but her mind kept returning to her near miss on the porch.

Had Travis truly been about to kiss her or had her imagination got the better of her? And what would have happened if she hadn't turned and run like a scared rabbit? Would he have kissed her with the same passion as before?

At the thought of their first electrifying encounter, Fiona sighed dreamily. Kissing was a much more pleasurable activity than she had imagined—at least with Travis it was. His mouth had been firm and yielding at the same time, while his arms about her had felt so—

She sat up with a jerk. *Stars and garters! What am I doing thinking about Travis Paine?* She forced herself to concentrate on the silk dress.

Someone she knew had given the material to Bridget, but that could be anyone in town. Narrowing it down to Bridget's suitors still left a dozen men from which to choose. She hoped Bridget had revealed something about her benefactor to the dressmaker. She dreaded the thought of having to pander to Bridget in order to draw information from the twit herself.

At the sound of footsteps at the top of the stairs, Fiona turned to see Travis appear in the doorway. Over his white union suit he wore her father's blue striped dressing robe. His dark hair was tousled from sleep and his face was shadowed with new growth of beard. He grinned rakishly. "Good morning."

Fiona jumped up in surprise. "Mr. Paine! What are you doing up at this early hour?"

"I woke and couldn't get back to sleep." He produced the blue china teapot and two cups from the kitchen and set them on the chairside table. "I thought you might need fortification, though I wasn't sure I'd find you up here. I seem to remember you saying that it wasn't necessary to stay in the tower for the entire watch."

Fiona gave a little shrug. "Dee and Jamie are sleeping in my bed. I thought I might as well nap here." Feeling awkward, she sat stiffly in the brown chair, her hands clasped nervously on her lap. Had it escaped Travis's attention, she wondered, that she had on her nightclothes, too? She watched mutely as he poured tea into the cups and handed her one.

"How's Carvey?" he asked.

"Not well. I checked on him an hour ago. He's sleeping

fitfully and keeps moaning, though whether from bad dreams or pain I don't know.''

"I'm sorry to hear it.''

"So am I. With the new baby coming, Dee will need Carvey's help. And my father will need his assistance with the light. It won't be long before I'll be leaving.''

Fiona took a sip of tea and contemplated her last remark. Only a short time ago, her plans had seemed all-important. Now she could scarcely drum up the enthusiasm they had once aroused. With a sigh, she set the cup on its saucer. "What has you so sleepless this night?''

Travis pulled up a wooden stool and sat on it, taking time to sip his own tea before replying. "My brother Jordan is coming to New Clare.''

Fiona stared at him in surprise. By the tone of Travis's voice, she could tell he was far from pleased about it. "Is he now? For what reason?''

"To aid the incompetent, I suppose.''

"The incompetent being you?'' she asked.

"The one and only.''

"When did you learn of this?''

"I received a telegram earlier today.''

Fiona wondered why he had waited so long to tell her. "When will he arrive?''

"Tomorrow.''

"Tomorrow!'' Fiona frowned in deep thought. Had the brother been sent to help Travis find the missing cargo? She rubbed her forehead. Just when she thought there could not possibly be any more complications in her life, another one arose.

"Jordan will take a room in town,'' Travis assured her. "You won't need to put him up. In fact, I'll take one there myself. I've been a burden long enough.''

Travis not stay at the lighthouse? When would she see him? "Oh, but you needn't do that!'' she exclaimed, then instantly wished she could take back her words. *Devil's knees, Fiona, why not just proclaim your interest in him?* At Travis's raised eyebrows, she said quickly, "What I meant was that there's no need for either of you to spend money for rooms when we can put your brother up here. He'll be helping you with the ship's repairs, won't he?''

Travis's gaze hardened and a muscle twitched in his jaw. ''I believe it's to be the other way around.''

Fiona set her cup in the saucer with a bang. The injustice of the whole situation infuriated her. Travis was a competent man. Why did his father treat him so cruelly?

''I suppose your brother will also be helping you locate your missing goods.''

For a moment, Travis stared at the floor, as though lost in thought. Finally, with a sigh, he closed his eyes and rubbed them with his thumbs. ''Jordan doesn't know about the loss yet. In fact, none of my family knows. I had hoped to recover the cargo without having to tell them about it. Now, of course, it's too late. I suppose I should have informed them immediately.''

Fiona raised her cup and sipped her tea. In the same circumstances she would have reacted just as Travis had. After all, he had only wanted to prove himself capable. But because of someone in New Clare, that chance was lost. And she felt responsible.

Fiona pressed her lips together. She would have to find a way to keep Travis's brother from finding out about the missing cargo. It was her duty to help Travis, if only to protect the good name of New Clare, Indiana.

''Does your brother have to be told?'' she asked.

Travis studied her curiously. ''What are you getting at?''

''Since he doesn't know about the loss, why not wait until we find the goods to tell him?''

''Because my father has probably given him instructions as to what to do with the merchandise upon his arrival.''

''Oh.'' Fiona set her cup aside, rose from the chair and went to stand at one of the windows. ''What if we tell him the cargo has already been sent on by train?'' she said, turning.

Travis shook his head. ''No good. The Paine Shipping Company has probably been deluged with telegrams from merchants wanting to know when their goods will be delivered. Those won't stop until all the orders have been received.''

Fiona chewed her thumbnail as she paced to the doorway and back again. ''There has to be something we can do to stall your brother.'' She continued to pace for several more minutes, then began to think out loud. ''I know what I'll do. I'll talk to Tommy about it. He might have an idea. In fact, I'll call a family meeting. I'm certain among all of us we'll come up with a plan.''

She glanced at Travis and found him smiling, as though he found her wryly amusing. ''This is hardly the time to make sport of me, Mr. Paine. I'm trying to help.''

''I was not making sport of you, Miss Cleary. I was admiring you.''

Embarrassed, Fiona sat down again and picked up her cup. ''Go on with you.''

''Look at it from my standpoint. I've done nothing but make your life difficult—granted, it's through no fault of my own—yet still you're trying to help me. I find that admirable, even though I don't understand it.''

''Well, it just isn't fair, is all,'' Fiona said. ''A father pitting one son against another? I've never heard of the like. The man needs to be taught a thing or two.'' She huffed indignantly, took a sip of tea and muttered, ''Wouldn't I love the opportunity to set him straight about a few matters.''

Travis knelt before her and took one of her slippered feet in his hand. ''Yes, I think you would.''

Fiona sat forward. ''What are you doing?''

''Something occurred to me on the porch this evening.'' He removed her slipper and ran his palm across the bare sole of one foot, sending pleasurable tingles throughout her body. ''You have very pretty feet.''

Fiona drew in her breath as his thumb traced the curve of her arch. Whatever he was up to, she had to put a stop to it immediately. ''A foot is a foot, Mr. Paine. Now please let *my* foot go.''

''I remember the first night I saw you walking on the beach,'' Travis told her, running his thumb back and forth over the arch until Fiona felt as though the very bones in her body were melting. "You had on a light-colored dress and you were barefoot."

Fiona's heart beat faster as he looked up into her eyes with a smile. "Mr. Paine," she protested weakly, "This isn't seemly."

"Your hair was loose." He reached up and removed the comb from the back of her head, spilling her long, dark hair onto her shoulders. "Like that."

Fiona's insides quivered as Travis bared her other foot and began to massage it as he had the first.

"I heard you singing," he continued, rubbing slow circles into the sensitive underside of her foot. "That's what drew me to the window. I didn't know who it was at first, but I thought that whoever she turned out to be, she was enchanting."

Fiona had no will to either stop him or reply. Her greatest desire at that moment was to lean back in her chair, close her eyes and enjoy the delicious sensations, yet she was afraid to let down her guard, not for fear he would take advantage of her, but for fear she would let him.

Travis lifted her foot to his mouth and pressed a kiss on the top of it, his breath warm against her skin. Fiona clutched the armrests of the chair until her knuckles turned white, but she couldn't bring herself to stop him. His lips brushed over her toes, then he gently took one in his mouth and sucked it before moving on to her arch, where he ran his tongue up the curve. Fiona drew in her breath, trembling so hard her teeth nearly clattered, yet still she did nothing to stop him.

When Travis slid his hand up her ankle to her calf and down again, she bit her lower lip to keep from whimpering. When he cupped her face between his hands and rose to kiss her, her heart pounded in anticipation, and when his tongue delved inside her mouth, exploring its soft contours, stroking her own tongue, she moaned with a mixture of passion and fright. Yet she did not stop him.

Every instinct warned her that such foolishness could easily get out of hand. But at that moment Fiona was disinclined to listen to her instincts. She wrapped her arms around Travis's neck and kissed him back until they were both breathless with need. He pulled her from the chair and gently laid her on the floor beneath him.

"Ah, Fiona," he murmured, pressing hot kisses against her forehead, her eyelids, running his tongue down her slender neck, nibbling her ear, until she was nearly delirious. He lay on top of her, his swollen groin hard against the apex of her thighs, his kisses so ardent that Fiona lost the ability to think rationally. His hand gripped her bottom through the thin cotton of her nightclothes, pulling her tightly to him as he moved rhythmically against her.

"Travis," she cried mindlessly, arching her back to press closer against him.

As though her needy cry had penetrated the fog of passion surrounding his brain and awakened his conscience, Travis suddenly stilled. Fiona opened her eyes and stared at him as he lifted himself from her with a tormented groan. Her body still throbbing, her mind befuddled, she reached out a questioning hand toward him. He took it and, without a word, helped her to her feet.

Embarrassed, bewildered and hurt by his abrupt change in behavior, Fiona hastened to straighten her clothing. Hadn't her kisses been good enough for him? Had she been too forward? She watched wretchedly as he walked to the doorway and paused with his back to her.

"I'm sorry, Fiona. I behaved badly. That should never have happened."

As Fiona listened to Travis's receding footsteps, angry tears sprang to her eyes and she pressed a hand to her mouth to hold back a sob. He was sorry it had happened, but no sorrier than she. Why had she trusted him? Why hadn't she followed her instincts? What barmy thoughts had pervaded her mind?

Never again! she told herself. By all the saints in heaven she would not let her heart rule her head again. She had to take care of herself. No one would do it for her, least of all Travis Paine.

Fiona dashed away the tears on her cheeks and returned to the safety of her father's chair. For a time she stared out through the large windows into the night, too emotionally and physically drained to do more than wish for the comfort of her bed. Suddenly, with a gasp, she checked the clock.

What could she have been thinking of? It was past time to refill the beacon. Springing from the chair, she hastened to do the task and found solace in the familiarity of it.

·16·

FOR HOURS, TRAVIS lay awake on his bed, his arms behind his head, staring at the ceiling as he recounted each second of his meeting with Fiona in the tower. He was drunk with the taste and smell of her, drunk with his need for her, and so aroused he had to grit his teeth against the pain of it.

He could have made love to her there on the floor—she had been as aroused as he—and yet his conscience would not have permitted it. Fiona was too trusting, too innocent. She deserved a man who would marry her, care for her, treasure her strength of spirit and bask in her love, not a man who would pleasure himself with her, then sail away.

And yet how many times had he done it before? Ten times? Twenty? Had his conscience stopped him on those occasions?

Ah, but none of those girls had been Fiona.

Travis rolled onto his side. His problem was that he had never had to consider a woman's feelings before. Basically, he was a loner, a selfish bastard, going where he pleased, behaving as he pleased, answering to no one—with the exception of his father, and that had gotten him nowhere.

The question was, what did he want to do about it? Would he keep striving to please his father while continuing his life as a lone wolf? Or did he want something more for himself?

Travis twisted onto his stomach. He knew what he wanted, yet he was afraid to reach for it for fear of being rejected again. Fiona had her own dreams and they didn't include marrying a sailor.

With a frustrated groan, Travis flipped onto his back and covered his eyes with one arm. His best bet was to turn the ship and the problem of the missing cargo over to Jordan and leave, his own ambitions be damned. It went against his grain to do so, but at least he would bring no more harm to Fiona or her family. His one regret was that he had nearly taken advantage of her. Thank God he had stopped himself in time.

When Fiona awoke later that morning, it was nearly nine o'clock. With a heavy sigh, she turned on her side and curled her knees to her chest, remembering the scene in the tower. What had transpired between them had forced her to admit the strength of her feelings for Travis. There were no two ways about it: She was in love with him, though she would never put it into words. And, though it was painful, she also realized he didn't feel the same about her. His own words had confirmed it. For Travis, what had transpired between them had been merely a matter of animal lust.

With a sigh, she rolled to a sitting position. At least when she got down to the kitchen Travis would be gone, having taken the train north into Michigan to oversee the repairs to the ship.

Suddenly, her eyes widened and, with a gasp, she threw her legs over the side and hopped out of bed. *Mother Mary! Travis's brother is on his way!* Fiona dressed quickly, splashed water over her face, fastened her hair into a knot with her comb and flew down the stairs.

"Dee!" she cried.

"Shhh!" Deirdre waddled into the kitchen from the pantry, her finger to her mouth. "Carvey is asleep."

Fiona poured herself coffee from the pot on the stove. "Is he better this morning?"

Deirdre heaved a sigh designed to gain Fiona's sympathy. "Don't I wish I knew? He's been asleep since I got up. He seemed quieter, though, when I checked on him."

Fiona took her sister's arm and led her to a chair. "Dee, sit down and listen to me."

Deirdre gave her a puzzled look as she lowered her swollen body into a chair. Fiona took the seat next to hers. "Travis's brother is coming today and Travis needs our help."

"But if his brother is coming, why do we have to help him?"

"I'll explain everything later. Right now I've got to go to town to get Aunt Tullia, Tommy and Pegeen. Tell Da we're going to have a family meeting just as soon as I get back."

"What about Ena and Murph?"

"Never mind them." Fiona glanced at the watch pinned to her bodice, set her cup in the sink and took her straw hat from the hook by the door. "Don't say anything to Carvey about this. There's no sense giving him anything else to worry about."

"Anything *else* to worry about? Is Carvey worried about something?" Deirdre asked, rising halfway from her seat. "Is that why he's ill? Is it me? Is he worried about the new baby coming?"

Fiona shook her head in consternation. "That's not what I meant, Dee. I'm sorry I brought it up. Just tell Da what I told you."

"Fiona?" she heard as she started out the door. "I forgot to tell you I invited Bridget to visit today."

And it's only morning, Fiona thought with a sigh.

An hour later, Pegeen, Tom, Tullia, Finn, Deirdre and Fiona sat at the kitchen table, chins resting on palms, frowns of concentration on their faces as they considered the facts Fiona had laid before them. Cups of cold coffee sat in front of each.

Fiona rose to make a fresh pot. "What are we going to do?"

"Certainly we have no time to find the missing goods before Jordan Paine's arrival," Tullia declared.

"Can we buy this Jordan fellow's silence?" Tom asked.

Pegeen brightened at the idea. "It can't hurt to try, can it? He may not be any fonder of his father than Travis is."

"I doubt it would work," Fiona told them. "From the

sound of it, the brothers all jump to do their father's bidding. No one dares go against Jefferson Paine."

Tullia huffed disgustedly. "What a crime it is to turn brother against brother."

"The crime is that the cargo was stolen," Fiona admonished, "and by someone right here in town."

"I still find that hard to swallow, Fiona," Tullia retorted. "None of our lads would do such a terrible deed."

"The fact is, Auntie, that Travis's shipment of silk, woolens and bourbon disappeared *after* the ship struck the sandbar and there's no way it could have gotten out of the hold except to have been carried out."

"Maybe pirates took it," Deirdre suggested.

"*Pirates,* Dee?" Fiona repeated incredulously. "Pirates who just happened to be in the vicinity immediately after the ship struck?"

Finn Cleary leaned back in his chair and rubbed his eyes. "Could we put dummy crates in the warehouse to make it look full?"

"Jordan would probably want to inspect them," Fiona said as she gathered the cups from the table.

"Too risky," Tom agreed.

"Just a minute," Tullia said, holding up her hand. "I can't believe I'm saying this, but I think Finn may be on to something." She gave her nemesis a sidelong glance, and seeing Finn's look of surprise, she smiled cagily. "While we can't lie to Mr. Paine, perhaps we can alter his perspective of the truth. With luck we'll be able to find the missing cargo before he's on to us."

Deirdre made a scoffing sound. "You'd have to get him drunk to do that."

Fiona stopped pouring fresh coffee and turned to stare at her sister. "Why, that's it, Dee!"

Deirdre looked surprised. "It is?"

"Of course!" Tom boomed. "We'll get him corned, take him to the warehouse and show him the dummy crates."

"We can even open a few for him," Fiona elaborated. "Pegeen, there's enough woolen and cotton at the store to fill a few crates, isn't there?"

"I'm certain there is."

Fiona's excitement soared. "Tommy, if we empty the crates of ruined merchandise already in the warehouse, we can put the new goods in them so they'll be marked with the ship's name."

"Leave it all to me, Fiona. I'll get the rescue team together and we'll get on it right away."

Tullia slapped her hands on the table. "We can get some whiskey from Devlin. He's bound to have set in a supply for his grand opening next week."

"And don't forget some for dinner tonight, too," Pegeen reminded.

"Dee, you, Peg and I will make supper so Fiona will have time to go to town and talk to Mrs. McDonnell about the silk," Tullia ordered. "And I don't want you to say a word about that to Bridget!"

Deirdre gave her a mutinous glare. "Why do we have to go to all this trouble for a stranger?"

"Stop whining like a child, Dee," Tullia scolded. "You'll do as we say and I don't want to hear a word of complaint out of you!"

"Now see here, Tullia," Finn began.

"Da, Auntie, please! This is no time to argue." Fiona handed out the fresh coffee and sat down. "Let's go over the plan one more time. Once Tommy takes care of the crates, we'll stall Jordan Paine until supper, then we'll refill his glass until he can't see straight, take him to the warehouse and show him the phony cargo. With any luck we'll have a few days to find out what happened to the real merchandise. Tommy, can I leave Jordan in your care afterwards? We have rehearsal this evening."

"Don't worry about a thing, Fiona. I'll tuck him right in bed."

"I wonder what Travis will have to say about your plan," Finn said to Fiona.

"Faith, Fiona!" Tom said. "What if he won't go along with it?"

"Why wouldn't he go along with it?" Fiona replied. "It

will save his hide, won't it? And there doesn't seem much love lost between the brothers anyway.''

Finn gave her a long look. "You might consider what it will do to his pride." He pushed back his chair and got up. "I'm going to the tower. Let me know when our visitor arrives."

Fiona walked into the warehouse as the rescue team quickly and efficiently emptied crates and refilled them with new goods. Tom spotted her and started across the floor toward her.

"Any luck with the seamstress, Fiona?" he asked.

"None." She and Tom stepped outside into the bright sunlight and began walking slowly along the pier heading back to the lighthouse. "Mrs. McDonnell knows only as much as I know," she explained. "It looks like the only way I'll find out anything is to pry the information from Bridget herself." Fiona kicked a stone out of her path. "It was probably her very own father who gave the silk to her."

"Even so," Tom said, "the question is, where did John Riley come by the material?"

"There's more, Tommy. Someone hid several bottles of whiskey in a crate in the stable. The crate was marked with the name of Travis's ship."

"Holy Mother of God!" he exclaimed. "Where is it now?"

"I got rid of it."

"Jesus, Fiona! Why would anyone hide stolen whiskey in your stable?"

"I wish to heaven I knew. Carvey was the one who found it first. He claims he doesn't know how it came to be there."

"Do you believe him?"

"I have to believe him, Tommy. If I didn't, I'd be saying he knows something about the theft of the whiskey."

"You're right, Fiona. Carvey is no thief." Tom ran a hand over his face. "Does anyone else know about this?"

"Only one person." Fiona gave her cousin a sidelong glance. "Travis found the whiskey before I did, Tommy. Luckily, when he took me to the stable to show me, I had already gotten rid of it, so he had no proof. But now he's convinced someone in the family is responsible for the theft. The only way I was able to stop him from going to the sheriff was to promise to help him find the thief as well as the rest of the cargo." She let out a heavy sigh. "It's a promise I have yet to keep."

"I'll help you in every way I can."

Fiona gave him a grateful smile. "I know you will, Tommy, and I thank you for that." She shook her head as they walked along. "How do I get myself involved in such messes?"

Tom put his arm around her shoulders. "It comes from having a caring heart, Fiona."

"Caring heart, indeed," she groused. "Maybe it comes from being stupid, as Mr. Paine once said."

"Speakin' of stupid," Tom said, and nodded toward the lighthouse.

Fiona glanced in the same direction to see Bridget climbing the stone path, holding a violet-colored parasol over her head with one hand, and lifting the hem of her violet-colored dress with the other. "Bridget Riley," Fiona muttered. "The bane of my existence."

Tom returned to the warehouse to supervise his crew while Fiona continued home, planning how to go about questioning Bridget about the silk without the girl being any the wiser. As Fiona stepped onto the porch she heard Deirdre's and Bridget's voices coming from the open sitting-room window. She paused outside the door to listen as Deirdre regaled Bridget with news of their unexpected visitor.

"No, Dee!" she whispered in dismay. Tullia had ordered her sister not to say anything about the silk, but she had not ordered Deirdre to keep quiet about anything else. Once Bridget knew about Jordan Paine's impending arrival, nothing would pry her out of the house. She'd latch onto him like molasses on wheatcakes.

With a resigned sigh, Fiona opened the door and stepped inside. She would only make herself barmy worrying about it. As her mother would say, Bridget was as unstoppable as a steam engine going downhill at full throttle.

Through the arched doorway to the kitchen, Fiona could see Pegeen and Tullia preparing supper. For a moment she stood quietly and watched them working side by side, their backs to her. It was a grand feeling knowing her family could always be counted on to help. Her heart filled with love for them, and then with sorrow as she realized that what she was looking at would soon be only a memory. She blinked back the prickle of tears and tried to burn the moment into her mind so she could hold it forever.

Pegeen glanced around and gave a start of surprise. "Fiona, I didn't hear you come in!"

"I didn't mean to startle you, Peg. How is Carvey this afternoon?"

"Right now he's sitting up reading."

Tullia lowered her voice to add, "In my opinion, Fiona, this stomachache of Carvey's comes from bad nerves. I don't think he has the backbone to be your father's assistant."

"Now how can Fiona leave New Clare with a clear conscience if you tell her that?" Pegeen scolded.

"It's all right, Peg," Fiona said. "I've been thinking along those lines myself, though I think it's a collection of worries that's causing Carvey's pain."

Tullia turned back to her cooking. "Time will tell."

"Did you find out anything from Mrs. McDonnell?" Pegeen asked.

Fiona shook her head as she took her apron from the hook by the door and tied it around her waist. "No more than I already knew. Did anyone remember to get whiskey for our supper?"

"I did," Tullia replied, "though I had to answer a hundred questions before Devlin would let me have it. He doesn't think much of our plan. He says we're fools for trying to find the missing cargo."

"And what would he do instead?" Fiona asked crossly.

"Nothing," Tullia replied. "He says that's why shipping companies have insurance."

"Well, I don't much care what Dev thinks. I only hope Travis gets here before his brother does so I can tell him of our plan. I wouldn't want him to say something at dinner and spoil it.''

But just as Fiona finished setting the table, there was a heavy knock at the door. ''Stars and garters!'' she muttered. ''That's sure to be Jordan Paine.''

She started across the kitchen, tucking stray wisps of hair into the knot at the top of her head. When she pulled the door open she knew instantly that the man standing before her was, indeed, Travis's brother.

Jordan Paine stood as tall as Travis and had the same build—wide at the shoulders, lean at the hips. His hair was as dark as Travis's but cut shorter, except for the sideburns which were long and thick. He had Travis's eyes, but of a lighter brown color. His mouth was a copy of Travis's as well, but his face was softer, lacking his brother's more angular features. And as Travis had done on his first days at the lighthouse, Jordan, too, wore a stern, forbidding expression. She guessed it was an inherited trait.

''Come in, Mr. Paine,'' she said with a cordial smile. ''We've been expecting you.''

Jordan stepped into the house and glanced around, as though appraising its worth. ''Is my brother here?''

''Not yet. I'm Fiona Cleary.'' She held out her hand.

Jordan seemed surprised at the gesture and took it hesitantly, as if unsure of whether to kiss it or shake it. He ended up giving her hand a squeeze and dropping it. It was easy to see he wasn't comfortable around females. He'd probably been on board a ship since he was old enough to stand. There was no doubt in Fiona's mind but that he was a bachelor.

''Your brother should be here any time.'' Fiona led the way into the kitchen. ''This is my aunt, Tullia Brody,'' she said, ''and my cousin, Pegeen Brody.''

''How do you do?'' he said stiffly.

''Will you have coffee?'' Fiona asked.

Jordan declined with a shake of his head and a frown that reminded her of Travis. ''I didn't mean to interrupt your supper. I can wait for my brother outside.''

Saints in heaven, he's bound to run into Travis outside! As Jordan turned and headed for the door, Fiona cast an alarmed

look at Pegeen and Tullia, but they merely shrugged helplessly. Fiona chewed the end of her thumbnail and stared at
Jordan's broad back. Somehow she had to keep him away
from Travis until she had a chance to speak to Travis pri-
vately.

Just then, the sound of girlish giggles erupted from the
direction of the sitting room and Fiona smiled in relief.
Bridget!

"Mr. Paine," she called quickly, "there's someone I'd like
you to—"

Before she could finish, the door opened and Travis
stepped inside.

❖ 17 ❖

Travis TOOK ONE look at his older brother and came
to an abrupt stop. For a moment he and his brother did nothing but regard each other as though they were strangers instead of kin. In truth, they might as well have been strangers,
Travis decided, for all the affection he felt for his brother.
Had it been his own house, he would not even have let Jordan
in. But it had not been his choice. He shut the door and
walked forward.

"Hello, Jordan," he said stiffly, offering his hand.

Jordan shook it. "Hello, Travis."

Travis immediately walked away from him, making it clear
how he felt about Jordan's presence there. "Hello, ladies,"
he said, walking over to see what Tullia and Pegeen were
preparing. "Could I trouble one of you for a glass of water?
The train ride was hot and dusty."

"Wasn't I just saying your brother was due back any moment?" Fiona said cheerfully to Jordan, as though embarrassed by Travis's behavior. To Travis she said with a quick
warning look, "I've set an extra place at the table for your
brother. You both can wash up at the sink."

"Excuse me, Miss Cleary," Jordan said, staring at Travis,
"I don't see any need to stay for supper. I'll just speak to
my brother outside."

Leaning against the counter, Travis watched Jordan turn

and stride to the front door. A confrontation was coming and there was nothing he could do but see it through. He took a sip from the cup of water Pegeen handed him, set it on the table and followed his brother outside.

"God's teeth!" Fiona muttered as she started after them. She had to keep Travis from telling Jordan about the missing cargo.

"What are you going to do, Fiona?" Pegeen called.

"I'm going to alert the molasses that the wheatcakes are on the porch."

"She's gone barmy!" Tullia whispered.

Fiona dashed across the hall and burst into the sitting room, startling both Bridget and Deirdre. "Supper is ready, Dee. Bridget, you're invited to join us. Travis's brother has arrived, a handsome devil, by the way. He's outside right now talking to Travis. What a shame I couldn't convince him to stay for the meal." She turned, walked to the front door, counted to five and opened it.

Bridget sailed through.

"Yoo-hoo! Mr. Paine!"

Both Travis and Jordan turned to see Bridget hurrying down the porch steps toward them. Normally Travis would have groaned at the sound of that grating voice, but this time Bridget was a welcome distraction. As Travis had suspected, his father had sent Jordan to oversee the ship's repairs. Travis resented being interrogated about the matter as though he were a child, especially by a brother only four years older. He was glad for an excuse, any excuse, to put an end to it.

Behind Bridget, Travis caught sight of Fiona in the open doorway, a look of satisfaction on her face. He narrowed his eyes at her, wondering what she was up to.

"Oh, Mr. Paine, it's so good to see you," Bridget said in her high little-girl voice. She glanced at Jordan and batted her eyelashes at him. "How do you do, sir?"

"Miss Riley, this is my brother, Jordan Paine," Travis said. "Jordan, Miss Bridget Riley."

Even as stiff and somber a person as Jordan couldn't resist

Bridget's blatant flirtations. Jordan took the dainty hand shoved under his nose and gave her a semblance of a smile. "How do you do, Miss Riley?"

"Oh, ever so much better if you'd consent to dine with me, that is *us,* this evening."

With a forbidding expression Jordan opened his mouth to decline, but at her pretty pout he hesitated, glanced at Travis, then back at Bridget. "Well, I—"

"Oh, I'm delighted you've changed your mind! It will be ever so pleasant having two such delightfully handsome gentlemen to talk to."

Before Jordan had a chance to protest, Bridget tucked one hand through his arm, the other through Travis's and started them toward the house. "You'll have to tell me all about yourself, Mr. Paine, or should I call you Jordan? I suppose it would be more proper for me to call your brother by his first name since we've been acquainted for some time. It's *so* awkward having two Mr. Paines in the same room."

Travis rubbed his jaw to hide a smile. There'd be two pains in the room all right—Bridget and Jordan.

The diminutive pain paused at the top of the steps to turn her baby blues on her newest prey. "You're not married, are you, Jordan? I'll wager you have your own ship, too. You seem the strong captain type. We're going to have a festival in a few days and I just know you'd have a wonderful time there. You will come, won't you, Jordan? I'd be just devastated if you didn't."

"Well, I—"

"Oh, I'm so excited! You must bid on my lunch basket. I know Travis will. My basket is always filled with the best food at the festival."

If Travis hadn't resented Jordan's presence so much he would have pitied him. Travis stepped back and allowed Bridget to lead his befuddled brother into the house. But as he started in after them, Fiona stepped out of the sitting room, grabbed his sleeve and pulled him back outside.

"I need to speak with you," she whispered.

With a puzzled frown, Travis followed her around to the back of the stable, where they were out of sight of the house.

She shaded her eyes to look out at the lake, avoiding eye contact with him. "Don't say anything to your brother about the missing cargo. We've stocked the warehouse with dummy crates and we're going to—"

Travis stared at her in disbelief. "You did *what*?"

"—get him drunk and take him down there this evening," she finished quickly.

Travis raked his fingers through his hair. "When in God's name did you have time to stock the warehouse?"

"This afternoon. Tommy had the rescue team help him empty the crates already there and fill the ones in front with goods from the store. I hope that will stall your brother long enough for us to find out what happened to the cargo."

Travis was dumbfounded, imagining not only the work involved but the planning and manpower needed to make it happen. He saw immediately that there were flaws in her plan, but she gave him no time to point them out.

Fiona spun about and set off at a rapid pace, calling over her shoulder, "We've got to get back before your brother gets nervous and changes his mind."

What the hell, he thought, it might be fun to watch her attempt it.

Travis shook his head as he started after her, still surprised by the sudden turn of events. After the way he had behaved in the tower he was even more surprised that Fiona would be so eager to help him. He could more easily accept that she had another reason for tricking Jordan, such as protecting whoever it was who had stolen the cargo.

Of course, that was it! He should have thought of it sooner. Fiona was merely doing what came natural to her—looking out for her own. His anger flared at the thought of it, but instantly cooled when he realized the cause behind his anger.

It was envy.

"Come on, brother, wake up." Travis shook Jordan's shoulder insistently until his brother moaned and turned on his side.

Travis shook him again, thoroughly enjoying the torture he was inflicting. "Can't let you sleep. We'll miss our train."

"Don't mention trains," Jordan rasped, squinting his eyes and pressing his fists to his temples. "My head feels as though it were run over by a train."

"You had a lot to drink last night. Listen, if you don't feel like going with me—"

"I'm getting up," Jordan snapped.

Travis smiled to himself. "I'll be in the kitchen. There are biscuits and ham on the stove if you're hungry."

"Dear God, don't mention food either!"

With a chuckle, Travis left the room. He hadn't believed Fiona's plan would work, but so far it had. After a supper of lamb shanks, roasted potatoes and too many glasses of bourbon, Jordan had been taken to the warehouse, propped up by Tom Brody, shown the crates of what he believed to be the ship's cargo, and delivered safely back to the lighthouse none the wiser.

By the time Travis and Fiona had returned from rehearsal, Jordan was snoring drunkenly in Travis's bed. Travis whistled as he jogged down the stairs. It was only what his dear brother deserved.

Fiona was sitting at the table reading a book when he entered the kitchen. Their eyes met momentarily, then she looked away. "Good morning," she said coolly.

Travis's good mood vanished. He muttered a reply and poured himself coffee. Ever since their passionate embrace in the tower, Fiona had taken great pains to avoid looking at him. At rehearsal, she had been polite but distant, and on the walk home had done little more than give him perfunctory replies. Travis knew why she was behaving in such a manner but was at a loss as to what to do about it. He had already apologized. What more did she want?

"How is your brother this morning?" she asked, keeping her nose buried in her book.

"Not well. You'll see for yourself in a minute. He insists he's taking the train with me."

"Do you think he'll go back to Erie soon?"

"I have no idea."

They heard slow footsteps on the stairs and waited silently for Jordan to appear.

"Good morning, Mr. Paine," Fiona said with a polite smile, rising to greet him.

Jordan glanced at her through bleary, bloodshot eyes and muttered, "Morning."

"Would you care for some breakfast?"

He shook his head, his pale lips pressed together. "Just coffee, please."

Travis glanced at the clock on the shelf as Fiona handed Jordan a cup. "Drink it down quickly. We've got to get to the depot." He walked to the door, then stopped to look back at Fiona, hoping for a smile from her or some form of acknowledgment, but she had already gone back to her book.

"Damn it anyway!" he snarled as he started down the stone path with his brother close behind.

"My sentiments exactly," Jordan muttered.

"You're crazy as a loon is what you are!" Devlin advanced across the empty saloon towards Fiona, his fleshy face an angry, mottled red, his heavy hands balled into fists.

Fiona stood her ground. In her hand she held the whiskey bottle that Tullia had brought for their supper the night before. Fiona had noticed the familiar label at once and, without telling anyone, had emptied the liquor into a decanter and hidden the bottle in the pantry.

Now she held it out in front of her. "You can't bully me, Dev. I know where you got this whiskey. You bought it from the thief who stole the cargo. I recognized the bottle right away. It's the same brand as the liquor that Travis was carrying on his ship."

Devlin tried to grab it from her, but Fiona snatched it back. "I bought that whiskey in Chicago," he sneered. "Old Grand-Dad is a common enough brand. Would you care to see my receipts?"

"Yes, I would."

Hitting his fist against the bar's polished wood surface, he cursed loudly, "Divil take you, Fiona! I don't owe you anything. Get out before I toss you out."

Fiona glared at her cousin. She had hoped to startle him into a confession, but Devlin was holding firm. In truth, she had no evidence, only an instinctual feeling. If Devlin knew he could make good profit from stolen whiskey he wouldn't hesitate to buy it. She hoped she was mistaken about Devlin, but she doubted it. With an icy glare, she turned and marched out.

The sky was overcast and the air was heavy and damp when Fiona left the saloon. It added to her feeling of depression. She had spent another long night in the tower, and had not relished having to confront Devlin. Her relationship with Travis was strained and she was frustrated at being no further along in finding the thief than she had been the week before.

Window shoppers crowded the sidewalks. The Festival of Lughnasa was just around the corner and the excitement was palpable. But Fiona barely noticed as she threaded her way through the crowd and slipped into the cooler interior of the general store.

"Hi, Peg," she called listlessly.

Pegeen turned from dusting the shelves behind her counter and smiled, but seeing the bleak look on Fiona's face, her own took on a look of concern. "Poor Fiona, you look like something the cat dragged in. Come on in the back for some coffee and tell me what's wrong."

Fiona followed her through the curtained doorway. While Pegeen went to pour coffee for her, she took a seat at the small pine table and sat with her chin in her hand, staring vacantly at the floor. Not wishing to repeat her conversation with Devlin, she said, "I can't stay long, Peg. I still have to get over to the church to see how the scenery is coming. I only stopped by to pick up some material to fashion a knapsack for—*St. Christopher's knees!*"

"For St. Christopher's knees?" Peg turned around to see Fiona kneeling beside the low bin used to store kindling for the stove. Fiona took a thin slat of wood off the top of the pile and jumped to her feet.

"Peg! Look at this!" she exclaimed.

Pegeen gave her a puzzled look. "It's just kindling, Fiona."

"But look at the black paint on it. What do you make of it?"

Pegeen took the strip of wood and examined it. "It looks like bits of letters."

"Yes, Peg! See how this one curves, like the lower part of an *S?* And this could be part of an *E.*" Fiona picked up another. "Where did you get this wood?"

"From shipping crates. We break them up and use them for kindling."

Fiona fitted two pieces together and reached for a third. As the word *Thomas* began to take shape her heart raced. Had they found the remains of a crate from the *Thomas E. Paine*? "How long has this wood been here?"

"I can't say for sure, but I know the bin was empty three days ago because that was when I swept the floor last."

"Who fills the bin?"

Pegeen twisted her fingers together, as though suddenly afraid to answer. "Tommy and Devlin," she said hesitantly.

"Where do they keep the wood before it's chopped for kindling?"

Pegeen led her to the rear of the storeroom and opened the door onto the narrow yard behind the building. "In that shed."

Fiona stepped into the shed and raised a piece of canvas covering what appeared to be a large pile of wood. Underneath the cover was a tall stack of knocked-down crates. She lifted one section of a crate and saw the name of Travis's ship in bold black letters on the underside.

"Mother Mary!" Fiona whispered, dropping the cover back in place. Either Devlin had purchased the entire lot of whiskey from the thief, or Devlin *was* the thief.

With Peg standing behind her wringing her hands, Fiona wrapped several pieces of wood in brown wrapping paper and tied the package with string. "Please say nothing about this to anyone, Peg."

"Oh, Fiona, I know my Tommy's no thief," Pegeen blurted. "Please don't think it's him."

"Of course I don't think it's Tommy," Fiona said gently, putting her arm around Pegeen's plump shoulders. "I just think it's best not to say anything until I can find out who it is."

"You think it's Devlin, don't you?" Pegeen asked in a trembling voice.

"I can't say one way or the other until I have more proof."

"Please be careful, Fiona. You know how mean Dev can be when he gets angry."

"And I learned long ago not to be frightened of him."

Fiona hurried down the sidewalk toward the church, her thoughts spinning wildly. What she had uncovered pointed directly to Devlin's involvement with the stolen cargo, but to what extent she wouldn't know until she had more proof than an empty whiskey bottle and a few pieces of wood.

Fiona's grip tightened on the package in her hand. How could her own flesh and blood be so without conscience? Devlin deserved to be caught, just as Travis deserved the chance to redeem himself. She would see to it that both got what they deserved.

As Fiona stepped into the serene interior of the church, however, she was suddenly struck by a wave of guilt. If she exposed Devlin's involvement to exonerate Travis, it would reflect directly on her own family and they would be forever shamed.

Could she do that to them?

❖18❖

TRAVIS GRITTED HIS teeth during the trip back to New
Clare. Once off the train, he strode rapidly through town, not
even bothering to see if Jordan was keeping pace with him.
The sky was thick with gray rain clouds, matching his disposition. He had endured several long, humiliating days following Jordan around like a dog at his heels, watching his
brother issue commands to *his* crew as they repaired the ship.

By the time they reached the lighthouse, Travis was still
in no mood for even the slightest conversation. The thought
of having to sit across from Jordan at supper disgusted him.
Fortunately, the Clearys were able to keep the conversation
going without him.

To add to his frustration, Fiona was still avoiding his gaze.
She seemed deeply preoccupied as well, and he caught her
several times staring at her plate, a worried frown on her face.

"Looks like a storm coming in," Travis commented as he
and Fiona walked to the church for rehearsal that evening.

"Yes," she murmured absently.

"Do you still have to take the night watch?"

She gave him a quick, apprehensive look, as if she were
afraid he was planning to make another appearance in the
tower. It cut him to the quick. "I imagine so," she said.

Travis clenched his jaw. "Damn it, Fiona. I apologized for
what happened. What more do you want from me?"

"Nothing."

He took a deep breath. "Look, it's difficult enough having Jordan here stepping on my toes without you slighting me."

"To slight someone, *Mr. Paine*," she said in a cool, clipped tone, "one would have to have either a grievance against that person or a disdain for him, which I do not. I understand you were behaving in a typical male fashion. I'm simply using my head now. However, if you'd prefer a mindless female, I suggest you try Bridget. In fact, there she is waiting for you."

Travis glanced at Bridget standing in front of the church and cursed under his breath. He was getting nowhere with Fiona. He didn't believe for a moment that she had no grievance against him. He'd acted like a cad and he knew it, but he had apologized for it. Why wasn't it enough?

He stuck his hands deep in his pockets and frowned at the ground. What the hell was wrong with this woman anyway? What more proof did Fiona need that he cared about her? He was leaving New Clare for her sake and he couldn't even get her to look at him without glaring.

Out of frustration he blurted, "I'm leaving town tomorrow."

His words had the desired effect. Fiona halted abruptly and stared at him, disbelief written on her face. "Your ship isn't ready! You can't leave."

"On the contrary, Jordan is in charge now. There's no reason for me to stay."

"So you'll tuck your tail between your legs and slink off to lick your wounds, is that right?"

"If that's how you want to see it, yes."

She planted her hands on her hips. "And who do you suppose will play Rip Van Winkle when you leave?"

It wounded Travis to think replacing him in the play was her only concern. "Ask my brother," he snapped. "He's a quick study."

Fiona shook a fist at him. "You're a coward, Travis Paine, an ill-mannered, inconsiderate, selfish coward!"

"Yoo-hoo, Travis!"

In a low, furious voice, Fiona offered her parting shot.

"You deserve the likes of Bridget Riley!" With a huff, she left him in front of the church to fend off the blue-eyed cyclone alone.

"Goodness!" Bridget exclaimed as Fiona hurtled past her, yanked open the church door and stormed inside. "Whatever has gotten into her?"

Smarting from Fiona's angry words, Travis glared past Bridget as the heavy wooden door swung shut. Fiona had called him a coward, a selfish one at that! Wasn't he risking his father's wrath by leaving New Clare to spare her further pain? How much more unselfish could he get?

Granted he was leaving Fiona in the lurch with *Rip Van Winkle*, but he was certain someone could step in for him. And granted, her family had gone to a lot of trouble to help him out with his brother, but considering that they had caused his problems in the first place, Travis figured they owed him that much.

"Why aren't we going inside?" Bridget whined. "We should go inside. . . . Travis, you're not paying attention! Rehearsal must have surely started already and they'll be wondering where we—Oh!"

Grinding his teeth, Travis grabbed Bridget's wrist and pulled her into the church. Damn it, Fiona just didn't understand him. What he was doing wasn't cowardly, it was honorable, and it was the *only* thing he could do to protect her.

Fiona was close to tears throughout rehearsal. Nothing seemed to go right. Mr. Tucker, the narrator, had developed a cough and could barely get his words out. Bridget couldn't remember her lines to save her life. The scenery was nowhere near finished, and the festival was only days away.

And, of course, Travis was walking out on her.

No! she thought angrily. That was wrong. He wasn't just walking out on her. He was also deserting the cast members, his brother and his responsibilities. Couldn't he see that by walking away from it all he was only hurting himself?

Personally, Fiona thought with a sniff, she would not be affected in the least. Her life would go on exactly as she had planned. So why did she feel so hollow inside? So bereft?

The truth is you love him, Fiona, and there's no denying it, her conscience whispered.

"And what good is that, I'd like to know," she said aloud, "when I will never marry a sailin' man?"

With a heavy heart, Fiona locked the church and crossed Kilkenny Street. For once she was relieved that Travis had escorted Bridget home. Her emotions were too close to the surface to be near him. She didn't trust her control.

A strong gust of wind blew the first drops of rain against her face. Fiona glanced upward, dismayed by the thick, black clouds rolling across the night sky, obliterating the stars. A storm was coming in, to be sure. She stepped up her pace, a knot of worry already forming in her stomach at the thought of having to take the watch on such a night.

"Fiona!"

Shielding her eyes against the rain and blowing sand, Fiona paused at the bottom of the stone path and turned. Travis held up his hand and yelled above the escalating wind, "Wait."

She steeled herself, determined not to let him see how hurt she was by his leaving, nor to let him read the love in her eyes. When Travis reached her, he was out of breath, his dark hair windblown.

"I want to explain something to you."

Fiona looked away. "If it's about your decision to leave, you've told me all I need to know."

"I'm not a coward."

She lifted her chin and looked him in the eye. "Letting yourself be bullied is cowardly. Leaving when the going is rough is cowardly."

"I'm leaving for *your* sake, Fiona."

She stared up at him in surprise, but it was instantly replaced by anger. How dare he put the blame on her shoulders! The rain began to fall in large drops, quickly soaking through her clothing. She turned, picked up her damp skirt and started up the stone path.

Travis caught her and blocked her path. "Didn't you hear what I said?"

"I heard you," she retorted. "*I'm* to blame for your leaving!"

"No, damn it, that's not what I meant!" Travis raked his fingers through his wet hair. He gripped her arms and gave her a pleading look. "What I mean is that I'm not leaving because I'm afraid of Jordan or of disappointing my father. Hell, I've already done that. I'm leaving because I don't want to hurt you. Do you understand what I'm trying to say?"

As Fiona searched Travis's face, she finally understood his meaning. He wasn't leaving out of cowardice but out of concern. He was giving up his hope of redeeming himself in his father's eyes so that the search for the thief could be halted and her father's good name could be safe.

As lightning streaked across the sky, illuminating Travis's earnest face, Fiona's heart swelled with love for him and for the sacrifice he was making. But at the same time she was filled with regret for a love that could never be realized.

How far Travis had come, she marveled, from the imperious, aloof stranger she had first brought home. Yet one thing had not changed: he was not a coward, and Fiona was ashamed for having accused him of it.

Chagrined, she looked down. "I thank you for your concern," she said humbly. "I know my family will, too."

"It's not just out of concern that I'm doing this, Fiona."

The wind swirled fiercely around them as Travis reached for her hand and pressed his lips against it. Fiona glanced up in surprise. His gaze as he stared at her was dark and intense and his voice was husky with emotion. "I love you, Fiona," he said simply.

For a moment she was so overwhelmed by his declaration that all she could do was stare, but then she pulled her hand from his grasp. "And what good will it do me to know how you feel when nothing can come of it?" she cried, half in anger, half in torment.

Travis started to answer her, then changed his mind and looked down. In a voice tinged with regret he said, "If that's how you feel, then it's for the best that I leave."

As thunder reverberated across the lake, Fiona blinked back tears and clenched her jaw in determination. She had resolved to use her head, not her heart, but she hadn't realized how much it would cost her to do so. Now she had to restrain herself from throwing herself in his arms, from begging him to stay, for if he stayed, it would mean the loss of both their dreams.

In a voice devoid of feeling, Travis said, "I'll catch an early train tomorrow. Please express my appreciation to your family for all their help."

Watching him stride up the path to the lighthouse, his back stiff and proud, Fiona felt as though her heart were shattering into tiny, unmendable pieces.

Fiona closed the door against the driving rain and paused to wipe the tears off her face. With a heavy heart she walked into the kitchen, where Deirdre was making a pot of tea. "I'm back, Dee," she said listlessly.

When Deirdre turned, Fiona could see at once that her sister had been crying. "What is it? Is Carvey worse?"

Deirdre nodded and began to sob, covering her face with her hands. Fiona put her arms around Deirdre's shoulders and held her. Taking great gulping breaths, Deirdre responded, "And I thought—Carvey was doing so much—better!"

"What did he have to eat?"

"Noth—nothing unusual. Only goat's milk and bread, just as the doctor said."

"Sit down, Dee. I'll pour you some tea." Fiona urged her sister into a chair and filled a cup with the steaming beverage. Outside, the wind blew with such force that it rattled the windows and sent a shiver of apprehension down her spine. "Have you sent for the doctor?" she asked.

Deirdre took a sip of tea, then nodded her head. "He was here just a little while ago. Devlin went for him."

Fiona stiffened. "Devlin was here?"

Deirdre nodded. "He came by about an hour before Carvey took ill." She shivered violently. "Devlin was in a terrible temper. The way he was acting you'd think Carvey was sick on purpose! I was almost afraid to ask him to fetch the doctor."

The knot of worry in Fiona's stomach grew larger. Carvey had taken ill after speaking with Devlin, just as he had before. For the first time she considered the possibility that Devlin was poisoning Carvey. But what possible reason could her cousin have for wanting to hurt Carvey?

Fiona thought back to the day she had found Carvey and Devlin talking in hushed voices in the storeroom, both of them looking as guilty as sin. Was it possible Carvey knew about the stolen cargo?

She poured herself a cup of tea and carefully posed a question to her sister, trying not to alarm her. "Did Carvey have anything to eat while Devlin was here?"

Deirdre shook her head. "No, he ate before Dev came."

Then Carvey's setback had to be the result of the conversation he had with Devlin, Fiona decided. But what was she to do about it? She wished she could confide in Travis, that she could lean on his strength, but she wisely knew that anything she did to draw him closer to her would only make his leaving that much more difficult to bear.

Deirdre took several more sips of tea and it seemed to calm her down. "The doctor gave Carvey some laudanum to help him sleep," she told Fiona. "He'll be back again in the morning."

"Where's Jordan?" Fiona asked.

Deirdre sniffled and wiped the tears off her cheeks. "He retired early. Da's up in the tower."

Fiona drained her cup and stood up. "As long as Carvey's resting, I'd better go up to relieve Da. Let me know if you need me, Dee."

"I'm sorry you have to take the night watch again, Fiona," Deirdre said.

"With the weather as bad as this I wouldn't sleep well anyway."

Finn Cleary was standing at one of the large windows in the circular tower room, his hands in his pockets, his shoulders slumped.

"Hello, Da," Fiona called without enthusiasm.

"Looks like we're heading into a gale," he remarked.

Fiona sighed as she sank into his chair. "Did you hear about Carvey?"

Finn sighed and his shoulders seem to droop even lower. "I heard."

"I'm uneasy about it, Da. Something is troubling Carvey—I'm sure that's why he's ill—and I suspect Devlin is involved."

Fiona expected her father to chide her for her fears, as he always did. Instead, Finn remained silent. Fiona sat immobile, her heart pounding in dread. He knew something.

She went to him and put a hand on his shoulder. "Do you know the cause of Carvey's illness, Da?"

Finn let out his breath. "I know what's troubling him, Fiona."

"Will you tell me?"

He shook his head and was silent, as though he couldn't bring himself to speak of the answer.

"We have to help Carvey, Da," she said firmly.

His shoulders slowly rose and fell. "It's a terrible burden I've been carrying, Fiona."

Fiona felt suddenly weak-kneed with apprehension. "Tell me," she whispered tersely.

"It was on the night of Mr. Paine's shipwreck," he began after a moment. "The storm woke me about four o'clock in the morning. I couldn't sleep after that and went down to the kitchen for a cup of tea. It was there that I heard the ship's distress call and rushed straightaway to the tower." He shook his head, as if he still couldn't believe it. "The light was out, Fiona."

Fiona stared at him aghast. "Out?" she repeated incredulously. "But where was Carvey?"

"Passed out on the floor—dead drunk."

Suddenly dizzy, Fiona braced her hands against the window. "Mother Mary!" she whispered. Travis had spoken the truth.

"I still don't understand it," Finn admitted. "There was enough kerosene to last at least another hour. I relit the beacon, but the damage had been done."

And a crew of twenty had been lost. As the storm raged outside the tower, Fiona shut her eyes against the dreadful images she carried of that night. She wanted to weep for the terrible waste of human life and curse the heavens for the injustice of it. And all along Travis had been telling the truth, though she had stubbornly refused to believe him. She pounded a fist against the window in helpless fury. "Damn Carvey!"

"Carvey was beside himself when he learned of the shipwreck," Finn continued. "He wept and begged for forgiveness. He swore by all that was holy that he would never let the light go out again nor let another drop of liquor touch his lips."

"And what of the families of the dead sailors?" she retorted sharply. "His vow is too late for them."

Her father gave her a tormented look. "We can't be angry with him now, Fiona. What's done is done. We have to trust that Carvey will keep his vow."

"Save your trust, Da. He's already broken it."

Finn studied her grim countenance. "Tell me the truth of it, Fiona."

"I found him out by the stable in the middle of the night a few days ago drinking whiskey."

"Whiskey!" he exclaimed in dismay. "By all the saints, Fiona, he didn't get it from me."

Fiona made a quick decision not to tell her father about the whiskey hidden in the stall until she had positive proof of Devlin's involvement. Her father had enough burdens without adding one more. "He must have gotten a bottle from Devlin's saloon."

Finn shook his head in bafflement. "Carvey's not a drinking man. Why would he suddenly take to the bottle?"

"I don't know, Da, but it explains his stomach problems."

"No, Fiona," Finn said in a voice heavy with regret, "it's not the liquor causing Carvey's problems. It's the guilt of what he's done."

Fiona searched her father's craggy features and saw the remorse he still carried for his own transgressions. She returned to the chair and wearily leaned her head back, knowing Carvey would suffer just as her father had. Finn was right. What was done was done. She had to let her anger die.

But for the life of her she could not understand why Carvey

had gotten drunk the night of the shipwreck. When she thought of the tragedy he had caused she wanted to weep. And Travis had suffered all along thinking he was responsible.

"How could you have let Travis accept the blame for the shipwreck, Da?" she asked sadly.

"Don't you think I've hated myself for it, Fiona? Do you know what it's like to watch a man go through the agony of blaming himself for his crew's death because the truth would cause your own family to suffer? I have five mouths to feed, soon to be six. I couldn't risk losing my position here. So I made a choice and I've suffered greatly for it. But I'd make it again to protect my family."

Fiona stared at him pityingly. Could she blame her father for the choice he made? What would she have done under those circumstances?

"If you want to tell Travis the truth," Finn said with a heavy sigh, "I won't stop you, Fiona. Follow your conscience."

"Travis is planning to leave New Clare in the morning," she replied in a flat voice. "There's no use telling him now."

Finn looked surprised at the news. "He's turning his ship over to his brother?"

"They both thought it best," Fiona answered vaguely. She yawned and rubbed her eyes.

"You're weary, daughter. Go down to bed. I'll stay the night."

Fiona shook her head. "You're weary, too, Da, and as Aunt Tullia always says, I've got youth on my side."

"There's truth in that, Fiona."

"I'll call you if I need you, Da."

Fiona sat in her father's big chair and listened to the wind wailing outside. To think that one slip had affected so many lives and caused so much sorrow. It was no wonder her father looked haggard and Carvey was in such agony. Neither one had been the same since the night of the wreck.

One question still bothered her. Why had Carvey become worse after speaking to Devlin?

An answer presented itself instantly. Carvey had confided

in Devlin and now Devlin was threatening to reveal the truth about the light to Travis. It would explain why Carvey had taken ill after speaking with Devlin, but what would Devlin have to gain by threatening Carvey?

Again, a solution came to mind. Carvey had discovered that Devlin had stolen the cargo, and now Devlin was worried that Carvey's conscience would bother him until he told someone about the theft.

Fiona rubbed her temples as a headache began to form. Of all the questions she now asked herself, there was one for which she had no conceivable answer: Why would Carvey confide such a terrible secret to Devlin? It made no sense.

Fiona stood and began to pace, chewing her thumbnail as she walked. Because she now shared their secret, she carried the burden of it as well. Was it right, she asked herself, to let Travis forever take the blame for something clearly not his fault? Was it just to let Devlin get away with his crime?

Was it her place to decide their fates?

Fiona pressed her hands to her ears, not only to block out the terrible clamor of the wind but also the cry of her conscience. If she continued to let Travis take responsibility for the shipwreck, she would be as guilty of deceit as the others. Yet once Travis found out about the light he would surely report it. What was she to do?

There was one thing she could do and that was to make sure the thief was caught. It was no longer a matter of deciding anyone's fate; it was a matter of her honor. If she could not bring herself to tell Travis about the light, at least she could salve her conscience by bringing the thief to justice, even if it turned out to be Devlin.

Fiona gave a start when a tree branch hit the window. Lightning lit up the sky in jagged streaks and rain pelted the glass. Through the blur she could see the waves on the lake swelling to twice the height of the pier.

Her father had been right. They were headed into a gale.

Suddenly Fiona heard the low, mournful call of a ship in distress. "Saints in heaven, please, not again!" At the second blast of the ship's horn, she ran down the stairs to her father's room, but she had no need to wake him. Finn was already pulling on his pants.

"Sound the bell, Fiona, quickly!"

Her heart slamming against her ribs, Fiona raced through the silent house, pulled open the door and ran through the rain for the huge bell mounted on an iron stand behind the house. Pulling on the rope with all her might, fighting the powerful push of the wind, Fiona sounded the alarm that would rouse the rescue team.

Within minutes she saw lights in the town below, and shortly after that the bobbing motion of lanterns. The rescuers were headed for the lake. Soaked to the skin, Fiona hurried back inside to check on the beacon before changing into dry clothing.

In the kitchen Dee had already started making pots of coffee. Fiona grabbed her rain cloak by the door and called, "I'll be back for the coffee in a bit, Dee."

She hurried down the long pier, passing Brian Kelly, Kevin Malone, Jesse O'Keefe and Mick Doyle, who were getting ready to man the bright yellow rescue boats. Mrs. O'Donohue was there, too, along with Mary Sheridan, Father Patrick and Pegeen, swiftly and silently helping in any way they could.

Fiona found her father at the end of the pier with her cousin Tom Brody and two other men who were already climbing into a boat. Fiona didn't see their faces until they had taken their places on the wooden benches and then she ran to her father and clutched his sleeve, shouting above the storm, "Da, you can't send Travis and Jordan out there!"

"They asked to help, Fiona," he shouted back.

"But they've never done it before. It's too dangerous!"

"Don't worry. They're both experienced sailors."

Oblivious to the wind and driving rain, Fiona stood on the pier with her hands clasped tightly together, watching with her heart in her throat as the three rescue boats started out across the turbulent waters toward the stricken ship, which was little more than a ghostly shape in the distance.

Three men manned each of the long boats: one at the prow to carry a lantern and the other two at the oars. Tom Brody carried the lantern in the first boat, sitting at the prow to direct the rescue operation. Brian Kelly, Kevin Malone and Mick Doyle were in the second. On the last boat, Travis and Jordan each took an oar while John Delahanty, the baker, held the lantern. In a few minutes all that could be seen of the gigs in the darkness were the bobbing lights.

Each time one of the lights disappeared Fiona caught her breath and didn't release it until she saw it again. She was always sick with despair when a ship struck, but this time it was far worse. This time Travis was out there, fighting darkness, towering waves and terrible winds, struggling not only to rescue the ship's crew, but also to get safely back to shore.

What if he didn't make it?

Unable to watch any longer, Fiona turned and paced the length of the pier. She hadn't ever intended to fall in love with him. Indeed, she had tried mightily to protect herself from it. She had lived through these moments too many times to wish it upon herself again. Now the thought of losing that love hurt worse than anything she could ever have imagined.

Remembering the vow she had made the day of Travis's shipwreck, she paused to stare down at the inky water.

By every drop of blood that flows through my body, I'll never let you take my loved ones from me.

Only now did she realize how useless her vow was. She had no more power over the lake than she did over her heart. All she could do was wait, hope and pray.

❖*19*❖

FIONA SCANNED THE horizon, searching for a glimpse of the three boats in the murky grayness of the early dawn. The worst of the storm had passed, but the waves were still dangerously high. To the east she could see the first faint, pink glow of the new day. The men had been gone nearly three hours. Why was there no sign of them?

There was a cry from one of the women and suddenly two of the gigs came into view—tiny, fragile slivers of yellow against the backdrop of the seething black waters of Lake Michigan. There was still no sign of a third.

Fiona ran to the end of the pier and stood with the others. *Please, God, let Travis be safe.* She felt the clasp of a hand and turned to see Pegeen give her a wan smile.

Mrs. O'Donohue used a telescope to monitor the rescuers' progress. "Two of the gigs have sailors on board," she reported. "I don't see the last boat yet."

"Do you see Tommy?" Pegeen asked anxiously.

"Your Tom's on the lead boat, Peg."

"And Travis Paine?" Peg asked, squeezing Fiona's hand.

Mrs. O'Donohue looked again. "I don't see him."

Fiona's stomach twisted in dread. Where was Travis's boat? Standing on tiptoe, she strained to see over the immense waves. All at once, from far behind the other two, the third boat broke through the whitecaps, bringing forth a cheer from the group huddled on the pier. Fiona laughed and hugged Pegeen, her eyes filling with tears. Travis was safe.

But in the next instant disaster struck. A monstrous wave swelled beneath the two boats in front, tossing them over thirty feet in the air and dropping them suddenly into a trough just as deep. For several long moments there was no sign of either boat, then one of the vessels surfaced upside down. The other was carried upright toward the beach. Fiona could see the men aboard trying desperately to turn back to aid the others.

"Tommy!" Pegeen cried out in terror. She clutched Fiona's arm. "Mother of God, it's Tommy's boat that tipped over!"

They watched, horrified, as another wave struck the overturned boat. It floated deserted towards the shore.

"He's gone, Fiona!" Pegeen keened, turning to sob on Fiona's shoulder. "Tommy's gone."

"No, he's not! Look, Peg!" Fiona called, pointing out over the water. "They're all alive!"

The first boat had managed to turn back and was now attempting to rescue the men bobbing in the waters nearby. The third boat was rapidly approaching the same spot and within minutes was aiding in the rescue of the sailors.

"Brian Kelly is safe," Mrs. O'Donohue reported with joy as she peered through her telescope. "And there's Mick Doyle smiling as bright as the sun. They've picked up three, four, five more sailors as well."

"What about Tom Brody?" Mary Sheridan called.

Mrs. O'Donohue peered through her telescope again. Pegeen squeezed Fiona's hand so tightly that her fingers began to tingle. Both women held their breath.

But after several long minutes of searching the choppy waters, Mrs. O'Donohue lowered the instrument and slowly shook her head. Tom Brody was not among those rescued.

With a strangled cry, Pegeen crumpled onto the pier. Mary Sheridan instantly knelt to gather her in her arms, stroking her head and murmuring soothing words. With fists clenched to keep from crying herself, Fiona stood beside them and gazed into the distance, feeling Pegeen's torment. *Please, God, let Tommy be alive.*

At that moment she saw one of the men on the last rescue boat rise from his seat, take off his shirt and shoes and jump into the lake. "Saints preserve us!" she cried. "Someone's jumped in the lake! Mrs. O'Donohue, what do you see?"

"It's your Mr. Paine, Fiona," the woman relayed excitedly. "He must have spotted someone in the water."

Fiona's heart thudded in apprehension.

Pegeen began to sob. "It has to be Tommy he's spotted. It has to be! I'll die if anything happens to him. I can't live without him."

"Calm yourself, lass," Mary said in a soothing voice. "You must have faith that the Lord will watch over your Tom."

From where she stood, Fiona was able to see two of the men from the third boat reach down and pull a man from the water. "Who is it?" Fiona cried to Mrs. O'Donohue. "Can you tell? Is it Tommy?"

"It's not a face I know," Mrs. O'Donohue reported grimly. "It's not Tom Brody."

Travis hoisted the sailor out of the water into the waiting arms of his brother and John Delahanty. Drawing in three deep mouthfuls of air, he prepared to dive again.

"Travis, for God's sake!" Jordan called, leaning over the side of the boat. "You'll drown in these waters! Come back!"

Travis clutched the side of the boat as a wave swelled beneath him. For several moments he found himself under water, then his head broke the surface and he filled his lungs with air.

"Travis, give up! It's not worth risking your life." Jordan called again.

"There's still a man missing," Travis shouted back. He took another deep breath and dived beneath the waves. The water was cloudy with sand and his eyes burned as he strained to see through it. He ran out of air and surfaced again.

"Do you see any sign of Tom?" he yelled to the men in the gig.

"I see someone over there!" John Delahanty shouted, pointing across the boat. "On the other side of the boat."

Travis ducked under once again and used the boat as a springboard to launch himself through the water. He swam as far as he could on one breath, then came up to drag air into his starved lungs. He wiped the water from his eyes and looked around at the boat behind him. "How far now?" he called.

"Another three yards!" came the reply. In the few moments between waves Travis spotted a man flailing in the water and recognized him as Tom. Twice, he nearly reached him, but both times a huge wave separated them. "Hang on!" he called, but couldn't hear a reply.

Travis struck out again, but before he could reach Tom, the man disappeared under the water. Ahead Travis could see another gigantic wave heading his way. He quickly took a breath and dived. Through the murkiness he saw Tom and made a grab for his clothing. Holding on with all his remaining strength, Travis hauled him to the surface, his lungs nearly bursting from his efforts, the muscles in his arms burning from overuse. Sharp pains between his ribs made Travis fear he had reinjured them.

As soon as the two men surfaced, Tom began to struggle, pushing Travis under the water. He came up coughing and gasping for air. "Damn it, don't fight me, Tom," he ordered hoarsely.

"I can't make it," came the breathless reply. "Go on without me and save yourself."

"Just float, Tom. We can make it. I'll help you."

With his arm around Tom's thick neck, Travis kicked with his legs and pulled with all his might, yet it seemed they were making no headway against the waves. Out of breath, in pain and nearly out of strength, he feared they would drown. He began to pray silently for both of them.

Suddenly he heard someone shout his name and looked up to see the third rescue boat slowly approaching, Jordan at the prow. With renewed hope, Travis kicked hard and within a few minutes felt Tom being lifted from the water. Before Travis could grab for the side of the boat or even draw a breath, he was engulfed by another wave and pulled under.

In weakened condition, Travis struggled to right himself before what little air remained in his lungs gave out. He kicked his feet and aimed himself toward the light only to hit his head against something hard. Momentarily stunned, Travis glanced up to see the bottom of the boat hovering over him. He shook his head to clear his foggy brain, but it did no good.

At once strong hands gripped his arm and Travis turned his head to look dazedly into the eyes of his brother. Jordan hauled him from beneath the boat and helped the men hoist him into the gig. Travis collapsed on a bench, coughing and wheezing, too spent to sit or even talk. Someone put a blanket around his shoulders and he used the corner to dry his face.

"You did a good job, lad," John Delahanty said after Travis had rested a while. "You're a hero this day. You saved our Tom."

Wearily, Travis lifted his head to look at Tom, sitting opposite him, his large, meaty frame similarly covered by a thick brown blanket. Tom gave him a weak smile of gratitude. With a grin, Travis returned the smile. His smile faded when Jordan moved to the seat beside him, his features stiff, his lips pressed together in a grim line.

Knowing he was about to receive a lecture, Travis looked away. "I guess I owe you for getting me out of another scrape, eh, brother?"

"My God, Travis," Jordan said in a low, choked voice. "What were you thinking? You nearly drowned."

"Tom's my friend," he explained tersely, glaring at his brother. "I wasn't going to leave him out there to die."

Jordan stared at him almost as though seeing Travis for the first time. To Travis's immense surprise, his brother suddenly embraced him, holding him tightly for several long moments. When Jordan pulled away, his eyes were moist and his throat was working, as though he wanted to say something but couldn't for fear of being too emotional.

Touched by Jordan's unusual display of affection, Travis tried to make a joke about the situation. "All I can say is that it's a damn good thing I didn't drown. The Paine Shipping Company doesn't have any insurance on me, you know. If I drowned I'd *really* be in hot water with ol' Jefferson.''

Jordan stared at Travis with a look of incredulity, making Travis wish he'd kept his mouth shut. It was immediately obvious that his brother didn't find his attempt at humor at their father's expense amusing.

Travis was about to apologize when Jordan suddenly threw back his head and roared with laughter. Amazed, Travis began to laugh with him, until both men were holding their sides and shaking with mirth while the others looked on in puzzlement.

Travis grabbed his brother's arm and shook it, still laughing. ''Can't you just imagine what Mother would have to say about my drowning?''

Jordan gasped for air. ''No. Tell me.''

'' 'Travis *who*?' ''

At that they laughed even harder while the men in the boat shook their heads in wonder. Travis finally let out a long sigh and leaned back on his elbows. It felt good to break the tension of the past hours. It felt even better to share the moment with his brother. It was something he'd never done before.

They were still grinning when the boat docked at the end of the pier. Travis stood up slowly on wobbly legs. He clapped his brother on the back and turned with a smile to look straight up into Fiona's furious gaze.

He was laughing! She had just spent the worst three hours of her life worrying about him, and Travis was laughing! Fiona spun around and marched up the pier toward the lighthouse, cursing fate, the storm, the lake, the captain of the ship, her own folly and everything else that came to mind.

Using Mrs. O'Donohue's telescope, she had nearly fainted with fright when she saw Travis disappear under the waves, not once but three times. Each time she thought he had drowned she had died inside. Each time he had reappeared she had rejoiced, only to be thrown into despair once again.

If that was what love did to a person, Fiona thought angrily, she wanted no more of it.

"Fiona!" she heard Travis call.

Not this time, Travis Paine, she said to herself. *I'll not wait for you ever again.* When she reached the end of the pier she began to run. She didn't stop until she reached the lighthouse, then she hurried up the stairs to her bedroom and slammed the door. Muttering to herself, she tossed her rain cloak on the bed and began to pace back and forth, too distraught to sit for even a moment.

How she hated Travis for making her worry. How she wished she could cause him such misery in return. He certainly deserved no less.

Fiona found herself wishing she could pack her bags and catch the next train east. Leaving New Clare had never looked as good as it did at that moment. She wanted to be finished with the vengeful lake forever.

She tried to call to mind the vision she had carried with her for so many years. She pictured herself on a train bound for the East Coast, with all the wonders waiting there to be discovered: Philadelphia, Boston, New York—and of course Niagara Falls. But she no longer felt the same sense of excitement, the same thirst for adventure. What was wrong with her?

You know in your heart what the problem is, Fiona, her conscience scolded.

Concentrating harder, Fiona attempted to recall her fantasy of the handsome traveler whom she was supposed to meet and fall in love with on her trip east. But the stranger had Travis's face.

You love him. There's no turning away from it. "No!" she cried, holding her hands over her ears.

At a knock on the door she turned and said sharply, "Who is it?"

"It's me."

Travis. Fiona's heart leaped to her throat. A part of her wanted desperately to open the door and wrap her arms around his neck, to feel his arms around her, to know that he was safe. The other, rational part of her warned that she had to keep her distance to protect herself from any more such pain. She took a breath and said in a firm voice, "I'm busy."

The door opened and Travis stood there, the blanket still around his broad shoulders, his damp hair hanging over his forehead, looking as dashing as he did bedraggled.

He gave her a sheepish grin. "I don't think I'll make the early train."

As Fiona stared at him, a host of angry thoughts crowded her mind. How could he make light of such a terrible night? How could he return from near death *laughing*, when she had suffered every second he was gone? Her fists clenched in fury and her throat tightened. But all that came out were three words: "I hate you!" And then she burst into tears.

Travis was dumbfounded. He threw off the blanket and took her in his arms. "What did I do?"

Fiona clenched his damp shirt in her fingers and leaned her forehead against his chest. "How could you *do* that to me?" she sobbed.

"Do *what* to you?"

She gulped back her tears and raised anguished eyes to his face. "I was worried sick about you. You nearly died out there. And you were *laughing* about it!"

Stunned by her revelation, Travis was at a loss for words. Fiona had been worried about him. The enormity of her meaning hit him like a steam engine. She didn't hate him. She couldn't possibly be worried sick about him and hate him. What she meant and couldn't say was that she loved him. *Fiona loved him!*

Travis groped for something to say, some explanation to make her feel better. He stroked her head and hugged her close. "I had just made a joke for my brother's benefit, Fiona. Jordan and I were laughing about what I said, that's all."

"Stars and garters!" she exclaimed, pushing away from him. "You nearly drowned and then you made a joke about it?"

He gave her a crooked grin. "I didn't say it was a good joke."

She paced to the window and angrily swung to face him. "I spent the most miserable, terrifying three hours of my life out there this morning and—God's teeth, what are you smiling about now?"

Travis couldn't help but grin. Jesus, she was beautiful in her anger! "I apologize, Fiona," he said, walking toward her. "I didn't know you were upset."

"Of course I was upset," she retorted a little less angrily.

He lifted her chin with his finger and gazed into her eyes. "You had every right to be."

She gave him a skeptical look, as though she couldn't understand why he was being so agreeable. "What are you saying?"

"I'm saying that it was only natural for you to be upset. After all, you almost lost the man you love."

"The man I *love*!" she cried, but before she could protest further, he dropped his head and pressed his lips against hers, tasting the salty residue of her tears, enjoying the suppleness of her mouth. He felt her body stiffen and knew she intended to push him away. Before she could act, he slipped his arms around her, holding her steady.

"Travis!" she muttered against his mouth, struggling to free herself.

He tipped his head back slightly to gaze down into her eyes.

"Let me go!"

"Deny that you love me," he said and bent his head to claim her lips once again. He kissed her until he felt her body relax, then he placed his palms against the small of her back, drawing her against him.

The feel of her soft curves, the scent of her skin, the taste of her mouth, all combined to intensify the passion building inside him while her soft whimpers spurred him to greater heights. He pulled the comb from the back of her head to release her hair, then gripped the heavy tresses with his hands, tilting her head back to give him access to her throat.

She gave a small cry of pleasure when Travis ran his tongue around the inner shell of her ear and nipped the back of her neck with his teeth. Working the buttons of her bodice, he parted the material and slipped his hand inside, sliding beneath the lace edge of her corset to cup one silken mound. The velvety nipple hardened at his touch and made his manhood thicken with desire.

Before she could object to the intrusion of his fingers, Travis kissed her again, probing inside her mouth with his tongue as he stroked her breast. When he bent down and took the soft peak in his mouth, Fiona gasped and clutched his hair.

God, how he wanted her! Travis was so filled with desire that he scooped her up in his arms and carried her the three steps to the bed. Lowering her onto the quilt, he lay his full weight on her and kissed her with an intensity that left them both breathless.

He lifted his head and gazed down into her eyes. "Marry me, Fiona."

Fiona's mouth fell open in amazement. *Marry him?* Before she could reply he kissed her again, and despite her shock she found herself rising beneath him, arching to meet the hardness of his groin, striving to satisfy the heavy throbbing between her thighs. She wrapped her arms around his neck and met each thrust of his tongue with one of her own.

From somewhere within Fiona's passion-clouded brain, she suddenly registered the sound of footsteps coming up the stairs. With a gasp, she pushed him away. "Someone is coming!" she whispered, and slid off the bed, hastily fastening the buttons of her bodice with shaking hands. From the corner of her eye she saw Travis adjust his clothing and rake his fingers through his hair. At a soft knock she replied in a trembling voice, "Who is it?"

"It's Mary Sheridan. Fiona, dear, are you all right?"

Travis put a finger to his lips, warning her to silence. Fiona snatched her comb from the floor and quickly twisted her hair into a bun. "I'm fine, Mary."

"You ran off so quickly, dear. I was afraid something had happened."

Fiona darted a glance at Travis. Something *would* have happened, but thanks to Mary's timely arrival, it hadn't. "I just came up to get out of my wet clothing."

There was the sound of heavier footsteps approaching, then she heard whispering outside her door.

"Fiona?" her father called. "Have you seen Mr. Paine?"

Fiona couldn't look at Travis. "Isn't he down at the pier, Da?"

"I saw him head back this way. Maybe he's still outside."

She waited until two sets of footsteps had retreated to the lower floor, then she opened the door, peeked outside and motioned for Travis to leave. "Go, quickly, before someone else comes to look for you."

He stopped to give her a parting kiss, but she dodged his lips. He kissed her on the cheek instead. "I'll be back for your answer."

Fiona closed her door and leaned against it, still in shock over Travis's marriage proposal. She couldn't marry him! If she accepted his proposal she would be tied to the lake and all its disasters for the rest of her life.

She glanced at her bed and hurried over to smooth out the wrinkles where they had lain. Her movements slowed as she recalled vividly the feel of Travis's body on hers and of the driving passion he had aroused within her. The depth of her desire frightened her. What would have happened if Mary hadn't come up to find her?

She would have made love with him.

Fiona shivered and finished straightening the bed. She could not marry Travis. She had vowed never to marry a sailing man and the near tragedy of that morning only reinforced her determination to keep the vow. She would not live her life always fearing that Travis's next voyage would be his last.

Too weary to think further, she curled up on the bed and closed her eyes. Perhaps Travis had been overcome by passion when he asked her to marry him and was even now regretting it. Or perhaps he had not intended to marry her, only to use those words to seduce her.

Just to make certain, she would give him no opportunity to ask her again.

❖ *20* ❖

WEARING A VICTOR'S grin, Travis crossed the hall to his room and turned the knob. But before the door could swing open, his smile disappeared and the color drained from his face. "*Jesus*, I just asked her to marry me!"

"Then I suppose congratulations are in order."

Travis jerked his head to the left and saw Jordan standing near the pine bureau, fastening the buttons of a dry shirt. Travis shut the door and sat down on the bed, raking his fingers through his hair. "Jesus!" he muttered again.

He felt the bed dip as Jordan sat beside him to pull on a pair of clean socks.

"I assume the lady in question is Fiona?" Jordan remarked.

"I asked her to marry me!"

"We've already established that fact, Travis."

Travis stood and began to pace. "I can't ask Fiona to marry me. She has her own plans."

"Travis, you've already asked her," Jordan patiently reminded him.

"She'll say no. Fiona has made it perfectly clear that she will *never* marry a sailor."

Jordan tucked in his shirttails. "Then I suppose the logical thing to do would be to give up sailing."

Travis stopped in mid-pace and swung to stare at his

brother, whose expression was as placid as if he had just suggested that Travis get a haircut. "*What*?"

Jordan shrugged. "Give up sailing. You hate it anyway."

"Are you out of your mind? It's my profession. I can't give it up."

"Why not?" his brother demanded.

Travis was flabbergasted by his brother's cavalier attitude. "For one thing, Jefferson won't stand for it."

Jordan leaned back on his elbows. "What's more important, Travis, what Jefferson wants or what you want?"

Travis couldn't believe Jordan was telling him to pull out. He studied him warily, a lifetime of mistrust making him suspicious of his brother's motives. What would Jordan stand to gain if he did pull out?

As though he sensed Travis's suspicions, Jordan said, "It doesn't matter one way or the other to me what you do. What I'm trying to say is that you need to make a decision based on what *you* want to do with your life, not what Jefferson dictates."

Travis rubbed his jaw, then sat down on the bed again. "I want my own ship."

"You do?" Jordan asked skeptically.

"Yes!"

"You want to spend your life sailing the lakes?"

"As long as I'm master of my own ship, yes."

Jordan gazed at him thoughtfully. "Let me be the devil's advocate for the moment, Travis, and ask you this: What if you never make it?"

Travis clenched his jaw determinedly. "I *will* make it, damn it! I'm a good sailor. And someday I'll be able to prove to Jefferson that I'm as capable as you and Tyler are, that I *can* live up to his expectations!"

Jordan smiled at that and shook his head. He went to the window to pull back the curtain and gaze at the lake beyond. "No one can live up to Jefferson Paine's expectations, Travis. No one."

Travis stared at his brother's back. "But you and Tyler—"

"Have never been able to live up to them, either." Jordan

turned to look at Travis. "I've been striving to please that man since I was old enough to jump to his commands. Tyler, too. As soon as we'd meet one goal, he'd be on us to accomplish the next. Being captain of a ship wasn't even enough to satisfy him. Now he wants grandchildren. Christ, I'm so busy sailing, when does he expect me to meet the girl I'm supposed to marry?"

Travis stared at him in surprise. "I had no idea you and Tyler felt that way."

"Of course not. You were too busy resenting us for our successes. The difference between us, Travis, is that I *wanted* to be master of my own ship. I *thrive* on sailing and everything that goes with it, and I would do it whether Jefferson wanted me to or not." Jordan grinned. "You, on the other hand, hate sailing."

"That's a lie!"

Jordan folded his arms across his chest and gave Travis a forbearing smile. "Then why did you run away?"

Agitated, Travis ran his fingers through his hair. "I was young and foolish. I wanted to show Jefferson I could lead my own life without him telling me what to do."

"Why did you come back?"

Travis sighed. "Because I envied how much he respected you and Tyler for commanding your own ships. I wanted some of that respect for myself."

"He respects us because he knows we love sailing and he recognizes that we put our hearts into it. If you can't say the same thing about it, Travis, you'll never win his respect."

Travis rose suddenly and walked to the bureau, staring at himself in the oval mirror above it. He had always based his identity on what his father told him he should be. But all he'd been was a failure. So who was he? Was he a sailor? Would he ever be good enough in his father's eyes to be a captain?

God, how he hated sailing. Travis had never admitted that to anyone, not even to himself, yet Jordan had somehow known. It made him wonder if Jefferson hadn't also guessed it. The trouble was that if he gave up sailing, he didn't have a notion as to what he would do instead.

"You're right, Jordan," he said with a resigned sigh, turning to face his brother, "I loathe the thought of spending the rest of my life aboard a ship."

"Then, by God, do something about it," Jordan said, striding over to where Travis stood. He gripped Travis's shoulders and looked him straight in the eye. "Do you love Fiona?"

"Look, Jordan, Fiona has dreams—"

"Yes or no, Travis. Do you love her?"

Travis searched his brother's eyes. "Yes."

"Then marry her, damn it. Make a life for yourself here with her."

"And what am I supposed to offer her?" Travis countered. "If I quit sailing I'm out of a job. Shipping is all I know."

Jordan studied him a moment, then paced to the window and back, his head bent in thought. Suddenly he wheeled around, an exultant smile on his face. "Does New Clare have a freight transport company?"

"Not that I'm aware of."

"What comes in through the port goes out through the railroad, doesn't it? You know shipping, Travis. What would be more natural than for you to handle the cargo that the ships bring in?"

"You're saying that I should construct a tie-in with the main railroad line?"

"Exactly. Build a facility near the docks, tie into the railroad lines and you're in business."

Travis began to catch Jordan's enthusiasm. "New Clare has a lot of growth potential, Jordan. It's sitting in an ideal location at the southern end of the lake. But I'd need capital to get started."

"You've got it."

"From you?" Travis asked in surprise.

"I've managed to put aside a rather tidy sum. I think Tyler would want to help, too."

Travis rubbed his hands together as his thoughts whirled. If he had his own business, he could easily support a wife. His hands suddenly dropped to his sides. "I'm forgetting one small detail, Jordan. Fiona is dead set on leaving New Clare. She wants to see the world. It's been her dream for a long time. I can't ask her to give it up."

"You've already asked her to marry you, Travis. If she accepts, then it's her decision to give up her dream. If she turns you down, then there's been no harm done. You can go back to sailing or do whatever you choose." He paused to give Travis time to mull it over, then asked, "What do you say?"

Travis rubbed his face. "I'll speak to her about it after rehearsal this evening."

Jordan eyed Travis thoughtfully. "I didn't mean what I said about not caring one way or the other what you do with your life."

The two brothers looked at each other for a moment, then Travis gave him a nod of thanks, unable to express how much his brother's acknowledgment meant to him. To finally feel accepted by one of his own family was a priceless gift.

Travis bent his head and shoved his hands in his pockets, suddenly struck by an attack of guilt. "Jordan, there's something you need to know about that cargo you saw in the warehouse."

"Attention, everyone," Tullia Brody called, clapping her hands to gather all the cast members together. "Since tonight is our last rehearsal, I wanted to take a moment to thank each of you for striving to make our production a success again this year. Your costumes look wonderful, and for that we must thank our dear Mary Sheridan."

Tullia waited until Mary had been applauded, then added, "and a special thank-you to our director for all her hard work. Fiona, come over here."

Fiona groaned inwardly as the group cheered. With a blush of embarrassment, she walked to the center of the stage and accepted a bouquet of white daisies and black-eyed susans.

"I'd like to thank Mr. Paine, too," Tullia announced, "for being so agreeable about playing Rip Van Winkle."

Travis nodded to Tullia and graciously accepted the applause. He was dressed in his Rip Van Winkle costume—a flowing white shirt and tweed vest, knee-length tweed breeches, white stockings and black boots with large silver buckles. His dark hair curled onto his collar in the back and his face was tanned from working in the sun.

Fiona watched him with a mixture of love and regret. He was a fine figure of a man, handsome, strong and capable. He would make a courageous captain. *And a good husband,* her heart told her.

Travis turned suddenly and caught her staring at him. He winked and gave her a rakish grin that melted her insides. Instead of returning his smile, however, Fiona averted her gaze, hoping to discourage his attention. All day she had prayed that he had forgotten his impassioned proposal or at least had decided that he had erred in asking her. The perfect opportunity for him to ask her again would be on their walk home from the church, unless she could evade him.

From the back of the group came Bridget's little-girl voice. "Now, Tullia, don't you think Travis deserves more than a little hand-clapping for his fine efforts?"

Fiona looked up as Bridget elbowed her way to the front. Wearing Dame Van Winkle's costume of a frumpy muslin housedress, white apron and white mobcap over her golden banana curls, Bridget still managed to look adorable. She sailed straight over to Travis and tilted her head to gaze worshipfully into his dark eyes. Before Fiona could guess what the girl was up to, Bridget grabbed Travis's shirtfront, pulled him down to her level and kissed him fully on the mouth, drawing laughter from the men and a few shocked gasps from the ladies. Travis merely stiffened, but did not pull away.

Fiona clenched her fists at her sides and narrowed her eyes at the two of them. "Are we all to line up, then, Bridget, to express our appreciation to Mr. Paine, or may we proceed with our rehearsal?"

Bridget released Travis and turned to give her a smug smile. "I believe I've thanked him sufficiently, Fiona. You may proceed."

Fiona wanted to choke Bridget on her own apron strings. Turning to the group, she said tersely, "Please take your places."

Despite a strained beginning, the dress rehearsal went much more smoothly than Fiona expected. Even Bridget had her lines memorized perfectly. Fiona began to feel at ease about the next day's performance.

While the scenery was being changed, Fiona overheard Bridget again describing her new silk dress to one of the ladies. She watched for an opportunity to question Bridget and found it during the last act, when Dame Van Winkle had been declared dead and buried and Bridget had nothing more to do than stand at the dessert table off stage and nibble.

"Will you be wearing your new silk dress tomorrow, Bridget?" Fiona asked nonchalantly as she cut herself a piece of lemon pie.

Bridget licked the crumbs off her thumb and glanced at Fiona warily. "Yes."

"I've been thinking about ordering some silk, myself," Fiona lied. "I want to have a gown made to take with me when I leave."

"You're still planning to leave New Clare then, Fiona?"

"Oh, yes." Fiona gave her a sidelong glance. "And I hope you'll visit Dee often after I've gone, Bridget. The new babe will need an aunt, you know."

Bridget snapped at the bait, her blue eyes dancing with delight. "Oh, I'd be happy to, Fiona! I *love* babies."

Poor, unsuspecting little creature, Fiona thought.

"When are you leaving?" Bridget asked, fairly rubbing her hands together with excitement. Fiona could almost hear the wheels turning in Bridget's head as she made plans for the child's future.

"Just as soon as the babe is born and Dee's settled in. Of course, I have yet to start my travel wardrobe."

"I can get silk for your gown," Bridget blurted. "Just tell me the color you'd like and how much you'll need."

"Can you now, Bridget? That's very kind of you." Fiona put her arm around Bridget's shoulders and they began to walk back to the stage together. "I know we've not always gotten along, but I think it's time to put our differences aside—for the babe's sake."

Bridget slipped an arm around Fiona's waist and gave her a squeeze. "Oh, I quite agree, Fiona. I've always looked up to you as an older sister, almost a mother figure, in fact."

Fiona resisted the urge to tighten her arm around the girl's neck and instead forced a smile. "Why, thank you, Bridget. I'd appreciate it if you could get me some silk in a soft rose color. Seven yards will do. Let me know how much I owe you for it." She paused, then added coyly, "Do you have any idea how soon you'll be able to get it?"

"It shouldn't take more than a day. In fact, I'll tell Devlin first thing in the morning."

Very casually, Fiona asked, "Would he be able to get the silk that quickly?"

Realizing her slip, Bridget's eyes widened in alarm.

Fiona suddenly realized the rehearsal had stopped and the cast members were all watching them, waiting for her next direction. Travis stood only a yard away, a speculative look on his face. Before Fiona could think of what to do, Bridget suddenly began to moan loudly and limp on one foot.

"What happened?" Tullia called, hurrying over to Bridget's side.

"I twisted my ankle off stage," Bridget whined. She released her hold on Fiona and held her arms out to Travis with a pleading look. "Travis, would you be so kind as to help me?"

Leave it to clever Bridget to figure a way to avoid answering her question, Fiona thought with begrudging admiration as Travis stepped forward to help her. Bridget Riley had the uncanny ability to turn every situation to her advantage. But at least the question about the mystery silk had finally been answered. Devlin had supplied Bridget with the material. Now all Fiona had to do was find out where he was hiding the rest.

While Travis helped Bridget to a chair, Fiona called the cast together for last-minute instructions.

"We'll meet here at six-thirty tomorrow evening," she told them. "Our play will start promptly at seven-thirty. If there are no questions, enjoy the festival and I'll see you tomorrow evening."

"Ow! My ankle hurts so!" Bridget exclaimed, leaning on Travis's arm outside the church. "I think you'll have to carry me.'' She batted her eyelashes at him, her mouth forming a pathetic little pout.

Gritting his teeth to keep his temper in check, Travis bent and scooped her up. With a delighted squeal, she wrapped her arms around his neck and gazed adoringly at him. Ahead, Travis saw Fiona start up Wexford heading for the lighthouse.

Damn Bridget's blue eyes anyway! He had meant to walk home with Fiona so he could speak to her again about marrying him and had ended up with Bridget instead. Tomorrow Fiona would be busy with the festival. When would he have another chance? He started down the street at a rapid pace until Bridget's weight forced him to slow to catch his breath. For a tiny woman she sure was solid, he thought as he puffed along.

Briefly, he thought of introducing her to Jordan to get her off his back, but decided he wouldn't do that to his brother, even if they hadn't reached an understanding.

Travis struggled up the porch steps and used his elbow to push the door buzzer. When the door opened, her father gaped at the two of them in amazement.

''Hello, Papa,'' Bridget said with a coy smile. ''I twisted my ankle.''

Mama Riley appeared in the doorway beside her husband. ''Come in, Mr. Paine!'' they exclaimed in unison. Travis groaned inwardly as he stepped over the threshold, feeling like the proverbial fly in the spider's web. He carried Bridget into the parlor, lowered her onto a chair and straightened, massaging a kink in his lower back.

''Will you take some refreshments, Mr. Paine?'' Mama Riley was quick to offer.

Papa Riley hurried over with a rosewood cigar box and thrust it under Travis's nose. ''Care for a smoke, Mr. Paine?''

Travis hastily declined both offers. ''Thank you, no. But you might want to send for the doctor to look at your daughter's ankle.''

''Oh, she'll be fine,'' they both said, not even sparing her a glance.

Travis backed toward the door. ''Tomorrow's a busy day,

so I'd better take my leave. I hope your ankle is better for the festival, Miss Riley.''

Without waiting for a reply, Travis left, a shudder rippling down his spine at his narrow escape. He covered the distance to the lighthouse in record time, but he wasn't quick enough to catch Fiona.

❖ *21* ❖

Fiona STOOD BESIDE the window in her darkened bedroom and pulled the curtain aside a fraction of an inch to peer out. Below, she could see Travis sitting on the pier, his shoulders hunched dejectedly, his bare feet dangling in the water. He had been there the better part of an hour.

Fiona paced to her door and back, anxiously twisting her fingers together. Travis had tried to get her attention by throwing pebbles at her window, but she had not responded, hoping he would think she was not there. She knew Travis had planned to speak to her about his proposal on the walk home, and for that reason she had blessed Bridget and her feigned injury for preventing it. Telling Travis she could not marry him would be the hardest thing she'd ever done.

But now her conscience bothered her. What should she do? Leave him out there to mope? She glanced at the clock on her bureau. In half an hour it would be time to relieve her father in the tower.

"Devil's knees!" she muttered as she eased open her door. There was nothing to do but go out there and talk to him.

Her bare feet made little sound on the wooden planks of the pier, yet somehow Travis sensed her presence. He looked around, saw her walking toward him and quickly got to his feet. "I thought you were asleep."

"Why are you sitting out here?" she asked. "It's late."

"Will you walk with me?"

Travis's handsome face was so earnest, his gaze so hopeful that her heart ached with longing. Despite her vow to avoid him, she couldn't bring herself to refuse his request. "Yes, I'll walk with you."

A smile spread across his face. Travis held out his arm and waited. Reluctantly, Fiona took it and they began to walk down the dunes together, the feel of the sinewy muscles beneath his shirt making her pulse leap and race.

"And how is Bridget's ankle?" she couldn't resist asking.

"Better than my back."

Fiona smiled to herself. "Had to carry her, did you?"

"She just about jumped into my arms." He glanced at her as they walked. "Now if I could only get you to do likewise."

Fiona turned her head away from him to gaze out at the black waters of the lake, so tranquil now in the aftermath of the storm, the moonlight glimmering invitingly on its placid surface.

"It's beautiful, isn't it?" Travis asked quietly.

"As beautiful as it is deadly."

Travis stopped and turned to face her. Fiona kept her gaze averted, her heart thudding heavily, knowing what was to come.

"Fiona—"

"Travis, there's something I must say."

"No. Hear me out first."

Fiona searched his eyes, then gave a nod of agreement. She owed him the chance to speak his mind.

Travis led her back to a grassy area away from the beach and they sat down. Fiona plucked a stem of grass and wound it around her finger, waiting.

"I've made a decision, Fiona, and I think, that is, I hope. . . ." He stopped, shook his head in frustration, and began again. "I know you said you'd never marry a sailor, but what about a businessman?"

At Fiona's bewildered look, he hurriedly continued. "I've decided to give up sailing and open a freight transport business instead, right here in New Clare."

Fiona's mouth fell open in shock. "Give up sailing?"

"My brother has agreed to put up the capital, and once I have the business going, I'll be able to provide for a wife—if you'll have me."

Fiona's mind registered little beyond his first sentence. "How can you give up sailing? It's your life's ambition!"

Travis took her hands in his. "It was my father's ambition, Fiona, not mine. I never would have chosen it for myself." He smiled. "To tell you the truth, I hate sailing." He squeezed her hands. "Now what do you have to say?"

Fiona was speechless. If Travis gave up sailing, she wouldn't ever again have to fear the lake claiming him. But what of her own dreams? She watched mutely as he raised one of her hands to his mouth and kissed it, his gaze still on her face.

"I love you, Fiona."

Tears gathered in her eyes as she gazed at him. She loved Travis more than life itself, yet it would do no good to tell him unless she could honestly answer her own question: What of her own dreams?

She had only to look in her heart to know the answer: Her dreams had changed. She didn't have to leave New Clare to find herself. She had found herself in Travis's love. Indeed, she could not imagine a future without him. "I love you, too," she whispered in a voice thick with emotion.

Travis dropped her hand and pulled her into his arms. Fiona melted against him, kissing him as fervently as he kissed her, overwhelmed by her love for him. He put an arm beneath her to lower her to the grass, then removed the pins from her hair and fanned it out around her.

"You're a beautiful woman, Fiona."

Fiona reached up to touch his handsome face. "You mustn't say such things."

Travis lifted her hand and turned it palm up to brush his warm lips over the sensitive skin. "I'll say it again. You're beautiful." He lightly bit the fleshy part of her thumb, then nibbled her wrist, pushing the sleeve of her dress higher to run his tongue up the inside of her arm.

A shiver of delight raced through Fiona's body. Travis raised himself to kiss her again, unfastening the buttons on the front of her dress and parting the material, exposing her flesh to the cool night air.

He ran his fingers over one breast, strumming the tip with his thumb until it puckered, then he bent his head to draw it in his mouth. As his tongue tantalized her, Fiona threaded her fingers in his hair and closed her eyes, oblivious to everything but her awakening passion.

She felt Travis's hand slide down over the curve of her hip to her calf, then move slowly up to the junction of her thighs. As his fingers brushed intimately over her, Fiona bit her lip to keep from moaning aloud. Her desire for Travis was frightening, yet at the same time, she wanted him to touch her, to excite her.

Travis tugged the skirt of her dress up to her waist, then untied the cord of her drawers and slid them down over her hips. Leaning down to kiss her again, he ran his hand up the inside of her thigh until his fingers found the sensitive nub of her womanhood.

With a gasp, Fiona grabbed his hand and held onto it, suddenly fearful of what he was going to do next.

"I won't hurt you, Fiona," Travis whispered huskily. He placed her hand against his groin. "Do you feel my desire for you?"

She shook her head, her heart racing.

He pressed her hand down harder, until she could feel the long, thick outline of his shaft. "Now?"

Swallowing hard, Fiona nodded. Beneath her hand his manhood throbbed with life, stimulating her and terrifying her beyond measure. She pulled her hand away, staring up at him in apprehension. "I can't," she whispered hoarsely.

"I won't make you do anything you don't want to do," he reassured her. "I would never hurt you."

When he bent his head to kiss her again, Fiona wrapped her arms around him, her need for him burning inside her. She wanted him to make love to her, yet she feared it at the same time. When he touched her intimately again, she didn't stop him or suppress her moan of pleasure. Excited by his taste, his smell, his touch, she ran her hands down his back, under his shirt, suddenly needing to feel his naked flesh beneath her fingers.

She tugged at the buttons of his shirt until Travis stopped to strip it off. He jumped to his feet and took off his pants as well, then stood above her in all his masculine splendor, his manhood jutting proudly from his lean, muscular body.

Fiona shivered in apprehension at the size of him, yet as he knelt beside her and gazed at her with eyes full of love and desire, her fear slowly melted away. Travis used a skillful touch to make her gasp with pleasure, but not until she cried his name and reached out for him did he spread her thighs and gently cover her with his body.

At the first intrusion of his flesh, Fiona gasped and stiffened. In a low, soothing voice, Travis murmured against her ear, "I will be gentle, Fiona. I promise."

She whimpered as her maidenhead broke and clenched her teeth as he slowly moved deeper within her, whispering words of passion in her ear until she was able to relax. As he began a gentle, rhythmic motion, Fiona felt a growing tension deep inside, as of a spring being tightly wound, and soon she began to move in opposition to his movements.

As her desire built, she clasped his broad back and strained against him, desperate now for relief. The world around her ceased to exist as all her feelings were centered on the point of their joining. And then, as though she had been hovering on the edge of a precipice, she felt herself plunging over it, great waves of pleasure rippling through her, throbbing then subsiding, leaving her appeased and spent.

Suddenly Travis's body went rigid and he groaned as though in agony. Fiona stiffened, thinking she had somehow hurt him. Lifting himself from her, he fell back on the grass with his eyes closed. Fiona quickly pulled up her drawers and scrambled to her knees. "Are you hurt?"

He opened one eye and peered at her, then grinned. "Hurt?" He flung an arm around her neck and pulled her on top of him, kissing her soundly on the lips. "No, sweetheart, I'm not hurt. Far from it."

Fiona pushed back to a sitting position and studied him, this man she loved. The word *love* now felt inadequate to describe the profound feelings within her. She frowned thoughtfully, imagining what her mother would have said about her behavior. *Sinful*, she would have labeled it. But her mother had been in love once, Fiona reasoned. Surely she'd had the same feelings for Da that Fiona had for Travis.

Travis propped one hand behind his head, a look of concern on his face. "Are you all right?" he asked, reaching up to stroke her cheek.

Fiona blushed and looked away. "Yes," she replied, suddenly tongue-tied. She wished she could share her feelings with him, but how could she describe something that went beyond words?

He took her fingers and brought them to his lips. "I can make you happy, Fiona. And you needn't give up your dreams. We'll be able to travel. I'll show you the world a little at a time. I want you beside me, Fiona. I want to make a home for us here, with the people who love you, and whom I've come to love. I feel safe here with you. I trust you."

A moment before Fiona had felt on top of the world. Now she felt as though the world had suddenly caved in on her. Travis trusted her, he felt safe with her, not knowing she carried a secret that would destroy his trust. She hadn't wanted to tell him that Carvey had been responsible for the deaths of his crew. She had hoped he would leave New Clare without ever having to know.

Fiona looked into his dark, hopeful eyes and her heart felt as though it were shattering. She loved Travis more than she ever thought it was possible to love a man, but she couldn't be his wife and keep such a terrible secret from him. Yet, if she told him the truth now, Travis would realize that she had been hiding it from him, destroying not only his faith in her, but also in her family. She would lose him as surely as the sun rose and set.

Fiona dropped her gaze. What should she do? What could she tell him?

22

TRAVIS REACHED OVER and turned her chin toward him. "Fiona? Are you sure you're all right?"

Fiona quickly blinked away the first trace of tears before meeting his questioning gaze. If she told Travis the truth, would he ever forgive her? Would it be better to let him think her plans to travel meant more to her than he did? She searched her heart for the right answer but her emotions were too jumbled. She needed time to think.

In the town below, the church bell began to toll the hour. Fiona counted eleven gongs and jumped to her feet, silently blessing every saint she could think of for the reprieve. "It's eleven o'clock! I was due back half an hour ago."

Travis sat up and reached for his clothing. "You haven't given me your answer."

"I have to go! Da will be worried."

"Fiona!" he called, jerking on his pants, but Fiona was off at a run.

Damn it! He was going to have his answer that night or else! He slipped on his shirt, grabbed his shoes and ran after her. But he hadn't gone more than ten yards when he came to a stop.

If Fiona had decided to accept his proposal, she would have told him so before she left. Travis felt a sudden despair. Perhaps she had already given him her answer.

Festival day dawned sunny and warm. The bells in the church tower rang gaily as Fiona and her family, accompanied by Travis and Jordan, set off for town. Even Deirdre, who had ventured out very little during her confinement, had decided to go. Only Carvey remained at home, not yet well enough to participate in the day's festivities. Come evening, however, he would man the tower until the family returned.

Fiona wore a lightweight navy cotton twill skirt with a soft cotton blouse in narrow pink and white stripes, which she had made herself expressly for the festival. Under her straw skimmer she wore her hair in a Psyche knot with a fringe of ringlets framing her face.

She had expected to receive a compliment, or at least a look of admiration, from Travis on her outfit, especially after his fervent declarations of the night before, but to her surprise he had seemed not to notice her at all. Indeed, Fiona thought as they walked along, Travis seemed most preoccupied with his brother.

Instead of being relieved that he was not badgering her for an answer to his proposal, however, Fiona felt slighted. Wasn't it better that he had forgotten the proposal for the moment? she chided herself.

But it went deeper than just feeling slighted. What had happened between them on the beach had connected her to Travis in a way she could not describe. She had given herself to him and had received his love willingly. And though she now knew there was no hope of a marriage between them, her love for Travis would never die. With the way Travis was behaving now, however, Fiona was beginning to suspect she was the only one who felt so strongly about it.

Conferring with his brother, Travis strolled unconcernedly down Wexford, handsome in his collarless white cotton shirt, brown suspenders and pants with freshly shined brown boots, his dark hair washed and neatly combed. And though the day was bright, Fiona felt a pall over her, knowing that when it came time to give Travis her answer, she had to tell him the truth about the night of the storm. Her conscience would not let her do otherwise, though she knew it would destroy his trust in her forever.

Her only hope for redeeming herself was to prove that Devlin had stolen the cargo. To do that, however, she needed an opportunity to search his storeroom. The festival was her opportunity. She had only to wait until Devlin was involved in some activity, then sneak back to the saloon and take a look.

Kilkenny Street, barricaded on either end of a two-block area to keep out horse and buggy traffic, was crowded with townsfolk out to enjoy the holiday. Bright green bunting hung over storefronts, banners stretched over the street proclaiming the occasion, and colorful booths offering everything from applehead dolls to woolen sweaters lined both sides of the street.

Jamie, riding on Finn's shoulders, immediately spotted a booth of hand-carved wooden animals and excitedly pointed to them. "Gampa, look! Look!"

"Yes, Jamie boy, I see," Finn assured him and veered off toward the booth.

Deirdre, waddling along next to Fiona, grabbed her sister's arm. "Let's stop at that booth over there, Fiona, the one with the baby clothing."

As Deirdre marveled over each of the tiny handknit creations, Fiona watched Travis, who had stopped to admire the work of a tanner. Jordan picked up a pair of leather boots, and at his brother's nod of encouragement began to bargain. The tanner, who appeared to be highly offended at the price he had been offered, shook his fist and loudly voiced his objections. Fiona smiled to herself, knowing it was all part of the game. Soon Travis joined in the haggling, but before Fiona could learn the outcome, her father summoned her.

"Jamie wants to ride a pony," Finn said. "We'll join you girls at the auction."

"Ponies, ponies!" Jamie cried, kicking his legs excitedly from astride his grandfather's shoulders.

Finn laughed. "All right, Jamie, pony rides it is."

Wandering down the long row of booths, Fiona and Deirdre slowly made their way to the park next to the church, with Travis and Jordan following a short distance behind them. They ended up at the gazebo, where tables had been set up to hold pies for the pie-baking contest. Mrs. O'Donohue stood at the top of the steps, her hands on her hips, looking flustered.

"Oh, Mr. Paine!" she called when she spotted Travis. "I'm so glad you came today." She lifted the hem of her blue gingham dress and hurried down the three wide steps. "One of our judges took sick this morning. Would you please help us out?"

Travis glanced at his brother. "Do you mind?"

"Be my guest," Jordan replied. "While you're doing that I think I'll go back to that tanner and see if I can't talk him into lowering his price again."

As Travis was taken to the table where the four other judges waited, plates in hands and napkins tucked into collars, Fiona heard the nasal voice of the telegraph operator Edwin O'Banyon call excitedly from behind her, "Good morning, Fiona."

With a snicker, Deirdre elbowed her. "He's all yours, Fiona. Give me your lunch basket and I'll take it into the church for you."

"Not on your life," Fiona whispered, holding tightly to the handle as Deirdre tried to pry it from her hands. She turned quickly to smile at Edwin, who had decked himself out for the occasion in a brown derby, tan serge sack suit, white shirt and red bow tie.

He held his derby to his chest with one hand and stroked his handlebar moustache with the other as he rocked back on his heels and beamed at her. "You're looking exceedingly fine today, Fiona."

Behind him Deirdre pulled a face, then turned and waddled off toward the front door of the church.

"Thank you, Edwin," Fiona said politely. "Wait, Dee! Edwin, please excuse me. I have to drop off my lunch basket for the auction."

Before she could make her escape, Edwin hurried after her. "May I accompany you?" he asked eagerly.

"Do I have a choice?" she said under her breath.

"I beg your pardon?" he said, falling into step beside her.

Fiona gave him a forced smile. "I said I wouldn't want to *foist* myself on you, Edwin."

"Oh, you needn't ever fear of that happening, Fiona." He cleared his throat nervously, dodging people to stay beside her. "Mother was asking about you the other day, Fiona. She thinks very highly of you, you know. In fact, she was thinking that you and I should—"

"Will you look at that now!" Fiona exclaimed as they reached the street.

"Look at what?" Edwin asked, standing on tiptoe to see above the crowd on the sidewalk.

"Bridget Riley, that's what, and not a trace of a limp to be seen! After her performance last night you'd think she'd limp a little today."

"What performance?" Edwin asked in a puzzled voice. "I thought the play was tonight."

Fiona ignored Edwin to watch Bridget's regal procession down the sidewalk toward the park. She wore her new lime-green, full-skirted silk dress, completely inappropriate for a summer festival, yet on Bridget it seemed perfectly accepta-ble. The dress had a high collar and outsized cap sleeves trimmed at the shoulder with delicate pink lace. Her corseted waist was bound with a pink sash and the hem of the dress was finished with ruching of the same green silk. On her head of golden curls sat an elaborate pink hat laden with a generous amount of green ribbon and white silk flowers. She smiled and nodded to the people around her as though she were queen of the festival.

Bridget was accompanied by several of her beaus, all vying for her attention at once. But as they passed by Devlin's sa-loon and Devlin himself appeared, her suitors melted into the crowd as if by magic. Puffing his chest out, Devlin stepped up beside Bridget, took her arm and sauntered past Fiona, heading into the park.

"Oh, there's Travis!" Fiona heard Bridget exclaim excit-edly. Disengaging her arm from Devlin's hold, Bridget lifted her skirt above her dainty low-heeled pumps and hurried to-ward the gazebo, calling shrilly, "Yoo-hoo, Travis!"

Watching Devlin stalk after Bridget, Fiona knew trouble was brewing.

"As I was saying, Fiona, Mother thought that you and I should consider—"

"Edwin, would you please take my basket to the church and give it to Dee?" Fiona shoved the wicker lunch basket at Edwin, who grabbed it in surprise.

"But, Fiona—"

Fiona pressed a quick kiss on his cheek. "Thank you so very much, Edwin," she called, dashing after Devlin.

She arrived at the gazebo in time to see Devlin march up to Bridget, take a firm hold of her arm and lead her away. Protesting loudly at his rough treatment, Bridget yanked her arm out of his grasp, slapped his face and dashed up the steps of the gazebo straight toward the startled judges.

"Travis," Bridget said breathlessly, glancing over her shoulder to see where Devlin was, "would you be my partner in the three-legged race?"

"Bridget Riley!" Mrs. O'Donohue cried indignantly. "We are in the middle of judging the pie-baking contest. Kindly leave the gazebo at once and wait until after the judges have finished to speak to Mr. Paine."

"Oh, he doesn't mind." Bridget turned her little girl pout on Travis. "Please don't say no and disappoint me, Travis. The races will be starting in half an hour."

Red with embarrassment, Travis said quietly, "All right, Miss Riley. I'll meet you there as soon as I've finished."

Chewing her thumbnail, Fiona glanced worriedly at Devlin. Her cousin stood on one side of the gazebo glowering at Bridget, his large, heavy fists clenching and unclenching at his sides. As Bridget flounced down the three steps and sailed past him she lifted her nose in the air and sniffed in disdain. Devlin glared malevolently at her retreating back, then slowly turned his head to fix his small eyes on Travis.

"Mother Mary, what has Bridget started now?" Fiona muttered with a troubled frown. She saw Jordan strolling across the grass toward the gazebo and hurried to meet him.

"Mr. Paine, do you see that large, mean-looking man in the red suspenders and black derby?"

"Is that the fellow I saw Miss Riley slap a moment ago?"

"The same. Unfortunately, Devlin Brody is not one to take a slap with good grace. He's the jealous type and I'm worried that he'll take his anger out on your brother. Bridget has asked Travis to be her partner in the three-legged race, you see."

Jordan gave her a tolerant smile. "I'm sure Travis can hold his own."

Fiona saw her cousin start off toward the back of the park in the direction Bridget had gone. "Devlin's not a fair fighter, Mr. Paine. It would be best if you warned your brother."

"All right, Miss Cleary. But why not warn Travis yourself? I believe they're about to announce the winner of the pie-baking contest and then he'll be free."

"I would, but I have to find Dee," Fiona told him. "She'll be looking for me." With a quick backward glance at Travis, she hurried away, not to find her sister, but to follow Devlin.

Rubbing his distended stomach, Travis walked slowly down the steps of the gazebo and joined his brother. "I'm stuffed to the gills. What are you grinning about?"

"You and Bridget Riley running a three-legged race together, *that's* what I'm grinning about."

Travis grimaced as they strolled across the lawn. "How was I supposed to refuse her in front of all those people?"

"Do you know a man by the name of Devlin Brody?"

Travis gave Jordan a puzzled look. "He's Fiona's cousin. Why?"

"Fiona just gave me a message for you. She said Devlin is the jealous type and warned you to be careful."

Travis gave his brother a sly grin. "Does it sound to you like Fiona is trying to keep me away from Bridget?" He clapped his brother on the back. "I told you my plan would work."

"I don't know, Travis," Jordan said. "I sensed more than jealousy behind Fiona's warning; she seemed genuinely concerned about you. I saw this Devlin fellow. If I were you I think I'd take Fiona's advice and steer clear of him."

Travis scoffed at Jordan. "I can handle Devlin Brody. It's

Bridget who's going to be the problem. I trust you'll do your part?''

''I'll do it,'' Jordan said with reluctance, ''but I won't like it.''

Fiona stood in the cheering crowd along the sidelines and watched Travis and Bridget run the three-legged race to the finish line. Twice Bridget nearly fell, but Travis managed to keep her going, one arm around her shoulders to hold her. They came in fifth, but neither seemed to mind. In fact, Fiona thought irritably, Travis looked as though he were thoroughly enjoying himself.

''The devil take him,'' Fiona muttered. Only the day before he had made love to her—and proposed marriage as well! Today he was flirting with Bridget Riley. To think she had warned him to be careful of Devlin.

Fiona glanced at the faces around her, searching for signs of Devlin. She had successfully followed her cousin as far as the area set off for the races but then she had lost him in the crowd. Somehow, she had to get back to his saloon and do some investigating, but she couldn't do it unless she knew he was occupied.

On the opposite side of the field she saw Edwin bobbing up and down, searching through the crowd, and guessed he was looking for her. She edged farther back from the sideline and turned her attention back to Travis just in time to see Bridget grab his hand and lead him aside.

''The horseshoe-pitching contest is next, Travis,'' she heard Bridget say. ''You have to enter so you can win a prize for me.''

''Fiona, here you are!'' Deirdre called, weaving through the people around her.

Fiona turned with a jerk and put her finger to her lips. ''Shhh!''

''What are you doing?'' Deirdre whispered.

''Hiding from Edwin,'' Fiona whispered back.

Deirdre turned her by the shoulders. ''You didn't hide well enough. There he is and he's coming this way.''

"Stars and garters, Dee! He's going to ask me to be in the next race with him."

"Fiona," Edwin called, waving his hand in the air as he hurried toward her.

"Try to get out of this one," Deirdre said with a snicker. "And don't you dare send him on another errand to find me. My feet hurt. I'm going to sit down in a shady spot and rest."

Fiona considered using Bridget's ploy to feign a limp, but at the last moment decided she couldn't stoop to Bridget's level even to save herself from Edwin.

"Fiona, will you run the next three-legged race with me?" Edwin asked breathlessly, coming to a stop behind her.

Casting her eyes heavenward Fiona whispered, "Forgive me," and quickly crossed herself. Then she turned and exclaimed, "Oh, here you are, Edwin! I've been looking all over for you. The horseshoe-pitching contest is about to begin. I was hoping you'd enter so you could win a prize for me."

Edwin looked so exultant that Fiona feared she had damned her soul for all eternity. Removing his derby, Edwin pressed it against his chest and said in a reverent voice, "I would be honored."

With a guilty smile, Fiona took Edwin's arm and allowed him to lead her across the park.

When they arrived at the area staked out for the horseshoe-pitching contest, the first game was already under way. Fiona immediately spotted Travis leaning against a tree nearby, listening to Bridget, who was chattering animatedly. Travis looked up and met Fiona's gaze, but immediately turned his attention back to Bridget without so much as a flicker of recognition.

How dare he pretend not to know her! With a furious scowl, Fiona turned her back on him.

As soon as the first game ended, Mr. Tucker, who was running the contest, announced the start of the next game. Fiona glanced around and saw Travis casually saunter toward the playing field.

"Edwin would like to play," she called, and gave her hapless hero a push in Mr. Tucker's direction.

"Good luck, lad," Mr. Tucker told Edwin with a smile, handing him two iron shoes.

As Travis picked up his horseshoes and walked toward the pitching box where Edwin waited, Bridget sidled up beside Fiona to watch the game.

"Hello, Fiona."

"Bridget," Fiona returned coolly. "How is your ankle?"

"Much better after a night's rest." Bridget eyed Edwin with amusement. "I see you have a champion."

Fiona clenched her jaw and refused to comment.

"Get ready, boys," Mr. Tucker called. He flipped a coin and Travis said to Edwin, "Call it."

"Heads," Edwin squeaked as the coin was caught.

"Heads it is," Mr. Tucker announced. "Edwin is up first."

Edwin removed his suit jacket and handed it to Fiona. Moving up to the iron stake, he knelt to eyeball his target at the opposite end of the court, then rose to wipe his perspiring face with his handkerchief. He took aim, tossed the first shoe and missed the stake by a foot. The second one landed only a few inches closer.

As the midmorning sun beat down unmercifully on the two men, Fiona couldn't help but feel sorry for Edwin, who was clearly outmatched. Hearing Bridget's titters, Fiona was sorely tempted to teach her what a real limp felt like. The more Bridget cheered Travis on, the more Fiona valiantly cheered Edwin on, until the last shoe was pitched and Travis was declared the winner.

"Oh, Travis, I knew you'd win!" Bridget cried triumphantly, clapping her hands.

As Travis and Bridget strolled away arm in arm, Edwin walked toward Fiona, hanging his head in shame. "I'm sorry, Fiona."

Fiona helped Edwin into his jacket and patted his shoulder. "You did fine, Edwin. You tried very hard."

"But I wanted to win a prize for you."

From the corner of her eye, Fiona suddenly caught sight of Devlin sauntering toward the church, no doubt to get a place near the auctioneer so he could bid on Bridget's lunch basket.

Fiona checked the watch around her neck. Now would be the perfect time to search his storeroom. But first she would have to dispose of Edwin.

"What I'd really like is a glass of cool lemonade, Edwin."

Edwin brightened. "I'd be honored to get it for you. Why don't you find a cool spot nearby to wait? I wouldn't want you to get overheated."

"Thank you, Edwin. I'll wait over by the church."

As Edwin hurried off, Fiona glanced at her watch again. She had fifteen minutes before the auction began. How much time she had after that depended on whether Devlin was outbid for Bridget's lunch basket. If he lost, he would no doubt return to his saloon. Slipping quickly through the crowd, Fiona prayed that Bridget's basket would be one of the last to be auctioned.

❖ 23 ❖

WHEN FIONA ARRIVED at Devlin's saloon she found it jammed with men, talking, laughing and hoisting their glasses in celebration of the grand opening. Deciding it would be too risky to march straight through the saloon and into the storeroom as bold as brass, she cast about for another way to get in. For a moment she considered asking Donald Dugan, the barkeeper, to help her, but Donald had been a longtime friend of Devlin's and would probably stop her.

She glanced around and saw Kevin Malone, the man in charge of Travis's repair crew, striding jauntily down the sidewalk toward her.

"Good morning, Miss Cleary," he called with a big smile. His manner was in sharp contrast to the forlorn soul she had found sitting despondently in the general store only a few weeks ago. She hoped he would do her a favor in return for getting him the job with Travis.

"Kevin Malone, you're just the man I'm looking for."

As Kevin raised his eyebrows, Fiona linked her arm through his and walked with him to the corner, quickly describing the favor she needed. He nodded in agreement and turned back toward the saloon while Fiona slipped down the alley and waited. She glanced at her watch and nervously chewed her lip. Only ten minutes until the auction began. She had little time to waste.

In a few moments Fiona heard the sound of metal scraping against wood. Gently, she tried the door and found it unlocked. She peered inside, saw that the storeroom was deserted, and slipped through the door, quietly closing it behind her.

Devlin had hung a curtain between the saloon and the storeroom and it was from that vantage point that Fiona peered into the saloon beyond. Finding the barkeeper engrossed in a lively conversation with Kevin Malone, she began to search the boxes on deep shelves that lined two walls.

When she found no sign of the silk there, Fiona looked around and spotted a tall cabinet with a lock on it. Finding the lock securely fastened, she hurried to Devlin's battered oak desk, moved the chair aside and eased out a drawer, looking for a key. When that proved futile, she looked around again, chewing her thumbnail. A glance at her watch told her the auction had begun. Where was the key?

Devlin was not a brilliant man, she reasoned. He would not go to elaborate lengths to hide it. As she studied the tall cabinet an idea came to her. She set the chair in front of it, climbed up and felt along the top. Her fingers closed over a small metal object.

Her heart racing excitedly, Fiona stepped down, pushed the chair aside and inserted the key in the lock. To her relief, it turned smoothly and silently. But just as she was opening one of the narrow doors, she heard the barkeeper's voice boom out, "Rum it is. I'll need to get more from the back."

With a pounding heart Fiona crammed herself in the narrow cabinet, pulled the door shut and held her breath. Only a moment later she heard the sound of something heavy being moved, then retreating footsteps. From far off she heard Donald Dugan call, "All right, boys, belly up to the bar."

Fiona let out her breath and slowly opened the door. After peering out to be sure it was safe, she unfolded her legs and stepped out. When she saw what she had been sitting on, her eyes opened in surprise.

"St. Peter and Paul, it's the silk!" she whispered.

On one side of the cabinet, neatly stacked, were bolts of the costly material. The other side of the cabinet was piled clear to the top. What Devlin had done with the rest she had no clue, but now she had all the evidence she needed to convince herself Devlin was the culprit. She locked the cabinet, put the key in her pocket and slipped out the back door.

Before heading back to the church, Fiona ran to the saloon's front window and signaled to Kevin to lock the back door. As she hurried away, she glanced down at the watch around her neck. Half an hour had passed since she left the park. The auction was well under way.

Katie O'Banyon, Mary Sheridan and Tullia Brody, the three chairwomen of the charity auction, stood behind a long cloth-covered table at the bottom of the church steps and smiled at the crowd who had come to cheer on the eager bachelors. Wicker baskets of all sizes and colors decorated with ribbons and freshly cut flowers lined the steps behind them, while the baskets' owners gathered in small groups on each side of the steps, whispering, giggling and making eyes at the anxious men waiting to make their bids.

Travis leaned against a lamppost at the rear of the group and searched the crowd for Fiona, growing more frustrated by the second. He couldn't very well succeed in his attempt to make her jealous if she wasn't there.

Jordan came striding up to him, cradling a pair of shiny leather boots and wearing a victorious smile. "I knew the tanner would come down to my price eventually."

Travis looked around as Tullia rapped on the table and opened the bidding on another basket. "Have you seen Fiona?" he asked his brother.

"Not since the pie contest."

"Gentlemen, this basket of delicious-looking food belongs to none other than our Fiona Cleary," Tullia called. "You all know what a fine cook Fiona is. Who will start the bidding?"

"One dollar," came a squeaky voice from the crowd.

"Who is that little fellow?" Jordan asked.

"Edwin O'Banyon, the telegraph operator."

At someone else's bid of a dollar twenty-five, Edwin piped up, "One fifty!"

"Two dollars," Travis called.

Jordan nudged his brother. "I don't think Edwin liked that."

"Two twenty-five," Edwin cried, glaring at Travis.

Travis straightened as he caught sight of Fiona making her way through the throng to the church steps. She looked flushed and out of breath. Travis's eyes narrowed speculatively. Where had she been?

"Three dollars!" Edwin called out. He beamed at Fiona, but she didn't return his smile.

"Three twenty-five," Travis said calmly. Fiona's head swiveled toward him and he thought she looked relieved. He almost felt guilty about what he intended to do, but he decided that in the long run it was for the best.

Edwin called louder, "Four dollars!"

At a bid that high there were gasps of surprise from the crowd. Katie O'Banyon nodded approvingly at her son, while Fiona gave Travis a pleading look.

"Are you going to make Edwin squirm a bit longer?" Jordan asked him.

"I think he's squirmed long enough."

Tullia called out, "All right, boys, we have a bid of four dollars." Her gaze sought out Travis. "Four dollars for the opportunity to share this fine lunch with Fiona. Four dollars going once . . ."

Fiona's gaze remained on Travis.

"Going twice . . ."

"I feel like a heel," Travis whispered to his brother.

"Courage, man," Jordan whispered back.

Travis gave Fiona a shrug. An expression of disbelief crossed her face before she pressed her lips together and looked away.

"*Sold* to Edwin O'Banyon for four dollars." Giving Fiona a sympathetic smile, Tullia handed Edwin the basket. As she reached for another, Bridget shoved her own flower-and-ribbon-bedecked basket forward. Travis had to smile at the effort Tullia was making to refrain from scolding Bridget in front of the crowd.

"Next we have Bridget Riley's basket," Tullia announced tersely. "Who would like to start—"

Before she could finish her sentence, Devlin Brody boomed out, "Five dollars."

At the gasps and whispered comments from the people gathered in front of the church, Devlin hooked his thumbs in his red suspenders and glared at the faces around him, silently daring anyone to outbid him. Bridget narrowed her eyes at Devlin, then gave Travis an expectant smile.

"Don't disappoint her," Jordan whispered.

"Five fifty," Travis called.

"Six dollars," Devlin immediately countered.

"Six fifty."

Heads swiveled toward Travis, looks of amazement on their faces. Bridget beamed in delight and whispered to the girls around her. Travis noticed only one face, Fiona's. She was staring at him as if he had suddenly sprouted feathers.

Jordan nudged him. "Travis, perhaps we'd better rethink our plan."

"Not on your life. Fiona is as jealous as I've ever seen her."

"So is Devlin Brody."

Travis turned his head and met Devlin's furious glare.

"Seven dollars," Devlin sneered.

"Seven fifty," Travis countered.

Jordan glanced at Travis nervously. "Are you sure you want to continue this? I think you've made your point with Fiona."

"That bastard is not going to push me around," Travis replied, returning Devlin's stare.

"Eight dollars!" Devlin shouted, his face an angry red.

Tullia glanced from one man to the other, then quickly said, "Eight dollars going once, going twice . . ."

"Nine dollars," Travis said firmly.

Jordan ran a finger under his collar. "For God's sake, Travis, enough is enough."

"It's worth *ten* dollars to bring that buffoon down a peg," Travis replied.

"We have a bid of nine dollars," Tullia called, exchanging

nervous looks with her co-chairwomen. "Going once, going twice . . ."

Every face in the crowd was turned toward Devlin, waiting for his next bid. He glared at Travis for a long moment, then wheeled about and stalked off.

"*Sold* to Travis Paine for nine dollars," Tullia announced, mopping her upper lip with her handkerchief.

Travis shifted his gaze to where Fiona stood, only to find she had gone. His plan was working perfectly.

"This is turning out to be an expensive day for you, little brother," Jordan remarked dryly.

Travis smiled. "Someday I'll have to tell Fiona just how much she cost me. Right now you'd better prepare yourself to turn on the charm."

"Yoo-hoo, Travis!"

Jordan gave Travis a scowl. "I forgave you for letting the Clearys trick me, but I may never forgive you for this."

"Thanks, brother. I'll be forever in your debt." With a devilish grin, Travis ducked into the crowd, leaving Jordan to claim the basket.

Travis edged his way through the remaining bachelors and caught Tullia's eye. He motioned for her to meet him at one end of the table.

"Mrs. Brody, I have a favor to ask," he said in a low voice.

"If it's a loan you're needing to pay for Bridget's basket you've come to the wrong person," she whispered angrily. "You know Fiona was expecting you to win *her* basket."

"Can you get Edwin away from Fiona for a little while?"

Tullia pulled back to stare at Travis for a moment, then a grin spread across her gamin face and her eyes twinkled merrily. "I see your game now. All right, I'll do as you ask, but no one's to be the wiser about my part in it."

"You have my word on it."

Tullia pointed in the direction of the bandstand at the far rear corner of the park. "She and Edwin headed off that way. Give me ten minutes, then go after her."

"Thanks," he whispered, and with a wink, strode off.

* * *

Fiona sighed forlornly as she unpacked her basket and set the food on a small blanket. What a fool she had been to think Travis loved her, or even cared about her. She felt shattered and used, betrayed even by her own instincts. He had duped her and now he was on to another conquest. That he had chosen Bridget to be next was more salt in the wound.

She glanced at her watch, noting that ten minutes had passed since Edwin had been called away. She had hoped to get her luncheon with him over with as quickly as possible, but now that did not seem likely. From where she sat in front of the bandstand she could see some of the other couples laughing and flirting as they shared their food. She did not, however, see Bridget and Travis, and for that she was very thankful.

Travis's about-face had wounded her to the core. For one who claimed to love her he certainly was fickle. She smoldered inside, wondering if he were using the same lines on Bridget that he had used on her the night before. To think she had worried that she would destroy Travis's trust in her when he was the one who had destroyed *her* trust in *him*.

As the sun went behind a bank of clouds, a frown creased Fiona's forehead. The far western sky was a dark blue-gray, a sure portent of rain. Her gaze dropped lower and settled on a tall figure striding toward her. She peered harder at the figure. Surely that wasn't Edwin. Edwin shuffled. Suddenly, Fiona sat up straighter, her eyes coming into sharp focus. It was Travis!

With a racing heart, Fiona began to gather her food and shove it in the basket. As hurt and angry as she was, the last thing she wanted was to see Travis. She looked up at the figure growing closer and knew she would never finish packing the basket in time to escape him. Abandoning her food, Fiona jumped up and glanced around for a place to hide. Seeing that the bandstand was the only shelter nearby, she fled behind the wooden structure and pressed herself against the rear wall, her heart thumping loudly as she listened and waited.

When Travis did not appear after several long minutes, Fiona crept along one side of the shelter to the front and peered around it. Seeing no sign of Travis, she planted her hands at her waist and muttered, "Where the devil did he go?"

"Looking for someone?"

With a gasp, Fiona spun around and found herself face to face with Travis. "Certainly not for the likes of you!" she cried angrily.

Undeterred by her outburst, Travis walked over to the blanket and gathered everything up inside it.

"What do you think you're doing?" Fiona demanded.

"You'll see."

Reluctantly, Fiona followed Travis to the back of the bandstand, where he spread the blanket on the ground, rearranged the food and sat down. Patting the blanket beside him he said, "Care to join me?"

"*Edwin* won my basket, not *you*," Fiona said, crossing her arms in front of her. "*You* are supposed to be having lunch with Bridget."

Travis opened the basket, peered inside and pulled out a chicken leg. "At this moment Bridget is being heavily charmed by my brother."

Fiona could not understand what he was up to. "Edwin will be back any moment now and he won't take kindly to you eating his lunch."

Travis calmly took a bite of chicken. "Edwin will come halfway back, see that you are no longer here, then return to the church where he will be told by Tullia that you had a pressing engagement."

"That would be a lie!"

Travis laid the chicken aside, took her hand and tugged her down beside him. "That would be the truth," he said, pulling her into his arms. "You do having a pressing engagement— with me."

Fiona struggled to free herself. "Don't give me any of your malarkey, Travis Paine. I won't fall for it again."

"Did you really think I would let Edwin claim you?" he asked, gazing intensely into her eyes.

Fiona narrowed her gaze. "And what did you want me to

think when you let Edwin win my basket so you could bid on Bridget's?''

"I wanted you to be insanely jealous."

"Jealous over Bridget? Ha!"

Travis smiled. "Admit it, Fiona. You were jealous."

"Never."

He laughed and pulled her against him. "You don't need to admit it. I know it's true. And I love you anyway."

As his mouth came down on hers, Fiona closed her eyes, her heart singing with joy. Travis did love her! Her instincts hadn't been wrong.

He kissed her passionately, intensely, his arms like iron bands around her back molding her to his torso. She broke the kiss to draw in some air, then leaned her head against his. "Poor Edwin!" she chided. "That was an underhanded thing to do to him, not to mention what you did to me."

"So was running off without giving me an answer to my proposal." He kissed her forehead, the tip of her nose, her lips. "Will you give me an answer now?" he said huskily, nuzzling her neck.

Fiona's heart slowed its beating to a heavy thud. She looked down and said with a sigh, "I can't marry you, Travis."

Feeling him tense, she turned away. "I'm sorry," she whispered.

His hands dropped to his sides and his voice, when he spoke was flat, emotionless. "I thought you loved me."

Tears filled her eyes. "I do."

"But not enough to marry me."

Fiona wiped the tears from her face and lifted her gaze to his. It was time to tell him the truth. "The beacon was out on the night of your shipwreck, Travis. You were right."

His face registered profound shock, and then it turned to anger. "You swore to me that it was on all night," he said sharply.

Fiona wanted to tell him she had learned of it herself only two days before, but she knew it would put her father's position in jeopardy and she could not do that. She bent her head. "I was frightened. Carvey is still new to the job and I didn't want it to get out that he had made a mistake.''

"So you let me take the blame for the deaths of my crew."

Fiona raised her head and gazed at him through a watery blur. His face was stiff with anger, his eyes accusing. Just as she had feared, she had destroyed his trust.

Travis got to his feet and walked away.

❖ 24 ❖

REELING FROM THE shock of Fiona's confession, Travis strode blindly through the park toward Kilkenny Street, his only aim to get the hell out of New Clare. As he passed the deserted gazebo, a figure stepped out in front of him, blocking his path. Travis looked straight into the steely gaze of Devlin Brody.

"Going somewhere, friend?"

Travis clenched his jaw. "I've got no quarrel with you. Step out of my way."

Devlin grinned and slowly shook his head. "But you see, I *do* have a quarrel with you."

Before Travis had time to react, Devlin's fist shot out and met his jaw with a hard crack. "*That* is for stealing my girl."

Travis shook his head to clear his vision and barely had time to dodge the next blow. "I didn't steal your girl!"

Devlin swung again only to have Travis sidestep him. "No one outbids Devlin Brody," he sneered. His other fist came up to connect with Travis's midsection. "No one!"

Travis grunted as the air was forced out of his lungs. "You misunderstood my intentions," he gasped. "I was trying to make Fiona jealous, not steal Bridget from you."

Devlin's upper lip curled back. "No, *you* misunderstood, friend. I don't care what your intentions were. Don't ever bid against me again."

Travis noticed an empty crate on the ground behind Devlin, just in front of the steps to the gazebo. He lashed out with his right fist, knowing Devlin would take a step back to dodge it. The unlucky man fell backward over the crate and struck his head on the bottom step of the gazebo. Stunned by the blow, Devlin raised his head, looked at Travis through dazed eyes, then lowered his head with a groan.

With a satisfied smile, Travis stood above him. "Don't call me *friend* unless you mean it."

In the street in front of the park, dancers performed the Irish reel to the music of bagpipes while the impending storm filled the sky overhead with thick, dark clouds. Fiona, helping the women set food on the long tables for the pig roast, paused to watch the dancers.

She had never felt as heartbroken as she did at that moment. She hadn't seen Travis since lunchtime and wondered whether he would even come back for the play. She didn't regret telling him the truth about the shipwreck; she regretted the pain he had suffered thinking he had caused it. Even more, she regretted the loss of his trust.

By the time the feast was underway a light mist was falling, but it mattered little to the large, joyful assembly gathered under the canvas tent. Fiona kept a watch on the sky as she sat with her family at one of the long tables. "What do you think, Da?"

"With dusk falling it's hard to tell." He sniffed the air. "We're in for a storm, but how bad I can't say for sure."

Tullia shook her fork at him. "It never storms on festival day."

"There's always a first time," Finn countered worriedly.

Half an hour later the skies opened up and proved him correct. Those still under the canvas fled to the church basement to escape the torrents of rain and jagged bolts of lightning and to pass the time until the play began.

In the two rooms behind the stage, the cast of *Rip Van Winkle* assembled to begin dressing for the play. Fiona checked on the progress of the ladies, then knocked on the door of the men's dressing room.

"Has Mr. Paine arrived yet?" she asked Mr. Tucker, who had opened the door.

"Not yet, Fiona, but we've still got a good half an hour."

Fiona chewed her thumbnail as she paced nervously between the rooms. What if Travis failed to show up? Who would play the part of Rip Van Winkle? She finally went out to the large hall to see if there was any sign of Travis.

Wooden chairs were lined up in neat rows across the front of the hall. At the back the townsfolk gathered in groups, talking and laughing together. Fiona spotted Jordan standing with her father, Jamie and Deirdre, and hurried toward him.

"Might I speak to you for a moment?" she said quietly.

Jordan gave a nod and followed her out of the hall.

Fiona clasped her hands together at her waist. "Have you seen Travis?"

"Not since the auction. Is there a problem?"

"He should be in the back getting into his costume." Fiona glanced around nervously. "I'm afraid he's not coming."

Jordan gave her a tolerant smile. "He'll be here."

Fiona gazed up at him in consternation, twisting her fingers. "We had words earlier, you see, and he's very angry right now. That's why I fear he won't come."

Compassion flickered in Jordan's eyes. "Would you like me to find him for you?"

"Please."

With a sense of relief Fiona watched Jordan stride toward the door. She turned when Mary Sheridan hailed her.

"You'd better come quickly, Fiona. Bridget is in a state and we can't get her to settle down long enough to put her costume on."

Fiona followed Mary to the dressing room where Bridget was, indeed, in a state. Marching back and forth muttering angrily to herself, her full green skirts flouncing up and down, she looked furious enough to take a bite out of the next person to come near her. Her gaze fell on Fiona.

"Your cousin is the cruelest man alive!" she cried. "If I had a gun I'd shoot him!"

"Is this Devlin we're speaking of?" Fiona asked calmly.

"Who else would order me never to see Travis again? *Or-*

der me, mind you, as though I belonged to him! Who else would threaten to rough Travis up if I ever spoke to him again?'' She stamped her tiny foot in frustration. ''I hate Devlin Brody! Do you hear me? I *hate* him!'' And with that she collapsed into a heap of lime silk on the floor, sobbing pitifully.

''Bridget, you have to collect yourself,'' Fiona said in a stern voice, kneeling beside her. ''It's time to dress for the play.''

''I can't go on tonight!'' Bridget cried, raising her wet, swollen face to gaze despairingly at Fiona. ''How can I appear on stage like this?''

Fiona studied the girl's red-rimmed, watery eyes and puffy features. Bridget was right. She was not an attractive weeper. But the show had to go on. All Bridget needed was a little incentive.

''Well,'' Fiona said with a shrug, ''I suppose I'll have to play Dame Van Winkle myself. We certainly can't have Travis playing his part without a wife.''

Bridget's waterlogged eyes widened. ''Travis!'' she whispered. Picking herself up, she hurried to a clothes rack and began to hunt through the dresses for her costume. ''I can't abandon Travis! He needs me. Devlin Brody can go jump in the lake.''

''Now we just have to hope Travis hasn't abandoned *us*,'' Fiona muttered under her breath.

His travel bag in hand, Travis walked into the kitchen just as Jordan stepped in the front door of the lighthouse and quickly shut the door against the rain.

''Here you are!'' Jordan said. He walked to the sink, took a towel from the towel bar and dried his face with it. ''Fiona sent me to find you. She had some silly notion that you weren't going to show up for the—Good God, what happened to your face?''

Travis gingerly pressed his fingers against his bruised jaw. ''It came into contact with Devlin's fist.''

''I trust you evened the score.'' Catching sight of the travel bag, Jordan's eyebrows lifted in surprise. "Going somewhere?"

"That's my plan," Travis replied curtly.

"I thought your plan was to make Fiona jealous so she'd change her mind and marry you."

"It didn't work."

Jordan scoffed as he hung up the towel. "I know for a fact that she's jealous, so what didn't work?"

Travis glowered at him. The way his emotions were running, he didn't feel like explaining anything to anybody. "We're not getting married. That's all you need to know."

Travis started to pass him, but Jordan caught his arm. "So you're going to walk out on the play?"

"Jordan, at this moment I don't give a damn about the play."

"What about Fiona? Are you going to walk out on her, too?"

"That's right."

"I thought you loved her."

In a flat, emotionless voice Travis said, "I don't know how I feel about her. I have no feelings at this moment. I'm empty, hollow."

"Care to tell me why?"

"She lied to me, that's why. Fiona let *me* take the blame for the deaths of my crew knowing the beacon was out that night."

Jordan looked stunned. "When did she tell you this? Today?"

Travis's gaze shifted to the window, which was now blurred with rain. He pictured the blanket behind the bandstand and Fiona sitting with her back turned away from him. "After the auction." He shook his head slowly, still unable to believe she had lied to him about the light.

Jordan stepped to one side. "I won't stand in your way, Travis. She hurt you and you've every right to be angry. If you think it's best to leave, then by all means leave."

"Thanks," Travis said dryly, moving past him.

Jordan waited until Travis reached the door, then he called, "It's what Jefferson would do, in any case."

Travis froze in his tracks. "What *Jefferson* would do?" he repeated through gritted teeth.

Jordan followed him into the front hall. "You're a chip off the old block, Travis. Jefferson would be proud of you."

Travis dropped his bag and wheeled around, his teeth bared. "Damn you, Jordan, you don't know what the hell you're talking about."

Jordan folded his arms across his chest and leaned against the door frame. "What I know is that Fiona loves you enough to realize she can't marry you and carry such a terrible secret. So she risked losing you to confide it and what did you do? Turned your back on her just like Jefferson has been doing to you all these years. Like I said, a regular chip off the old block."

"She lied to me, damn it!" Travis countered. "From the beginning she swore that the light had not gone out that night. Then suddenly she says that Carvey made a mistake and she was too frightened to tell me. For weeks she let me believe my error had caused the wreck. Do you know how much I suffered thinking I was responsible?"

"Look, Travis," Jordan said angrily, "there's no doubt that what happened was a tragedy and that you suffered because of it, but what's done is done. Stop wallowing in self-pity. Fiona didn't cause the shipwreck, she only tried to protect her family from the consequences of it. But because of her integrity she had to tell you about the light knowing she would probably lose you. And you proved her right. She *is* losing you."

Jordan paused for a moment, then said in a kinder voice, "Why don't you consider how hard it must have been for her to keep such a terrible secret from you and how much courage it took for her to finally tell you? You profess to love her, Travis, but as soon as she angers you, you turn your back on her. I don't claim to be an expert on love, but that's certainly not my definition of it."

As thunder rumbled outside the lighthouse, Travis sat down on a kitchen chair and rested his head in his hands. He *was* behaving like his father. Because Fiona had angered him he had withdrawn his love. It was a childish and shallow thing to do. After all the misery he had suffered each time Jefferson had turned his back, Travis couldn't believe he had inflicted that very pain on the woman he loved.

And by God, he *did* love Fiona. There was no doubt in his mind that she loved him, as well. At the risk of losing him, as well as of damaging her family's good name, she had confessed the truth because her integrity would not let her keep such a secret from the man she loved. Travis pushed back the chair and stood up.

"Where are you going?" Jordan asked, following him out the door.

"To find Fiona. And this time she's going to say yes."

Behind the closed curtains of the stage, Fiona made a last-minute survey of the scenery and props, then checked the dressing room to see if Travis had shown up. Told that he still had not arrived, she went back into the hall to look for Jordan. Instead she found Devlin.

He was standing near one of the double doors at the rear of the hall, thick legs braced apart and arms folded across his chest. He was greeted politely as people passed him, but no one stopped to chat, nor did he encourage their conversation. Only his eyes moved as he looked from one side of the room to the other.

Suddenly his gaze met Fiona's and his upper lip curled into a sneer. Fiona clenched her fists, wishing she could confront him about the stolen cargo, but decided now was not the time to do it. She could, however, put a halt to his intimidating threats.

"Come to watch the play," she asked blandly, "or just to bully my actors?"

Devlin turned his head to look at her, his eyes hard and cruel. "I came to watch the play, if it's any of your business."

Fiona's gaze narrowed. "It *is* my business. I'm the director and I don't appreciate your threats to Bridget about Travis Paine. Only a cowardly man threatens a lady."

Devlin gave Fiona a snort of contempt. "I fear nothing and no one, *little* Fiona, not you, and especially not your Mr. Paine. And you can tell him for me that if I ever meet him again I'll break him in two.'' With those words he turned his back on her and walked away.

.

With only five minutes to go before the play was to begin, Travis arrived backstage dripping wet from the storm.

Tullia gasped when she saw him. "Saints be praised! Dry yourself, boy, and get your costume on! Mr. Tucker will help you if you need it."

"Where's Fiona?" Travis asked.

"Don't worry about Fiona now," Tullia scolded. "The curtain is about to go up. Hurry!"

"I have to talk to her, Mrs. Brody."

"There'll be time to talk between scenes," Tullia said firmly, pushing him toward the dressing room.

In the men's narrow, cramped quarters, Travis quickly slipped into his costume, glanced in an old, cracked mirror to run his fingers through his hair, then hurried into the wings. He spotted Fiona on the opposite side conferring with Tullia and his heart flip-flopped. He wondered how he had ever thought he could leave her.

"Yoo-hoo, Travis!" he suddenly heard from behind. "Here I am, much recovered now and ready to play your wife, you'll be relieved to know."

Travis gave Bridget a cursory glance and dismissed her. He had no time for her travails.

Bridget grabbed his arm and pulled him around to study his face. "Oh, you poor thing! You do have a bad case of hives."

Travis flinched as she reached up to stroke his bruised jaw. "Hives?" he asked, puzzled.

"Yes, silly! From the strawberry pie. Jordan told me all about it while we ate lunch."

Travis's eyes widened in understanding. "Oh, *those* hives."

"Do you have other hives?" she asked in bewilderment.

At that moment Fiona called the cast to take their places on the stage. Travis cursed his luck. He would have to catch her between scenes.

His opportunity didn't come until only two acts remained.

As Fiona slipped past him on her way to the back, Travis caught her wrist and pulled her aside. "I need to talk to you."

She looked around, as though afraid someone would hear. "I can't speak to you now."

"It's important, Fiona."

Apprehension flickered in her eyes. "It will have to wait until after the play," she told him, pulling her hand away.

Clenching his jaw in frustration, Travis watched her hurry off.

Fiona stood at the back of the hall observing Travis as he performed. Something about the intense way he had looked at her when he spoke to her in the wings frightened her. She could only imagine the worst, that he had decided to inform the authorities about Carvey's blunder.

Fiona knew her father would be held responsible. Carvey was, after all, his employee. What would become of them then?

On the verge of tears, Fiona left the church for some fresh air. Standing on the steps, sheltered from the rain by the eaves, she gazed out into the misty darkness and wiped tears from her cheeks. She wished she had never met Travis Paine nor learned the agony of love.

Out of habit she turned to look at the lighthouse, but found it obscured by the fog. Even the beam seemed diffused by the low, gray clouds, and almost appeared to be flickering, as though the fuel were running low or a gust of wind had blown across it. A glance at her watch told her it wasn't yet time for Carvey to replenish the kerosene. She couldn't imagine what would cause it to behave so.

Thinking her eyes were playing tricks on her, Fiona began walking toward the lighthouse. But just as she started up Wexford, the beam disappeared completely.

"Mother Mary!" she whispered, and began to run the half mile to the lighthouse through the fog. Out of breath and sodden from the rain, Fiona stumbled blindly up the stone path and burst inside the lighthouse calling, "Carvey? Where are you?"

There was no response.

Fiona took a lamp from the kitchen and held it in front of her as she dashed up the tower steps. "Carvey?" she called as she neared the top. She prayed she would not find him drunk.

Without stopping to glance around, Fiona rushed immediately to the huge light in the center and set down her lamp. Her first concern was to get the beacon lit.

Suddenly a heavy hand clamped over her mouth and Fiona was dragged backward across the floor. She clawed frantically to get free until her hands were gripped in a bone-crushing hold. She froze as a menacing voice whispered in her ear, "You've come at the wrong time, *little* Fiona."

❖ *25* ❖

At THE SOUND of her cousin's voice Fiona began to struggle anew. Her fury erupted in a stream of angry words which were muffled by his hand. Devlin released her, but immediately pulled both of her arms behind her back and began to bind them with a rope.

"What are you doing?" Fiona cried, wincing as the hemp cut into her wrists. "Why is the light out? Where's Carvey?"

"You always were too nosy for your own good," Devlin sneered as he pulled the rope tight.

Fiona twisted around to face him. "I don't know what you're up to, Devlin Brody, but if I don't light the beacon soon, we'll have another shipwreck on our hands."

Devlin's eyes glittered maliciously. "Now wouldn't that be a pity?" He gave her a shove toward the staircase. "Down to the kitchen with you."

Fiona stumbled and caught herself. She backed against the window, staring at her cousin in disbelief. "You put out the light, didn't you? You *want* to cause a shipwreck! By all the saints in heaven, Dev, how could you do such a thing?"

"Shut up, Fiona," he growled, taking a threatening step toward her. "I've no time for your questions. Get down to the kitchen."

Fiona backed away from him as the whole ugly truth dawned on her. "You caused Travis's shipwreck! *You* are to blame for the deaths of his crew—and the theft of his cargo besides.''

Devlin's mouth twisted into a cruel smile. "Fanciful thinking, Fiona, but you can't prove it."

"Did you force Carvey to help you," Fiona demanded, "or did you get him drunk and put out the light yourself?"

"Carvey is a weakling," Devlin scoffed. "He couldn't stomach the deaths of those sailors."

"But you wouldn't leave him alone, would you? That's why he's been ill. You've driven him to it."

Devlin glowered at her. "As I said before, you can't prove a thing. I'm losing patience with you, Fiona. It will go much easier on you if you do as I say."

Fiona's thoughts spun madly. The play wouldn't be over for at least fifteen more minutes and it would be another half hour before her father returned home. She had to stall for time.

With false bravado she taunted, "I can prove you stole Travis's cargo, Devlin."

"You're full of blarney. You have no proof."

"Only a crate full of whiskey and a cabinet full of stolen silk," she countered, lifting her chin defiantly.

Rage burned in Devlin's eyes as he glared at her. "You're lying! If you have proof, why haven't you gone to the sheriff, or told your Mr. Paine?"

Behind her back Fiona worked the ropes, trying to slip her hands free. "Because no matter what you've done, you're still family. I wanted to hear your side first."

Devlin shook his head. "You've always been loyal to the family, you little fool, but not me. What have they ever done for me?" He grabbed her arm and shoved her toward the stairs. "I think I'll have that inscribed on your tombstone: 'Little Fiona, loyal to the end.' ''

Fiona's stomach lurched in fear. "What are you going to do?" she cried, trying to twist out of his grasp.

"You'll see soon enough."

He surprised her once again. Instead of turning right to go to the kitchen, Devlin opened the narrow door at the top of the stairs that led out to the widow's walk. Giving her a shove, he pushed her through.

The wooden planks were slippery and the rain slanted on her face, making it difficult to see where she was going. Fiona tugged futilely against the ropes. Gathering her courage, she turned to face him. "What will you do, Dev? Push me off? Will you have another death on your conscience?"

"I'd never push you off, *little* Fiona," he said with an ugly sneer as he jerked her around and untied her wrists. "You're going to fall all by yourself."

"Have you seen Fiona?" Travis asked Tullia as the stage-hands hurried to change the scenery for the last act of the play.

"No, and I can't understand where she could have taken herself off to," Tullia said with a worried frown. "She'd never leave before the play was over."

Travis asked other cast members but each had the same response. No one had seen her since before the third act. Growing more concerned, he slipped off stage, entered the hall through a side door and searched the faces for the Clearys, thinking she might have joined them. He caught Jordan's eye and motioned him into the vestibule outside.

"I can't find Fiona."

Jordan shrugged. "Can't help you there, Travis. I haven't seen her since before the play."

Travis looked around. "Something's not right."

"Have you had a chance to speak with her yet?" Jordan asked.

Travis shook his head. "There wasn't enough time." Hearing his name whispered, he turned to see Tullia signaling to him from the stage door. He swung back to Jordan and began to strip off his vest and shirt. "You've got to take over for me."

"Play Rip Van Winkle?" Jordan held up his hands. "Not on your life. I'm not an actor and I certainly don't know the lines. Besides, I still haven't forgiven you for making me eat lunch with Bridget."

"Please, Jordan. This is important. You can read the lines straight from the script."

"Mr. Paine," Tullia whispered, motioning frantically.

At Travis's pleading look, Jordan gave him a scowl. "All right, I'll do it, but you owe me, brother." He grabbed the shirt and vest and stalked toward Tullia.

Quickly pulling on his own clothing, Travis made a hurried, useless search of the church. With mounting concern, he pushed open the heavy wooden doors and stepped outside into the rain. The street around the church was deserted and beyond that he could see only fog. He raked his fingers through his hair. Could Fiona have gone home?

As Travis started up Wexford toward the lighthouse, it struck him suddenly that the beacon should have been visible through the fog. "What the hell?" he said aloud. Had the light gone out? Was that where Fiona had gone?

Travis was just passing Mrs. Quinn's house when he heard a woman's screams coming from the direction of the lighthouse. His heart leaped to his throat. He knew that voice. Fiona was in trouble.

As Travis ran up the stone path, he heard the scream again and looked up. On the widow's walk at the top of the tower were two blurry forms struggling against the railing. Instinctively, he knew one of them was Fiona but he couldn't identify the other.

"Fiona!" he shouted, but didn't wait to see if he had been heard. He raced through the house and took the stairs two at a time. Bursting into the tower room, he scanned the windows ringing the walk. Fiona was no longer visible.

"You should have died with the rest of your crew, Mr. Paine."

The hair on Travis's neck lifted. Quickly, he swung around to see Devlin Brody standing in the doorway, an ugly, hulking form dripping rain and smiling like the devil himself.

"Where's Fiona?" Travis demanded.

Devlin moved slowly forward, his small eyes glittering like a madman's, his voice like cold steel. "You should have drowned like the rest of them."

Travis clenched his fists, his eyes narrowing in fury. "What have you done with Fiona?"

Devlin jerked his head in the direction of the staircase. "She met with some bad luck. She insisted on climbing out to the walk. I tried to stop her, but you know how headstrong she can be."

Rage filled Travis's soul. "You son of a bitch!" He lunged at Devlin and both men fell to the floor. Travis wrestled Devlin beneath him, but before he could pin the larger man down, Travis was flipped onto his stomach with all Devlin's weight on his back.

"Won't it be too bad," Devlin sneered, pressing his knee into Travis's back, "when they find both you and Fiona missing?"

Suddenly the harbor bell began to toll. With a great bellow of rage, Devlin jumped up and ran toward the staircase. Wincing in pain, Travis rolled to his feet and followed, his heart pumping excitedly. It had to be Fiona ringing the bell. She had to be safe!

He saw Devlin stop to glance from one of the narrow tower windows, then continue down, swearing viciously. Travis ran to the same window, but it was Carvey standing in the yard ringing the heavy bell, not Fiona.

Quickly, Travis looked around and spotted the door to the widow's walk. Jerking it open, he stepped through and raised his hand to shield his eyes from the rain. "Fiona!" he shouted, but his voice was carried away by the wind. He circled the slippery wooden walk, stopping every few feet to glance over the iron railing to the ground below, his heart gripped by strong tentacles of fear.

What would he do if he lost her? Travis had never known love before, and until that moment had never realized how necessary to his life Fiona had become. He could not imagine living without her.

"Fiona!" he shouted again, helplessly. *If Devlin has pushed her over I'll kill him with my bare hands.*

Suddenly he heard a faint cry and looked down to see slender fingers clasping the lower horizontal bar of the railing. "Fiona!" he cried in relief. "Thank God!"

"Travis, hurry!" she pleaded, gazing up at him, her face ghostly white.

He leaned over the top bar, stretching as far as he dared without falling himself, but she remained inches out of his reach. He looked around for a rope, anything he might use to haul her up.

"Travis," she gasped, "It's slippery. I can't hang on."

His heart slammed against his ribs. "Yes, you can, Fiona! Hold on, sweetheart." He threw a leg over the top bar and climbed onto the outside rim of the wooden walk, searching for a secure foothold. Holding onto the railing with his left hand, he lowered himself into a squatting position, bending at the knees until he could reach down and grasp her wrist.

"I've got you!" Travis called. He gritted his teeth as he pulled her up, his arm muscles quivering from the strain, the cords in his neck taut. With a groan, he lifted her over the bars and climbed after her. He opened his arms and she fell into them, sobbing, clinging tightly to him.

"Travis, I was so frightened."

"You're all right, sweetheart. Thank God, you're all right." Travis stroked her back, fighting to keep his own tears at bay. "I love you, Fiona," he whispered through a throat choked with emotion. "God, how I love you."

Her arms tightened around him. "I love you, too," she wept. "Hold me."

Travis pressed kisses against her wet hair, her cheek, her mouth. "I've got you, sweetheart. You're safe now."

Gripping his arms, Fiona raised her head and gazed at him through tearful eyes. "Devlin's the one who put out the light and stole your cargo. He'll get away if we don't stop him!"

Travis turned and saw a figure running toward the pier. "Light the beacon, Fiona. I'll take care of Devlin."

"Travis?" she called. "Who rang the bell?"

"Carvey," Travis replied as he ran for the stairs.

With shaking hands, Fiona relit the huge beacon, then hurried down the stairs and outside to the back yard. She gave a cry of dismay when she saw Carvey slumped over on the ground beside the bell, blood mixed with rain streaming down his face.

He stared at her through dazed eyes as she knelt down beside him. "Did Devlin do this to you?" she asked, wiping blood from his eyes.

Carvey's gaze shifted toward the lighthouse. "I tried to keep him out of the tower. I knew what he wanted to do." He swallowed hard. "Dev tricked me the first time, Fiona. I didn't know he was going to put out the light. He said he wanted to share a bottle with me. The next thing I knew Da was shaking me, telling me about Mr. Paine's ship. . . ." With a strangled sob, Carvey bent his head, unable to finish.

"It's all right, Carvey," Fiona assured him. "You don't need to explain now. Save your strength."

He slowly shook his head. "I'm ashamed, Fiona. I'm so ashamed."

"But you tried to stop Devlin, didn't you, Carvey, and you called for help, even with your injury."

At the sound of distant voices, Fiona looked around and spotted the glow of lantern lights as the rescue team made their way to the lake. Always before the sight had filled her with dread; now she felt only gladness. She jumped to her feet and waved her arms to attract their attention. "You see, Carvey?" she said joyfully. "They heard your summons."

Tom Brody was the first to reach her. "Mother of God, Carvey! What happened?" he asked breathlessly as he crouched beside them.

Fiona quickly filled him in as the others gathered around. Listening to her tale, Tom's features hardened and his face turned deep red. "Where's my brother now?"

"Travis followed him to the pier," Fiona answered.

Tullia pushed her way to the front of the group and immediately began giving orders. "You, Brian, go get the sheriff. Kevin, fetch the doctor. Pegeen, go back for Dee and tell her what happened. Tommy—" She stopped and stared at her younger son.

Tom had risen and was standing with his fists clenched at his sides. "I'll fetch Devlin," he said bitterly.

Fiona ran after Tom as he strode down the dune toward

the lake. He said nothing and she knew better than to talk to him. Devlin had proved to them that day what they had tried to deny for so long, and as Fiona looked back upon his numerous incidents of cruelty, she knew she should have been alerted to his true character: Devlin was a bad seed. The whole family would now suffer for what he had done. But at that moment, Fiona's concern was for Travis.

By the time they reached the boat dock the storm had lessened. They found one of the rescue gigs gone, but there was no sign of either man on the pier.

"Damn it!" Tom swore. "Dev must have sailed for Trenton Harbor."

But where was Travis? With a racing heart Fiona searched the choppy waters, lit only by the beacon. If Devlin was capable of pushing her off the tower, then he wouldn't think twice about killing Travis. She paced up and down the pier, shielding her eyes from the rain.

Suddenly she spotted an object and called excitedly, "Tommy, isn't that the boat?"

Squinting his eyes, Tom stared at the object. "It's the boat all right, and they're both in it."

Fiona stood on the edge of the pier and watched in terror as the two men wrestled with each other and struggled to keep their balance. As each wave smashed against its frail hull, the boat pitched violently beneath them. Fiona gasped as a rogue wave crashed over the boat and swept both men into the seething waters of Lake Michigan. For a heart-stopping moment they disappeared from view, then they broke the surface once again, locked in a battle that Fiona feared neither would survive.

Folding her hands she bent her head to whisper a desperate prayer, then crossed herself and looked up again. But though she desperately searched the water, she could find no sign of either man. "Where have they gone, Tommy?" she cried.

Tom shook his head. "I've lost sight of them."

Tears rolled down Fiona's cheeks as she stared dismally at the foaming whitecaps. Suddenly, just down the beach one of the men rose from the turbulent water and slowly waded to shore half carrying, half dragging the other. From a distance it was impossible for Fiona to tell which was Travis. She grabbed Tom's sleeve and pointed, crying, "Over there!"

Tom stared for a moment, then ran up the pier toward the beach. As Fiona followed, she saw the first man stagger onto the sand and fall to his knees. She felt a sob rise in her throat. "Travis!" she cried.

Slowly, the man on his knees raised his head. As he struggled to his feet Fiona ran toward him, sobbing. He opened his arms and caught her. While Tommy helped Devlin to his feet, Fiona smiled up at Travis with tears of joy. "Let's go home."

The early morning sun glinted brightly on the surface of Lake Michigan. Overhead, herring gulls screeched, dipping and soaring on air currents. Far out on the water a tall white sail billowed in the wind. It was a perfect August morning.

Sitting atop the dune beside the lighthouse, Fiona snuggled her back against Travis's chest, closed her eyes and sighed in contentment.

Travis's arms tightened around her. "Don't you dare go to sleep!"

Fiona turned her head to gaze up at him. "And if I did what would you do about it?"

He bent his head to kiss her mouth. "This."

As their lips met and their tongues intertwined, Fiona wrapped her arms around Travis's neck and let him lay her back on the sand. "What punishment!" she scoffed as he nibbled her jaw.

"Punishment is it?" he said, and began to tickle her.

Laughing, she grabbed his hands, pushed him away and twisted out from beneath him. "Travis Paine!" she said, straightening her clothing. "What would Da think if he found us doing this?"

Travis rolled to a sitting position. "After spending the rest of last night manning the beacon," he said, leaning against the wall of the lighthouse, "I believe you'll find your father snoring soundly in bed."

"Well, then what if Jamie comes out?"

"Dee is bathing Jamie," Travis replied, and before Fiona

could counter, he added, "Jordan is just getting up and hasn't even had his breakfast. And Carvey won't be going anywhere until his head is better."

Reminded of her brother-in-law's injury, Fiona sighed. "Poor Carvey. To be carrying such a secret and living in fear of Devlin, besides. Is it any wonder the man was ill?"

Travis put his arms around Fiona and pulled her against him. "At least you know the first shipwreck was an accident and not caused by Carvey or Devlin."

"Not caused by him, perhaps, but Dev still took advantage of it. I can't believe one of my own family is capable of such a monstrous crime. He's brought shame on us all."

"He's brought shame on himself, Fiona, not the family. He'll pay for what he did," Travis assured her, "along with his crew from Trenton Harbor. Look at the bright side. With Devlin in jail, Tom is in charge of his own shop now and no longer under his brother's thumb."

Fiona sighed. "I suppose you're right."

"I'm always right," he said seriously. "You might as well get that straight now. It'll save us a lot of future arguments."

With a gasp of indignation, Fiona turned to face him, only to find him smirking. "Why, you conceited, muleheaded oaf! What have you been right about?"

"The light, for one thing."

Fiona had to concede that Travis *was* right about that. "Name another," she demanded.

"That someone in your family was involved."

Fiona decided not to press her luck. "We'll stop at two, thank you."

With a laugh, Travis drew her back into his arms. "How about a third? That I'm madly in love with you."

Fiona put her arms around his neck and laid her head on his shoulder. "Three will do nicely."

"There's one more."

She lifted her head to gaze at him curiously. "What's that?"

Travis brought one of her hands to his lips and kissed it. "That I want to marry you."

A lump came to Fiona's throat and her eyes filled with

tears. After all they'd been through, she hadn't been sure he still wanted her.

He squeezed her hand in his. "Will you marry me, Fiona?"

She wiped a tear off her cheek, smiled and nodded. "Yes."

Travis studied her expression closely. "No reservations? You don't mind giving up your dreams to live here with me?"

Fiona sniffled, then gave him a sidelong glance. "Well now, I didn't say I'd give up my dreams."

A puzzled look crossed Travis's face. "But I thought you said—"

Fiona pressed her fingers against his lips, silencing him. "My dream has been to see the world. But you're a part of that dream now." She leaned forward and kissed him lightly on the mouth. "I'd planned to travel by rail, you see. With your ties to the railroad, it will make it that much easier."

"*That's* why you said yes?" he asked incredulously.

Fiona gave him a mischievous smile. "It *was* a consideration."

He ran his hands down her arms and up again, slowly, sensually. Lifting one eyebrow he said, "But not the *only* one, I trust."

Fiona leaned forward to nibble his lips. "*Definitely* not the only one."

With a deep growl, Travis pulled her against him and kissed her hard, making her quiver with desire. She ran her hands up his chest, exploring the hard muscles beneath her fingertips, imagining the feel of his warm, bare skin against hers.

"Yoo-hoo, Travis!"

"Mother Mary!" Fiona muttered crossly as she pushed away from Travis and adjusted her clothing. "Bridget always did have perfect timing."

Travis helped Fiona to her feet. "I think that little bluebird needs to have her wings clipped."

They turned as Bridget sashayed up the stone path toward them, her bright yellow parasol unfurled, the full skirt of her yellow and white striped summer dress billowing in the breeze.

"Morning, Travis," Bridget chirped happily. "Fiona," she said with a curt nod in Fiona's direction.

"Bridget," Travis said with secretive smile.

Bridget looked from Travis to Fiona. Her eyes narrowed suspiciously. "What's going on?"

Travis glanced at Fiona and winked. "Bridget, you may be the first to congratulate me."

Bridget looked confounded. "What may I congratulate you on?"

"My engagement to Fiona."

Biting her lip to keep from laughing, Fiona watched Bridget struggle to control her emotions.

"Well," Bridget said with a stiff smile, "Since you asked, I suppose I must congratulate you." She stood on tiptoe and kissed his cheek. "I hope you and Fiona will be—" she paused to consider her conclusion, "—as happy as possible." With that, she sailed blithely toward the house.

Travis grabbed Fiona's arm as she started after Bridget. "Where are you going?" he asked.

"To clip her wings," Fiona retorted.

Travis pulled her back. "Don't worry about Bridget. She's off to greener pastures."

"And by that do you mean your brother?" Fiona asked.

Travis took her by the hand and led her toward the beach. "That's who I mean."

"Stars and garters, Travis, aren't you going to warn Jordan?"

He led her into the shelter of a blowout and sat down, patting the sand next to him. As Fiona cuddled up beside him, he said, "Bridget has her own built-in warning system. Listen."

Fiona turned her head toward the lighthouse as Travis nuzzled her neck. "I don't hear anything."

"Be patient, love," Travis murmured huskily as he laid her back on the sand.

"Yoo-hoo! Jordan!"

At her familiar cry, they both laughed. Fiona put her hands on either side of Travis's face and gazed up at him, her heart filled with more love and happiness than she had ever known.

"How lucky I am to have found you," she said, running her fingers through his hair.

He rubbed his nose against hers. "Must be the luck of the Irish."

"Why, you muleheaded oaf!" She grabbed his hair and tugged, making him wince. "What of your own luck?"

"I'll let you know in an hour."

As Travis kissed her, Fiona wrapped her arms around his neck, closed her eyes and sighed in contentment, silently thanking all the saints in heaven.